THE WIDOWING

Book II of The Detectivists

Melanie Bacon

This is a work of fiction. All characters,
organizations, and events portrayed in this novel
are products of the author's imagination or are used
fictitiously.

DEL SOL PRESS.
ISBN: 978-1-7344900-7-7
THE WIDOWING
Copyright © 2024 by Melanie Bacon.
All rights reserved.

Printed in the United States of America.
Del Sol Press, 2020 Pennsylvania Avenue, NW,
Washington, D.C., 20006.
delsolpress.org

Cover Art by Mila

Please contact Del Sol Press by
e-mail at editor@delsolpress.org.

First Edition: August 2024
10 9 8 7 6 5 4 3 2 1

For Michael

*Thanks to Ben Marx for his faith
and perseverance.*

Chapter One

I had hoped to never again feel obliged to kill another person. Unfortunately, someone had just slid a knife into my right side. He'd been momentarily stymied by the thick twill and whalebone of my corset but was now just a split-instant from pushing the weapon forward into an organ.

Needs must when the Devil drives. Gripping my heavy oak cane in both hands, I twisted back using my casted left foot as the fulcrum for my weight and lashed out at the miscreant like a cricket batsman striking at a ball. The man fell, and I followed through with a smash at his head. I continued pounding on him until I noticed blood puddling by his ear and trickling down the sidewalk, a sight which brought me back to myself. I shuddered to a stop and bent over to see what damage I had bestowed on the wicked creature.

The vile assailant still breathed, but just barely. I relieved him of the knife. Dull and rusty, it could nevertheless have done serious damage had he more time, muscle, or evil will to complete the nefarious deed. I looked around the narrow street, eyeing others of his ilk who remained squatted on the sidewalk or leaning against nearby buildings, watching the entertainment with surly amusement.

"Do any of you know this man?" I inquired in a loud voice.

One old lady shrugged. I say "old", but she could have been any age from 20 to 70. It's a rough life, living on the streets of Whitechapel.

"I seen him around," she said.

I nodded. "Does he have any family? Or friends?" I was concerned about just leaving him here bleeding to death on the street. I may be a killer, but I am not a monster.

"That's his haybag," she said, pointing to another wizened crone hunched on the ground. "Ask her."

I walked over to address the woman in question. "Is that your husband?"

"Aye," she said. "He dead?"

"Not yet," I said. I opened my purse and handed her a half-dozen shillings, money I had intended to use to buy coal for the police horse infirmary. Her eyes gleamed at the rich insurance payout. I was aware of the irony of voluntarily donating all the funds in my purse to the wife of my would-be robber.

"You can hit him again, if you want," she offered. "He's a right old bastard."

"No, I'm done," I said. "I'll leave him in your loving care."

She tried to hand one of the coins back to me. "I'll pay."

I shook my head and turned away from her. I had thought no one was disturbed about my attack, but much to my surprise a police constable came running down the street, whistle blowing, followed by the urchin who must have gone for assistance.

"Hello, Archie," I said when the constable stopped beside me.

"Good afternoon, Maddie," he said, eyeing me curiously. "Are you the giant woman who's brutalising innocent men just minding their own business?"

I glared at the brat who had reported me to PC Froest. A moment ago I had planned to reward him for going after help; now I itched to give him a smack on the ear. He ran off, no doubt horrified to realise that I was friendly with the police.

"The man tried to stab me," I said, touching my hand to my side. It came back red with blood.

"Looks like he succeeded," Archie said with concern, reaching a hand toward me, worried that I was about to swoon. "Are you going to be all right, Maddie?"

"I'm fine," I said, though in truth I had no idea whether I was or not. "But I should probably get back home to bandage myself up."

He frowned, then smiled in relief as he saw a familiar hackney headed toward us. "Miss Astraia can take care of you," he said. "I'll handle things here, then I'll come to the stables and get your statement."

As John the coachman pulled up beside me I heard Archie Froest inquiring of the street crowd if anyone knew who the bleeding man was. No one seemed to be offering him any information. I turned back and pointed to the ungrieving spouse.

"She told me she is his wife," I told my friend. The woman gave me an angry look, but in my view cooperating with the police was the least she could do for the blood money I'd paid her.

Apparently John saw the blood running down my side; he climbed down from his seat to gently help me into the cab next to my friend and his employer, Astraia Holmes.

"Good God, Maddie, what happened to you?" Astraia said in concern.

It was a tight squeeze in the small cab, made worse by my ungainly foot cast. Usually Astraia and I ride in John's large carriage, not in the hackney he used to pick up extra money during the day while Astraia was at work. Clearly she hadn't intended to take me for a ride this afternoon.

"I just killed a man," I said. "Again." And I couldn't even blame this one on her.

"That's the least he deserved, after stabbing you," she remarked, looking in distaste at the blood-coated knife still in my hand. "An attempted robbery?"

"So I assume. There was no discussion. He stabbed me; I walloped him; I gave his widow money." My side ached. I hoped I would not be called upon to perform any horse surgeries today. I needed to care for my own wound first. "Do you have a handkerchief, Astraia?"

She took one out of her reticule, a dainty, lacy thing. Astraia is a milliner's doll of a woman, a tiny delicate redhead with a prodigious brain. I pressed the bit of lace to my side and winced.

"As it happens I was planning to stop to see you on my way home anyway," Astraia said. "Luckily John noticed you in that crowd." I am not hard to notice, being nearly six feet tall.

"I stepped out to see the coal-man," I said. "The bucket is low." Now that my assistant Susie was living with me, I tried to keep the place tolerably warm. We'd already gone through this quarter's allotment, and it was only the beginning of February. Sergeant Wilson would not be happy if I asked him for more coal so soon. "What did you want to see me about?"

"The Fabian Society lecture is the night after tomorrow. I was wondering if you would like to ride with me."

The Fabian Society is a socialist debating group and offspring of the Fellowship of the New Life, the pacifist organisation of which I am a member. Last month

George Bernard Shaw had given a lecture on why it would benefit landlords and capitalists with excess wealth and land to give away to the deserving poor the property and riches they themselves didn't need. I had eagerly anticipated attending the next lecture in the series, and a half-hour ago my answer to Astraia's offer would have been a resounding yes. Now I was not so sure. "I need to see how bad my wound is," I said. "Can I send you a message tomorrow morning at the library?"

"That will be fine."

As I held my hand out of the side of the cab to wring out the blood from Astraia's almost-useless handkerchief I thought about Letty, my friend's companion. That good woman would have proffered a more utilitarian piece of cloth.

"Where's Letty?" I asked.

Astraia waved her hand in dismissal. "She's been in a pother lately. I told her to stay home if she was going to be that way."

This was punishment indeed. Letty loved spending her days in the new Whitechapel library. Astraia was the only paid employee, but the board of governors got double their investment because Letty was usually the person working at the desk. Astraia liked the books but did not enjoy assisting people. She had been offered the job through the intervention of her brother Mr Mycroft Holmes. I doubted Astraia was paid any more for working at the library than I received as a police horse doctor. But happily for her (though she never seemed to appreciate it), Mr Mycroft and her other brother, Mr Sherlock, managed Astraia's small trust and paid her expenses, including the wages for Letty and John.

I was panting a little by the time John assisted me down from his cab, I think more from the shock of the thing than from blood loss, and barely had the strength to wave good-bye to my friend. When I opened the door of my stable infirmary in the police yard, it was a relief to breathe in the consoling warm horse fragrance of home.

My young assistant Susie came over to see why I had returned so soon from my errand. She noticed the blood dripping down my side and the gore that coated my cane, and tears came to her eyes. "Oh, Miss Maddie, oh no!"

"I'm fine Susie, really, don't worry," I said in a soothing tone. I might have hugged the girl in comfort but didn't wish to get blood on her too. "I'm just going to change—you could do me a big help if you'd pour warm water into the bedroom basin and also find me some bandages."

Susie brought in the hot water, carbolic acid, surgical tape, and bandages. She asked if she could help. But I sent her on several errands to get her out of the stables for the rest of the afternoon, not wishing to distress her more than necessary.

The cut wasn't deep and the blood flow had decreased. Cleaning it stung much worse than the stab itself, and if I had been a equine patient of mine, I would have put in a few sutures. However, there are limits to what I'm willing to inflict on myself, so I just taped on a thick bandage over the cleaned wound and wrapped a few layers around my torso to ensure stability.

My friend Archie stopped by the stable later just long enough to inform me that my latest victim was indeed dead, and to say he'd get more information from me the following day when I was more refreshed. The rest of the day brought no emergencies to my door and I was able to relax. By the next morning I felt well enough to send Susie off to the library with a message to Astraia that yes, I would be glad for a ride to the Fabian Society lecture the following evening.

I was sitting at the old table in my office, dressed in a more-or-less clean dress, when PC Froest stopped by to join me for morning tea, as he did most days. Archie did not question my motives in my most recent incident of violence; clearly I was the victim in the altercation. "But some suspicion was expressed by the denizens of the street because no knife appeared in evidence at the scene," he said.

I handed him the weapon, still rusted although no longer coated with my own blood since Susie had rinsed it off at the same time she cleaned my cane. I wondered where the girl was. She'd returned from the library long ago, and seldom missed meals.

"I urge you not to return it to the family as a memento," I told Archie. "I don't doubt it would soon be used again for the same purpose."

He agreed to keep it in the police locker, which meant that it would eventually end up in some constable or officer's home. I didn't mind; I certainly didn't want to keep the thing here with me like some souvenir of battle. It was enough that I would have a new addition to my scar collection.

He also agreed to bring me some more coal, the second time in as many weeks he'd performed this service for me. I realised I would need to discuss the stable's coal allotment with the precinct sergeant, and sighed. I detested those types of conversations, where I had to beg for basics.

"So what else is going on with you, Archie?" I asked after we finished our first few silent minutes of tea and gingerbread. I settled down to listen to his tales of inept criminals and corrupt officers, drinking another consoling pot of tea and trying not to wince at the jabs of sharp pain caused by my newest injury whenever I twisted my body. Susie and the dog Old Vic appeared an hour later, both hungry and tired from whatever they had gotten into over at the regular horse stable, where they seemed to be spending more and more time these days.

***

Later that night, as I changed the bandage on my newest laceration, I thought about all the injuries inflicted and healed here in the Leman Street Police horse stables over the years. I had been an official horse veterinarian for the Metropolitan Police since the death of my father, the previous horse doctor.

I frowned at the growing pile of dirty and even bloody clothes on the floor. I did not have time to wash clothes anymore, and did not like asking Susie to clean up after me. I needed to find a laundry, preferably one that would trade services with me, doing my laundry in exchange for me taking care of their horses like the arrangement I had with Feinman's Bakery (money was always a premium, especially if I was going to start doling it out to every would-be-widow whose husband I clobbered).

I seemed to encounter a lot of dead or injured people for a horse doctor. I guess it was understandable, having lived the last fifteen years of my life in a police precinct and sleeping not fifty yards from the Leman Street gaol.

In truth though, these violent irregularities had become normalised in my life only since the day I saw my father kill Mary Kelly.

***

Susie spent most of the day in the regular stable, where apparently a new stableboy had started haunting the place, someone who was helpful and considerate toward her. "Would you like to meet my new friend Ruven some time, Miss Maddie?" she asked enthusiastically that afternoon.

"Of course," I said. I was relieved to learn that a nice boy had joined the ranks in the regular horse stables, and hoped the rascals Jamie and Little Teddy would not sway him down a darker path; those stableboys had behaved abusively toward me ever since my father had been the police veterinarian, and I never trusted them to assist Susie.

I was grateful she was there, because her presence in the building allowed me to take a nice refreshing nap that afternoon.

*****

Because of that nap, I felt alert enough to accompany Astraia to the Fabian Society lecture. I had started attending these lectures after hearing about them from Herbert George Wells. Mr Wells was another member of the Fellowship of the New Life, a group I had joined initially because of their focus on peace, an irony which had not escaped me during these recent months of repeated violence, much of it instigated by myself.

Although I had stopped attending the meetings of the Fellowship of the New Life (which besides discursions on peace also usually involved discussions about free love, a topic that did not enthrall me), I usually do attend the public lectures organized by the Fellowship's sister group, the Fabian Society, and Astraia had decreed these meetings moderately entertaining ever since her first experience when a debate on an important political issue had degenerated into two old men kicking and punching at each other.

Last year the Society had published its book *Fabian Essays in Socialism,* and I had been enjoying hearing the essay writers read and lead discussions on their pieces. So at five that evening, after feeding Susie, the dog, the cat, and the two sick horses in our care, I hobbled out to Astraia's carriage for the trip to the assembly hall where George Bernard Shaw, the editor of the essays, would regale us with more of his own thoughts on the evils of capitalism.

Astraia and I hadn't spent time together in over a week, and during the ride we talked about a case referred to us by her brother Mycroft, who worked in the government.

"Mykie still wants us to investigate the murder of Lady Deborah Peacham, Maddie."

"The wife of the industrialist Sir Peter Peacham?" When she had mentioned this to me before I had been preoccupied over the arrest of my nemesis for selling meat pies with human organs in them, and hadn't paid much attention.

"Yes. The society doyenne. Lady Deborah died in her own bed two weeks ago, apparently stabbed under suspicious circumstances. She was one of the most militant suffragists in the country. In fact, a week before she was killed she was arrested for interrupting a committee meeting of the House of Commons by pounding at the doors to the Chamber, leading a group of women in shouts of 'Votes for women! Votes for your wives! Votes for your mothers! Votes for your daughters!' and so on."

I nodded in the dark. "I read about that. None of their entreaties convinced the MPs, who immediately called in the police. Archie told me that several women were actually charged at Old Bailey with Threatening Behaviour and Breaking the Peace, although I believe that neither Lady Deborah nor any of the other noblewomen were charged."

The rich always received special treatment. I wondered if Mr Shaw would mention that fact tonight in his socialism speech.

"That's right," Astraia said. "Many of the other women were scolded by the judge, but no one spent any time in gaol over the incident."

"What does your brother expect us to do that the police can't do?" I asked.

"Mykie believes that the murderer was someone in the suffrage community," my friend said. "He wants us to infiltrate Lady Deborah's suffrage coterie and find out which one of them did it."

This seemed a stretch. Usually when a woman was killed, the husband was the first and only suspect. Astraia agreed with my assessment.

"I told him that in my opinion Sir Peter committed mariticide, perhaps fed up with his wife's suffrage antics as so many men are. But Mykie knew them both, and he disagrees. I think Mykie is simply taking extra precautions because of the political difficulties in arresting someone who has been awarded a knighthood by the crown, albeit decades ago."

"What does the post-mortem say?" I asked.

"That's another thing," she said, her annoyance clear in her voice. "Apparently the police have not yet completed their post-mortem report, even though the death occurred two weeks ago. All we know is that she was stabbed. We don't even know what the weapon was."

So Mr Mycroft Holmes wanted us to investigate a stabbing murder without details about how the death occurred or specifics about to whom we should speak, other than "suffragists".

"I'm not sure how to start with this one, Astraia," I said.

"I haven't figured that out either yet," my friend said. "That's why I hadn't reminded you about it before now. You can't just go up to a group of suffragists and ask if one of them killed their leader. Women get touchy about things like that. I haven't the first idea where to start, but I'm confident something will come to me soon."

Chapter Two

When Astraia and I arrived at the assembly hall for the lecture, Mr Havelock Ellis, the door greeter, tried to embrace me, as was always his wont at such times. I pushed past him as politely as I could. And when he tried to embrace Astraia, a woman he'd met only once before, she kicked his ankle. He quickly moved away from her to my side, then escorted us past the front of the queue and into the small room set with chairs and a lecture dais. I assumed this special attention was on Astraia's account, since when I came to these lectures by myself I was always expected to queue up with everyone else.

"Miss Holmes, how do you come to know our dear Miss Barquist?" Mr. Ellis asked politely, his eyes searching the room to find a place where we ladies could sit near the speaker.

His question was a reasonable one, and one that probably occurred to most people who encountered us together. Astraia was small, girlish, and delicately flounced in pastel and lace; I was large, plainly dressed, and no doubt redolent of the stables in which I worked.

"We met recently at the library," Astraia said, her usual answer when people asked this question; it would take too much time to explain that we had met over a puddle of blood from a prostitute eviscerated at the steps of an opium den. Mr Ellis nodded and led us to a couple of open seats in the front row.

The seats filled and eventually Mr Frank Podmore, a leader of the Fabian Society, walked to the dais. I looked around the room and frowned as I realized that George Bernard Shaw did not seem to be anywhere around. Annie Besant, who often accompanied Mr Shaw to these meetings and spoke with authority on the same topics herself, also seemed to be missing. In fact, as I studied the attendees, I saw few of the leading socialist thinkers.

Astraia noticed my frown. "What's wrong?" she asked.

"Bernard Shaw isn't here," I said.

She scowled. She enjoyed a minor flirtation with Shaw, a forceful man who found himself easily flummoxed around beautiful women. If she wouldn't have an opportunity to trifle with the heart of a bombastic man, she really didn't understand what the point was in being here. Unlike me, she had no actual interest in socialism.

"Maybe someone will start a fight," I said, trying to cheer her up.

"We can only hope."

Mr Podmore cleared his throat and began to speak. "Ladies and gentlemen, I'm sorry to announce that because of illness Mr George Bernard Shaw is unable to be present here this evening."

There were a few groans but not many, and I realized that most of the people who would have come to hear Mr Shaw had already known of his absence and had remained truant themselves. Unfortunately I do not socialise regularly with any of the Fabian or Fellowship people, and so often lacked current gossip. And the only socialist whom Astraia knew was me.

Mr Podmore continued. "But I hope that we can present you with an evening just as thrilling. As most of you know, I am the president of the Society for Psychical Research." He motioned to another man sitting at the front of the room. "My colleague Dr Richard Dryson and I are well known for our travels up and down the British Isles and even into the wilds of Europe, seeking truth and enlightenment whenever an opportunity arises to investigate claims of supernatural phenomena. We are happy tonight to be able to share with you some of our most recent astounding discoveries."

And with that introduction, the most boring and awkward speaker in the Fabian Society started droning on about occultism, spiritualism, mysticism, and other esoteric gibberish, with occasional interjections by his friend Dr Dryson spitting ejaculations of enthusiasm over a particularly memorable phantasm incident or tale of floating household trinkets.

After a moment of shared dismay and mutual sighs, Astraia and I settled into the thing. There was no way that two ladies, one hampered by cast and cane, could exit inconspicuously from the front row of a brightly lit public lecture.

I let my mind wander. I had a gentleman friend, Detective Inspector Samuel Rankin, and the two of us were planning to take a day trip to the Shoreditch music hall soon. I thought about what I might wear, and what kind of entertainments we might enjoy; I wondered where Samuel intended to take me to dine. My mind drifted along in such pleasant thoughts while Mr Podmore and Dr Dryson spouted their interminable nonsense.

I don't know what kept Astraia awake during the beginning of the lecture, but at some point she suddenly perked up and I was aware from that moment to the end that she was practically abuzz with excitement.

As soon as the lecture ended Astraia jumped up from her seat. I assumed she was in a hurry to leave the place, but I could not have been more wrong. She rushed up to the dais to grab Mr Podmore's attention before anyone else had a chance to congratulate him on his presentation. I stared at her in astonishment but followed as quickly as I was able.

"Mr Podmore, I was so thrilled to hear that you and Dr Dryson are planning to attend a séance at the home of Professor Henry Sidgwick in Cambridge on Saturday night!" she said in her most suspicious girly squeal.

Mr Podmore beamed at her enthusiasm. "We are indeed. As I said, the great American medium Valerie Tillis will be leading the séance. We are most grateful to Professor and Mrs Sidgwick for sponsoring this important event."

Dr Richard Dryson joined us. "Mrs Tillis and I have been corresponding for many years now, and I cannot wait to meet her in person."

"So exciting," Astraia said. "So exciting. As it happens, Nora Sidgwick is one of my dearest friends, and I haven't seen her for ever so long. Not since college graduation, in fact."

I hadn't known Astraia had graduated from college. She had never mentioned it. I wondered if this was one of her stories, a useful fiction put about to achieve a particular goal.

"Oh, are you a graduate of Newnham College, my dear?" Dr Dryson asked in an avuncular manner.

"I am indeed," my friend said. "And I would dearly love to see Nora again. And even more important, Maddie and I are fascinated by psychical research and we would be so thrilled to attend a séance. Wouldn't we, Maddie?" She looked up at me with a beatific smile.

"Um, sure. Certainly. We'd be thrilled," I said. I was surprised by her enthusiasm because psychical research seemed like the very last thing Astraia Holmes, a ruthlessly practical individual, would ever be interested in.

"Could we join your company, Mr Podmore? I could write to Nora this evening to let her know we're coming. Maddie and I could be on the train to Cambridge the day after tomorrow," she said. "I believe the séance is scheduled for that night?"

"Yes, yes, that would be fine," poor Mr Podmore said. Really, she'd given him no other choice. And soon he began to see the positives of adding two more people to his group. "The more witnesses to verify the existence of the psychical realms the merrier," he said, injecting a tone of jollity into his voice.

"Excellent!" Astraia said with her most obnoxious false squeal, then grabbed my arm to pull me away. "Come, Maddie—we need to go pack! And I have to write to Nora!"

As soon as we were in her carriage riding back to the police precinct she told me her true purpose for volunteering us to attend such a bizarre activity: she believed that Mrs Eleanor Sidgwick, the Vice-Principal of Newnham College of the University of Cambridge and friend to all the educated women in England, would be glad to give us letters of introduction to the leaders of the British suffrage movement.

"Nora is a brilliant woman, with only one failing," Astraia said.

"What's that?" I asked.

"She believes in spiritualism." My friend sounded disgusted. "Sponsoring a séance is exactly the sort of thing she and Professor Sidgwick would do."

***

I spent the next day getting everything sorted in the horse infirmary in order to take a few days off to go to Cambridge. Mycroft Holmes himself had made the arrangements a month ago with the police for me to have an assistant in the stables, and he did so specifically in order to give me freedom to accompany his sister on ridiculous errands like attending seances in distant counties. So mostly what I needed to do was inform Archie, Sergeant Wilson, and Susie herself that she would be responsible for the animals for a couple of days, and that if any emergencies arose another veterinarian would need to be called in. I thought about sending a letter to my personal friend, DI Rankin, but like a coward decided against it. Samuel did not approve of the work I did with Astraia, because he felt that civilians had no business being involved in police matters. He also did not approve in general of my friendship with Astraia, whom he had known since they were children together—he did not trust her not to lead me into trouble. But he didn't often work in my precinct and there was a good chance he wouldn't even notice I was gone, so why stir that hornet's nest up unnecessarily?

I was sitting at my office table, finishing the dregs of my tea and wondering if I had any clean clothes to take with me on the trip when Susie rushed in, dragging a boy behind her.

"Miss Maddie, this is Ruven," she said proudly.

Ruven was a small boy, considerably shorter than Susie even though the two of them were probably of an age, which is often the case with boys and girls who are ten or twelve years old. He was also a quintessential street urchin—filthy, clothes too small and falling apart, and without shoes. But I could tell by her demeanor that Susie felt attached to him. And I was grateful that she outweighed him by a stone or more, since she seemed determined to spend time with him and I would not be around for the next few days to assist her if the situation got out of hand.

"I'm glad to meet you, Ruven," I said.

He bobbed his head in respect, a strange gesture from a common ragamuffin. "I am very obliged to meet you, Miss Maddie," he said. "I think this must be the best place in the world. And you and Susie are the nicest people I ever met." And then he bobbed his head again.

I frowned. I did not understand what Susie found so enthralling about him. But as long as he treated Susie respectfully he was not my problem; the stableboys worked for Harry, the stablemaster in the regular stable.

"That's fine," I said. "Go away now." He bobbed again and left, and I spent the next hour instructing Susie on what she would need to take care of while I was in Cambridge. I promised that I would return as quickly as possible; that I would leave her with funds to buy food in my absence; that my friend PC Archibald Froest would check on her frequently; and that yes, I would take care to change the bandage on my new knife wound.

I was proud that she expressed concern over my wound care. I liked to think she had the makings of a fine veterinarian, someone who could someday step into my place here, treating police horses.

***

Eleanor Sidgwick was elated that her dear former student Astraia Holmes had decided to visit her in Cambridge, even if it was just to get letters of introduction from her.

"I did know Lady Deborah well," she told us the next afternoon as we unpacked from our trip. "I know most of the educated women in England, including most of the prominent suffragists and proponents of temperance."

"I assumed you did," Astraia said, giving her friend one of her rare genuine smiles of affection. "Unfortunately neither Maddie nor I know anyone from Lady Deborah's suffrage circle, suffragists at the upper levels of society or leaders in the national suffrage community."

Until our train ride to Cambridge, I had been unaware of Astraia's educational achievements. She explained to me during our trip on the rails that Nora was the Vice-Principal of Newnham College, married to Henry Sidgwick, himself a professor of moral philosophy at the University of Cambridge and one of the founders of Newnham—and Astraia herself was a graduate of Newnham College, where she had read literature and botany. She had sat for examination and received a Degree of Honour but not normal degrees in her fields of study, because graduates of the women's college at Cambridge were not permitted such degrees even though their education was the same as that of male students, a point of great annoyance to Astraia even four years later. During her time as a student, Astraia had worked with Nora on a number of projects promoting women's suffrage, and they had continued a close correspondence over the years since.

She also spoke of her frustration that none of her school friends—many of whom were socially prominent—had chosen to work for the suffrage cause, but instead were "wasting their lives and educations" managing households.

"Many of my friends expressed interest in suffrage while we were at Newnham, but I'm afraid they're all still too young to have reached any prominence or influence in the movement, because they're all more focused on husbands and babies, either the ones they have or the ones they're striving to obtain," she told me with an affronted sniff. Astraia was unusual among her friends for being not only still unmarried but having evinced no interest to alter this status.

I was not altogether uninterested in the concept, myself. Theoretically. Someday, perhaps.

I did not comment on the fact that to my knowledge Astraia had not been working for the suffrage cause since graduation either.

Astraia had telegraphed her friend that we would be joining tonight's séance but had not told her until now about our ulterior motive for the visit. Happily, Nora was fully supportive of our pursuit of justice. "I was shocked by Lady Deborah's death and will of course do everything I can to help you," she said. "Let me think for a while about how best to do that. In the meantime, I'm so glad you can participate in our séance tonight. Henry and I so enjoy our work exploring the potential of supernatural connection. We have the famous American psychic and medium, Valerie Tillis, staying with us. She will guide our explorations tonight into the etheric realms—isn't that thrilling?"

Astraia strained a smile. "Thrilling," she agreed. She respected Nora too much to give one of her fake squeals of excitement.

We spent the next half-hour talking about the treat facing us that evening. There would be eight at supper and the séance to follow—Nora and her husband,

Professor Henry Sidgwick; Frank Podmore and Dr Richard Dryson, my associates from the Fabian Society and psychical research colleagues of Professor Sidgwick; Mrs Tillis the psychic; Astraia; me; and the Sidgewick's neighbour Lady Agatha Sotheran.

***

"Your dear mother, your eternal guardian angel, is radiant with joy and pride, watching over you as she leans into the protective arms of your loving father," proclaimed the sonorous voice emanating from the vocal chords of mousy Valerie Tillis, our séance medium.

She was referring to me. To my parents.

Mrs Tillis's "spirit control" was a forceful 16th century French doctor named Phinuit, and minutes ago he had convinced Lady Sotheran, Nora's friend and neighbour, that he was in contact with her deceased husband. Lady Sotheran was delighted to converse with her late spouse again, even though the late Sir Lawrence Sotheran refused adamantly to bless her desire to remarry and in fact had gotten into quite a little argument with his widow about it. But I had found the spirit Phinuit less than impressive in his assessment of my own otherworldly relatives. For one thing, this French doctor did not appear to have any knowledge of either the French language or of medicine. For another thing, he had now assured me (also through Mrs Tillis's deepened voice) that my Papa—whom I admit the spirit apparently knew had been dead for just over one year—was standing arm-in-arm with my dear Mummy, warm celestial smiles shining on both of their faces as together they watched over me with parental pride and love.

Although I could not doubt my Mummy was my guardian angel, I also felt confident that my parents were not spending eternity in the same locale, she having been a sweet saint of a woman and he having terrorised the nation as the villainous Jack the Ripper. And even if God and Mummy had forgiven my father, I was confident Papa would not be watching over me with affection because the man would never have forgiven me for poisoning his tea. So I had good reason to doubt the veracity of Phinuit's claim. Which was unfortunate, because if he had been a legitimate all-seeing spirit we could have just asked him who had killed Lady Deborah Peacham, thus quickly solving our current detectivist murder investigation.

"What can you tell me about my dear long-lost brother Digbert?" Astraia asked breathlessly. To those of us holding hands around the table who did not know her very well, her question no doubt sounded sincere and excited. But I knew not to trust that yearning tone in her voice. I suspected there had never been a Digbert Holmes.

However, we were never to hear Phinuit's answer about the elusive Digbert, because Lady Sotheran, who had clung rigidly to Frank Podmore's right hand and Richard Dryson's left for all of this past hour, even during the argument with her deceased spouse, suddenly collapsed face-first to the table. The movement of her massive egret- and argus-plumed hat created a forceful breeze that snuffed out the candles when she fell, pitching us into darkness. Mr Podmore shrieked, an unexpected high-pitched sound that he quickly brought under control; then he ordered "Quick, turn up the lights!" in a manly voice, perhaps deeper than his usual (Mr Podmore has a reputation of authority to maintain, being a respected officer in both the Fabian Society and the Society for Psychical Research).

Astraia wrenched herself from my hand and from Professor Sidgwick's on her left, and when the first gas lamp ignited by the housekeeper finally cast its flickers by the door I could see my friend bending over Lady Sotheran's collapsed form. By the time the gas chandelier was fully illuminated above her, she had pushed Lady Sotheran back into her chair and was feeling for a pulse.

"Loosen her stays," Nora said. "Agatha always laces too tightly."

"Nora, really!" her husband exclaimed, no doubt embarrassed because ladies do not discuss corsetry in mixed company.

Astraia shook her head. "That would not help," she told her friend gently. She turned to Richard Dryson.

29

"I'm sorry, Dr Dryson. I know Lady Sotheran is a dear friend of yours—of all of you here. But I'm afraid she is dead."

"No!" Dr Dryson said in distress.

"Oh dear!" Mrs Tillis said, somewhat hysterically, Phinuit having apparently floated back into the ether.

"How?" Nora asked, her voice shaking. Tears streamed down her face.

"You'll want to call in the doctor," Astraia said, "but I believe the cause of her death to be digitalis poisoning. I suspected she was ingesting digitalis when I noticed at dinner that she kept tapping at her heart and sipping something she called her weight loss elixir from a little vial in her evening bag; I've known of others who misused the drug in order to lessen their hunger pangs. And I became convinced it had been a tincture of digitalis she had been consuming when she commented on seeing halos in the candlelight around Mrs Tillis's head, which is often a symptom of digitalis toxicity." She frowned, and I realised she was questioning whether or not she should have said something during dinner to halt Lady Sotheran's intake of the dangerous medication.

"Agatha has always been very sensitive to psychic vibrations," Dr Dryson insisted. "She could see the purity of Mrs Tillis's aura." He seemed unwilling to admit that the halos Astraia mentioned, that Lady Sotheran had rhapsodised over when Mrs Tillis had been doing her reading earlier, might have been the sordid symptoms of a drug overdose and not a spiritual reflexion of the medium's ties to the angelic realms. When we had arrived earlier today, Nora had told Astraia and me that Dr Dryson considered Mrs Tillis to be his particular friend, even though he would escort Nora's neighbour Agatha Sotheran to the séance tonight, as he often accompanied her to events when he visited his friend Professor Sidgwick.

"That may be," Astraia said noncommittally. "As I said, you should call in the doctor."

Professor Sidgwick hurried through the door to comply with Astraia's directive, and I stood. "I think we should all leave this room until the doctor arrives," I said.

"Why?" Astraia said. She had her magnifying glass in her hand, examining the table and around Lady Sotheran's chair for clues in case she had missed something.

"Because it is not seemly for us to continue our séance party with an actual dead person in the room," I said. "The only dead people allowed at a séance are those of the spirit variety, I believe." I did not intend to elucidate, but the current aura in the room made it clear the late Agatha Sotheran had released her bowels. There was also an unpleasant stain on the table from regurgitant; the deceased lady's face and bodice were besmirched with remnants of half-digested dinner. The psychic vibrations had been replaced by odiferous ones.

"Yes," Mrs Tillis, the medium, said in distress, standing with shaking limbs. "Let us go. I think I'm going to be sick." She grabbed at Dr Dryson's arm and then suddenly, violently, vomited on him.

"Oh God," Nora said. Visitors retching on one another are a hostess's second-worst nightmare, the worst of course being visitors who drop dead in the middle of a party. This was indeed a poor night for the good lady. She hurried to a sideboard and grabbed some napkins and table runners from the linen drawer. Handing some to the sopping Dr Dryson and to Frank Podmore, who had hurried over to help his friend, she wiped Mrs Tillis's face and helped her out of the room, calling to her housekeeper for assistance as she strained under the weight of the much taller Valerie Tillis. Dr Dryson and Frank Podmore followed after them, wiping regurgitant from their persons, and very soon Astraia and I were the only people left in the room besides the late Lady Sotheran.

Chapter Three

I was shaking a bit. Although I had seen a great deal of death in recent months since I'd met Astraia and become involved in her detectivist endeavours, I was still not quite inured to it. And Lady Sotheran had seemed a pleasant-enough woman, with much to live for. I was unlikely to start crying like the others, but I was sorry that she had died. Astraia was not unmoved either; her hands were shaking as well, something I could see clearly since she was running them over the dead lady's body.

"What are you looking for?" I asked. "I thought you solved this already. You said it was digitalis poisoning."

"And so I believe it to be. But I'm not so arrogant as to think I'm never wrong, unlike some members of my family. I just want to check everything to be sure. Here, help me go over Lady Sotheran's clothing."

I started feeling the poor dead woman's torso just as Astraia was doing. "What are we looking for?"

"A cut in the material, perhaps; maybe some blood. I don't want to say it's digitalis poisoning and then have the doctor inform us she was stabbed."

I could not argue with this, and even felt annoyed with myself that I hadn't thought of such a possibility given my own recent stabbing experience. I joined Astraia in running fingers carefully over Lady Sotheran's back. Soon we both felt comfortable that no outside trauma had killed her.

Astraia opened the dead woman's evening bag and took out a small blue vial. She held it in her hand, considering it.

"Aren't you going to sniff it, or taste it?" I asked. That was how people identified poisons in all the books I read.

"I know the symptoms of digitalis poisoning but I have no idea what digitalis smells like," Astraia admitted. "Or what it tastes like."

"Might this be your opportunity to learn?"

"I suppose," she said morosely. She opened the stopper, sniffed, then touched a fingertip to a drop at the lid. She nodded, then handed it to me. "Your turn," she said. "You should know too, probably."

I sighed, then lifted the vial to my nose. It smelled fairly innocuous; I doubted I would ever recognise it, should I smell it again. I touched the wet lid, then brought my finger to my lips to taste.

"What are you doing, you foolish woman?" a man yelled. I almost dropped the vial in my surprise, but

Astraia grabbed at it and safely stoppered it back as a gentleman of venerable years hobbled over to us.

"Give me that," he said, grabbing the vial from her. "What do you think you're doing, trying to kill yourself with that poison?"

Professor Sidgwick hurried into the room. "Miss Holmes, Miss Barquist, this is Dr Donald MacDougal, our neighbourhood physician," he said. "Donald, let me present Miss Astraia Holmes and Miss Madeleine Barquist, friends of my wife."

The old gentleman shrugged. "Fine, fine, now leave me alone to do my job." He gently pulled out two foot-long hatpins to remove the enormous hat from Lady Sotheran's head, something I confess to my shame had not occurred to Astraia or me to do. He caressed the lady's hair, and I realised he must have known her, may have even been her own family physician. He sighed. "Poor lassie. Didn't I tell you to be careful with it?" He took a handkerchief from his pocket and carefully wiped expellant from the corpse's face.

Astraia pulled at me. "Let's go, Maddie," she said. "There's nothing more for us to do here."

We closed the door behind us, and after a few minutes to visit the water closet (what a luxury indoor plumbing is!) we traversed the stairs to find our hostess. We found her tending to Mrs Tillis, in a second-floor bedroom I noticed was not quite as nice as the room down the hall assigned to Astraia and me. I'd had the sense from the beginning that although Nora was an enthusiast about psychical research, she was a sceptic about mediums. She was very polite to Mrs Tillis—and certainly very kind to her as well, especially now—but not perhaps as friendly as she was with Astraia and me. Of course, she had known Astraia for years.

Nora had assisted Mrs Tillis in removing her flowy green medium's outfit and was now buttoning her into her nightdress with the assistance of a maid. "How is she doing, Nora?" Astraia asked, politely, though it was as clear as the tears running down the medium's face and the mucous streaming from her nose that the poor woman was experiencing disquietude.

"I have asked Mrs Clark to bring up some tea and a few of the cakes that Mrs Tillis so enjoyed this afternoon," Nora said, helping the woman into bed. "I'll stay with her for a while, and then if you're still awake I'll stop to confer with you two in your room before I seek my own bed for the night. Is the physician here?"

"Yes he is," I said. "Would you like him to visit Mrs Tillis before he leaves?"

"Perhaps that would be best," Nora said. "Thank you."

Leaving, we bumped into Richard Dryson, pacing outside the medium's room, wringing his hands.

"How is she?" he asked apprehensively. "She's such a delicate lady, and she's had a terrible shock."

Ignoring the remnant of delicate lady vomit still stuck in his sparse grey side-whiskers even though he had changed his clothes, I assured him that Mrs Tillis was fine but might benefit from the attention of a physician. Just then Mrs Clark, the housekeeper, entered the hall, lugging a heavy tray set with an attractive tea service and two cups. I guiltily considered sending her back downstairs to get the doctor, since with my foot casted I had trouble going up and down stairs plus my wound from the recent stabbing was paining me after a long day of almost-constant movement, but Astraia spoke up.

"Are you a physician, Dr Dryson?" she asked.

"No, I have a doctor of law degree," he said.

"That won't help," she said, and peremptorily sent the anxious man downstairs to retrieve Dr MacDougal while Mrs Clark carried the soothing brew into the medium's boudoir. "You must rest, Maddie," she ordered me, and lead the way to our room.

I did not argue; I had made the trek up and down two flights of stairs in this house today at least a half-dozen times, and before that the trip from the Leman Street railway station to the King's Cross railway station to meet Astraia this morning had been its own struggle, what with one hand holding tightly to my cane while I also had to carry my portmanteau to make the train changes. And then once in Cambridge there'd been more walking while we arranged our transport to Professor and Mrs Sidgwick's home at Newnham College. Twice I had felt blood running down the skin of my side and had to excuse myself to rewrap my bandages. I felt wrung out and glad to seek my bed, even if only to rest up for a while until Nora could join us.

Astraia was writing notes at the desk and I preparing for bed when Nora appeared, followed by the housekeeper Mrs Clark carrying another heavy tray. I felt bad for all the extra work we were making for the poor woman, and hoped she had someone to assist her in cleaning up the vomit and death stains mess downstairs.

"I hope you two are not temperance suffragists," Nora said. "I find a nice hot toddy the perfect antidote to a troubled evening." She pointed to a variety of bottles on the tray.

"We concur," Astraia told her friend. "But if Dr MacDougal is still around, do you think he could look at Maddie's side? She was stabbed a couple of days ago by a villain on the street, and I'm wondering if she should get a suture or two."

Nora looked at me in horror. I smiled weakly in agreement, pointing to the bloody bandage I had just removed, and she rushed out of the room. A few minutes later I was being scolded, cleaned, drained, and sutured, a privacy screen separating Dr MacDougal and me from Astraia and Nora who spent the time during my examination and surgical procedure preparing an ambrosial beverage from the hot brandy, spices, and sugar water Mrs Clark had delivered to our room.

Soon I rested in the soft blankets of my warm bed, happily sipping at the fiery, sweet concoction as Astraia and Nora conversed, trying not to wince at the pain from the sutures and hoping the numbness of alcohol would overwhelm me soon. Temperance suffragists were idiots.

"We are sorry for the death of your friend Agatha tonight," Astraia said to Nora, and I think she truly meant it.

Nora nodded. "Everyone warned her she was flirting with death," she said. "But ever since Sir Lawrence died she has been determined to lose weight and find another husband. I think she was hoping Richard Dryson might be the one. He spent time with her whenever he was in Cambridge, and paid quite a bit of attention to her yesterday before Mrs Tillis arrived. Dr MacDougal should not have procured the digitalis for her. Her heart was not that bad. But she was persistent in her goal, and I suppose he felt she would do better consuming the drug under his direction." She sighed, then abruptly changed the subject to the reason why Astraia and I were here. "In the morning I'll give you letters of introduction to suffragist friends of mine in London," she said. "Florence Balgarnie, certainly. Florence is the secretary of the Central Committee of the National Society for Women's Suffrage and she knows everyone. Some suffragists are willing to compromise—for example, some would accept the proposal to give the vote to unmarried women while the franchise remains denied to married ones. Florence refuses any such concessions, which I find very admirable. On the other hand, she is a founding member of the British Women's Temperance Association, so don't ask her out to the pub."

"Maddie and I can teetotal with the best of them," Astraia assured her. I quietly snorted my disagreement.

"Another woman I think you should meet is Isabella Somerset, Lady Henry. She's another temperance feminist, I'm afraid—in fact, she focuses her attention more on the cause of outlawing alcohol than she does on getting women the vote. But she was a very good friend of Margaret Lucas, the president of the British Women's Temperance Union who has just died, sadly—and Margaret knew every reformer in the country. Isabella would make a good ally for you."

"Was Lady Deborah Peacham a temperance feminist?" Astraia asked.

"Yes, she was," said Nora. "She was also one of those imperialist-minded women who want British women to get the franchise so that we can use our votes to work toward civilising the rest of the world in our image. She was vociferously opposed to Irish and Scottish home rule, and was one of the drivers behind the split that occurred in the Central Committee of the National Society for Women's Suffrage a few years ago, when the women who support home rule and oppose imperialism broke off and started their own suffrage group."

"Interesting," Astraia said noncommittally. I wasn't sure how my friend felt about these issues, or if she had any opinion on the matter at all—other than her revulsion over the opium trade, I'd seldom seen her evince much interest in international topics. For myself, I did not think I would have cared much for Lady Deborah.

"And to give you a different perspective, I'll also write you a letter for Rebecca Ravenwood Thornapple. I believe she and Lady Deborah were not close—quite the contrary, I imagine—but certainly they would have known each other. Rebecca opposes temperance and imperialism and supports home rule. She's rather wild, but I like her. And she's an officer in the Central National Society for Women's Suffrage, the anti-temperance group that broke off from the Central Committee of the National Society for Women's Suffrage, so she'll be able to introduce you to suffragists you might not meet through Florence or Isabella. I believe the two groups do still occasionally work together on strategies to secure the franchise."

They spoke for a while about these three women, and then moved on to discuss a variety of other feminist issues. Nora was completing a years-long study called *Health Statistics of Women Students of Cambridge and Oxford and of their Sisters* in response to concerns expressed in the public press that too much study would sap women's physique, thus diminishing the nation's birth prolificacy. Her study used statistics garnered from past students on their health, exercise, marriage, and children to determine the distribution of change in the health of women students pre- and post-college, and compared their health with their non-educated sisters to give an indication what their health might have been had they not attained higher levels of learning. Her research showed that education provided no detrimental impact to women's health. Astraia was glad to learn the research project would soon be published. She had been happy to complete the lengthy schedule, identifying her health since graduation as "good to excellent" and much better than it had been before she ever entered Newnham.

"I am sorry I do not have a younger sister for you to include in your study for comparison," Astraia said.

Nora dismissed this concern and they spoke of school days for a while. I was just drifting off to sleep when Nora questioned me on my thoughts regarding this evening's events.

"What did you think of Valerie Tillis, Maddie?" she asked.

"She seemed a nice enough woman," I said guardedly. Actually, Mrs Tillis had struck me as a dull and mousy nincompoop, one of those tall women who are embarrassed about their height and presence and stoop to make themselves seem smaller and more inconsequential. Of course, I'm a very tall woman myself and tend to be rather judgemental toward others on this subject.

"No, I meant—what about her skills as a medium? Did you believe she had contacted your parents through her spirit guide, as she indicated?"

"Oh that. No. Not at all. She is a complete fraud."

Nora nodded. "I was afraid of that. My husband Henry is one of the founders of the Society for Psychical Research and we've worked very hard to shine a serious academic light on the study of spiritualism—but most mediums we've encountered have been charlatans, I'm afraid. I am sorry that Mrs Tillis appears to be one of those—we'd heard such good things about her from the Americans. And certainly Richard Dryson holds her in the very highest regard. They've been corresponding for years, you know."

I mentioned this correspondence to Astraia after Nora left us to check on the vomiting charlatan again.

"I wonder what Mr Tillis thinks of that," I said.

"Mrs Tillis is a widow," Astraia said, yawning as she prepared for bed.

"How do you know?"

"By the mourning ring she has on her finger. Widows often wear them, to let gentlemen know they're eligible." She extinguished the lamps, and we were both soon asleep.

***

"Maddie, wake up! You'll never guess what happened!"

I opened one eye, unenthusiastic. I don't often get a chance to sleep late, and had been enjoying the luxury. The moment I woke, my various injuries emitted jabs of pain. "What?" I groused.

"Mrs Tillis and Dr Dryson have got engaged!" Astraia said. Her red curls bounced around her little head in a halo as she quivered in glee. I was reminded of a child on Christmas morning. Her violet dress glowed, which seemed odd. Then I realised the sun was shining brightly on her through the window glass, creating an aura that was hard to witness after a night of pain and hot toddies. I squeezed my eyes shut at the piercing glare.

"You can't be serious," I muttered, pushing myself up with difficulty, my hand covering my eyes. "They only just met—didn't she just arrive from America two days ago?"

"Yes, but they've been writing letters to each other for a long time, apparently. And of course, their spirits have entwined repeatedly during their past lives throughout eternity. They've been telling us all about it. Get up—it's hilarious, and you don't want to miss it. Mrs Tillis is still a little upset with Dr Dryson from when he was Henry the Eighth and she was Anne Boleyn, but she's decided to marry him again anyway. You must ask her to tell you about the lifetime when she was Cleopatra and he was Mark Antony. Poor Frank Podmore's eyes almost popped out from the lurid details."

We caught the 1:20 from Cambridge Station back to London that afternoon. Frank Podmore travelled back with us, alone since Dr Dryson and his charlatan medium fiancé had decided to stay on in Cambridge for a few more days; and after watching me almost fall a couple of times when my casted foot slipped on icy ground Mr Podmore graciously assisted me with my portmanteau, which put me in enough charity with him that all the way back to London I listened patiently to his stories about the many spiritualistic successes celebrated by the Society for Psychical Research. Nora had given Astraia the three letters she'd promised so my friend considered our trip to have been worthwhile. I did my duty listening to Mr Podmore's stories while she took the opportunity to nap on the train.

***

As he'd done so often over these last couple of months, John, Astraia's coachman, retrieved me from the police stables the following afternoon so that Astraia and I could begin our investigation of the suffragists. I had spent the morning showing my Susie how to make clay poultices for horses to treat hoof abscesses and reduce swelling in their legs. Now she was practicing her poultice application skills on the limbs of every animal in the stable, even the dog Old Vic, who would have bitten me if I'd tried any such thing but always seemed very tolerant of any treatment Susie used on him.

"Can I show Ruven how to do this too?" she asked me.

Susie had done a good job keeping the veterinary stable running during my absence in Cambridge, and I felt comfortable leaving things in her hands again today. I was also very glad she had found a friend who could help her.

"Of course," I said. I was about to hand her a few pennies so that she and Ruven could get lunch from a costermonger but at the last minute I handed her a shilling as well, in case Astraia invited me over to her house and I didn't return to the precinct by dinner time. "I'll come back as soon as I can," I said, perhaps untruthfully. I appreciated my work as a police veterinarian, but admitted to myself that I much preferred my detectivist adventures with Astraia.

Since Florence Balgarnie was the secretary of the Central Committee of the National Society for Women's Suffrage and the most likely of Nora's three friends to have been close to Lady Deborah, we decided to visit her first, at her home on Parliament Street.

Miss Balgarnie was home, luckily—apparently she was usually travelling, giving public lectures throughout the nation on everything from suffrage to temperance to the rights of women to work in the trades and professions to equal pay for women to the historic impact of women like Joan of Arc and the

Brontë sisters to the rights of prostitutes to not be locked up for having contagious diseases while their male clients remained free. She was home now both to celebrate and to mourn: she had campaigned hard for Miss Jane Cobden and Lady Sandhurst, who had each won election to the London county council recently despite being themselves unable to vote, and had attended a (non-alcoholic) congratulatory party for these two new officials last night; and she was also home to mourn the death of one of her mentors in the temperance movement, Mrs Margaret Bright Lucas, who had died just days before.

She told us all of this, and more, in the first five minutes of our meeting her and giving her our letter of introduction from Nora. In my entire life, I have never met a more energetic human being. It was as if one day God had enough life force for three people but only one body to put it all in, and so He made Florence Balgarnie.

"Please, join me for tea," she said, leading us into her sitting room. We had to move some books around to find a place to sit, but soon we were cosy, enjoying tea and biscuits together while Florence (we quickly adopted first names) told us about her own friendship with Nora Sidgwick who, like Florence, felt that men and women should have equal rights to the franchise whether or not they were married.

She slowed down enough to eat (Florence had a sweet-tooth) which gave Astraia and me an opportunity to share a little about ourselves. Florence was thrilled to learn that I worked at a police station, and urged me to become more involved with the women prisoners in the gaol. "There is a desperate need for police matrons in British courts and police stations," she said, and then told us a few horrific stories about incidents in which innocent women were arrested for prostitution in error, gaoled overnight under the supervision of male warders, and subjected to the grossest indecencies.

I confessed that I had never thought about all the implications to the fact that women prisoners did not have the assistance of someone of their own sex when they were imprisoned. I had often been asked to serve as police searcher when women were arrested and no police officer's wife or daughter was available to perform that duty, but after I had determined whether or not they had any weapons or drugs or alcohol on their person I returned to my stable and never thought about their inconveniences afterwards. I promised to be more alert to their situation in the future.

Astraia and I had decided on the train to not let anyone but Nora know that we were investigating the death of Lady Deborah. Our strategy would be to infiltrate the suffrage groups and just see what we could learn. This proved an easy approach with Florence who, as I've mentioned, loved to talk, including gossip about her friends. Though to be fair to her, we had been recommended to her by her ally Nora Sidgwick; I presume she would not have been so open with most strangers off the street.

She told us about a joint meeting to be held the following evening between the Central Committee of the National Society for Women's Suffrage and the Central National Society for Women's Suffrage, and invited us to attend as her guest. Both groups had participated in the recent rush on the House of Commons and were planning a similar event soon. Astraia mentioned that she had letters of introduction from Nora to Lady Henry Somerset and Rebecca Ravenwood Thornapple, and Florence said that the joint meeting would actually be held at one of the homes of Lady Isabella Somerset. She expected that Rebecca Ravenwood Thornapple would probably be there as well.

"Isabella and I discussed cancelling the meeting due to the death of Margaret Lucas; certainly everyone will be very forlorn—but we agreed that Margaret would want us to continue on. It was difficult enough anyway to get both suffrage groups back working together. We don't want to lose that momentum."

"Did you know the suffragist who died a few weeks ago, Lady Deborah Peacham?" Astraia asked.

"Lady Deborah, yes. I say 'Lady Deborah', because even her very closest friends used her title. She was 'Debbie' to no one. You might have been her dearest friend for twenty years; when addressing her you'd still say "My Lady." She was that kind of person. She was a strong force in both the temperance and suffrage movements, and very influential among the people who matter, because she was one of the daughters of the Duke of Belford. Her husband, Sir Peter, was knighted because of something he did in India."

"He was an army man?"

"I believe so. Or perhaps a merchant. I'm not really sure. I understand he inherited money. He's a notorious libertine and profligate, if you want the truth of it."

"Do you think he killed her?"

"No doubt about it, in my mind. I'm sure she found him a great embarrassment, with all of his affairs and wildness. Not that she ever discussed him with anyone, of course."

"Will she be badly missed?" Astraia asked.

"Oh, I should say so," Florence said. "She was a very determined woman, very focused in her goals. The temperance movement has lost years of momentum with the deaths of Margaret Bright Lucas and Lady Deborah Peacham. I am not sure who will take up their fallen mantles, who can lead us in their stead to victory against the pernicious disease of drunkenness. Isabella, perhaps. Yes, thank God for Isabella Somerset. She does not have quite the social influence of Lady Deborah, but she has influence enough—and she's far more tolerable to work with, much more likeable. People listen to her."

"We look forward to meeting her," I said.

"You said Lady Deborah wasn't as likeable—did she have many enemies?" Astraia asked innocently.

"I don't know if she had actual enemies," Florence said. "But she was very disdainful and even vengeful of people who held opinions different from her own. Even me—I was careful to never speak to her about my views on the unfairness of the way prostitutes are treated by the courts, for example, because Lady Deborah was also involved in the social purity movement. If I'd ever suggested to her that ending prostitution by focusing on the prostitutes instead of the men was impossible, and that just eliminating prostitution would not end all mistreatment of women, she would have shunned me ever after and maybe even railed against me in public. Which would have impeded my temperance and suffrage work."

She began to give us the details about the suffrage meeting a few nights hence, so the subject of Lady Deborah seemed to be over until Astraia found a way to bring her up again as we were leaving.

Florence's housekeeper—who seemed, by the familiarity between the two, to be an old family retainer—was assisting us with our coats while Florence stood by.

"Are you also looking forward to having the vote, Mrs Graven?" Astraia asked playfully (an approach which never appeared authentic to me, although strangers who didn't know her as an essentially dour person did not seem to ever question it).

Florence patted the older lady on the shoulder. "Of course she is," she said heartily, answering for her housekeeper. Mrs Graven just smiled at us and moved away to clean up the tea things in the sitting room.

"You can tell so much about a person by how they treat their servants," Astraia said. Astraia treated her own servants like members of the family—relatives whom she loathed but was forced to house against her will.

"Mrs Graven helped raise me," Florence admitted. "I don't know what I would do without her."

"Did Lady Deborah have that type of congenial relationship with her servants?"

Florence laughed. "Lady Deborah? Lady Deborah was adamant about the separation between the classes. If she could have identified a way to get the vote for herself and her society but keep the franchise out of the hands of lower-class women, she would have done so. I'm confident that any of her maids who ever dared to try to vote would have lost their jobs for it."

As we rode away in Astraia's carriage, she sighed. "That woman is exhausting," she said.

"I liked her," I said.

"Oh, I like her too," Astraia said. "But I've never met such a dedicated do-gooder. It quite wore me out. Shall we cross her off our list?"

"Our list?"

"Of suspects for the murder of Lady Deborah."

I laughed. "Yes, we should definitely cross her off that list," I said. "But I was a little unnerved by all the temperance talk. Will we need to shift our focus to people in the temperance movement, instead of suffragists? That sounds very dull."

"It sounds like they're all part of the same group," Astraia said. "Like the Fabians and the spiritualists."

"That's not fair," I complained. "I'm a Fabian but I'm not a member of the Society for Psychical Research."

She patted my hand. "I know, Maddie. And I'm sure there are sensible suffragists too. Like Nora. And that Rebecca Ravenwood Thornapple person doesn't sound like a temperance looney."

I noticed her coachman John seemed to be going in the wrong direction to drop me off at home. "Do we have another errand to run?" I asked. Truthfully, I hoped she was going to suggest we go to her home for evening tea. Astraia's companion Letty always conjured a very satisfying meal.

"We need to drive over to Baker Street," my friend said. "Apparently Sherlie has something he wants to say to you."

Chapter Four

Let me be clear: I did not hold Mr Sherlock Holmes in aversion. And he treated me as well as he ever treated anyone and better than most, so I presume he did not dislike me either. But do not infer from this that I felt any inclination toward spending time with the great detective. He knew my deepest, darkest secrets—details about my father and our relationship that I had not even confessed to his sister, my dearest friend. I could never feel comfortable in his presence.

Not that anyone ever felt truly comfortable in his presence, of course. Even Astraia spent as little time around him as possible, and she held actual affection for the man.

"What does he want to speak with me about?" I asked warily.

"I have no idea. John received a note from him this morning. I'm sure it won't take long—you'll be home in plenty of time for your supper," she said, thus crushing any hope for one of Letty's teas tonight.

In truth, meetings with Mr Holmes never took long. He was not a gregarious man. He always got right down to business, permitting few of the normal courtesies.

"Zhu Wei's spies are watching you, Miss Barquist," was the first thing he spoke when we entered his rooms.

"Good afternoon to you too, Sherlie," Astraia said. "Do you have any tea?"

She only asked for tea because she could see there was none prepared. She was not actually hungry, after our time enjoying Florence's ample hospitality.

"I can ask Mrs Hudson to bring something up," he said.

"Don't bother," his sister replied. "We don't want to put you to any trouble."

"Since when?" he said, but did not take his sister's bait. We would not be proffered tea here again today, nor any other social nicety.

Astraia sat down without being offered a chair. I followed her example.

"How do you know Zhu Wei is still interested in Maddie?" Astraia asked. "Surely he realises that he will never be given the Ya Zi weapons." Zhu Wei was a villain, a criminal leader in Limehouse whom we had encountered in our last case. He demanded possession of some items we had turned over to the British government via Astraia's brother Mycroft. The Ya Zi weapons belonged to protectors of the Chinese emperor, and their possession would have given Zhu

Wei a great deal of cachet in his community. One of the men I'd killed recently was a man I had clubbed with a mallet after discovering he'd tortured the mongrel Old Vic. My unfortunate victim had been Zhu Wei's cousin. Or perhaps his brother. The relationship was not clear.

"I'm certain he knows that the Ya Zi accouterments are forever beyond his reach," Mr Holmes said. "There is no indication he intends to follow up on his threats toward you, Astraia. But according to my sources he continues to keep a tab on Miss Barquist."

"Why?" I asked.

"Because you can identify him, Maddie," Astraia said. "You may even be the only non-Chinese person who knows what he looks like."

I knew what he looked like because he and a few of his henchmen had confronted me in my bedroom one night, tendering threats. I could certainly identify him to the authorities. Unfortunately I have a very good memory for faces.

But I did not understand why Mr Holmes had brought us here to tell me this. I already knew Zhu Wei was watching me—he had informed me himself that he would be doing so, to frighten me into delivering the ancient weaponry to him. His spy, a child named Chan, was a perennial fixture in the neighbourhood immediately surrounding the police stable where I lived and worked. In fact, I sometimes had food or tea sent out to Chan; and once, when it was very cold, took him a blanket. I had begun to think of the boy as one of my charges, almost.

Astraia guessed what I was thinking. "I imagine Chan is not the only one watching you now," she said. "Is that correct, Sherlie?"

"That does appear to be the case," he replied. "I understand you were stabbed by a thief on the street a few days ago, Miss Barquist? Apparently after that, Zhu Wei assigned at least two other people to spy on you. Both are foreigners, though not from the far east. So you are incorrect in your assumption that Miss Barquist is the only non-Chinese person who knows what he looks like, Astraia. But she is probably the only non-villain who might identify him. Have you noticed any suspicious foreign sailors around the stables recently, Miss Barquist?"

I shook my head. The Whitechapel neighbourhood was always full of foreign sailors. I never paid attention to any of them.

"The police force has been alerted to the situation," Mr Holmes said. This I did not doubt. And of course, as usual, none of my police colleagues had chosen to mention this newest threat to me. "Fortuitously, I had already decided to send a bodyguard to stay with you in the stables."

Astraia and I stared at him, then made the same expostulation at the same time.

"What?!"

"A bodyguard," he repeated.

"She works at a police station," Astraia said. "She doesn't need a bodyguard."

"You may recall that only a month ago she was thrice physically attacked, and gravely disturbed an additional time, and each of those incidents occurred on the police premises," he said. "The police do not seem to be doing a very good job of protecting her."

"I don't think the police are going to want a bodyguard around," I said. "They may find it insulting." This unquestionably understated what their response would be.

"Maddie doesn't need a bodyguard anyway," Astraia said. "She's perfectly capable of protecting herself. Which she did in each of those instances."

I smiled at my friend. It was such a change in my life to have someone around who had faith in my capabilities.

"Unless she tells them why he's there, the police will not realise Rutherford is a bodyguard," Mr Holmes said. "They will just think he is another local ragamuffin who has decided to hang around the horses."

I was confused, but Astraia figured it out straight away. "This is one of your Baker Street irregulars, isn't it? You're foisting one of your street boys on Maddie."

"Rutherford is a very intelligent lad," Mr Holmes said. "He has a promising future as an intelligence officer. I'm sure he will be of great assistance to Miss

Barquist. And being around the police will be educational for him."

"What if Maddie doesn't want another kid to take care of?" Astraia asked. "She already has Susie. And I need her to help me."

Her brother and I both looked at her strangely. "You know what I mean," she said crossly.

"I know you rely on her," Mr Holmes said. "I am hoping that Rutherford will become someone upon whom she can rely."

He turned his penetrating eye on me. "I'm sure you will do the right thing, Miss Barquist, and will accept Rutherford as your bodyguard."

This was as close as he was ever likely to get to threatening me with exposure. I took it seriously. "Do I have to take him everywhere with me?" I asked.

"Of course not," he said. "He doesn't need to be with you when John is with you both, or when you're with DI Rankin, for example. But when you're on your own, I would feel better knowing that Rutherford is watching your back."

"When do you propose that this should start?" Astraia asked. She was very annoyed, not least because her brother had mentioned DI Rankin, an old family friend who'd been spying on her for most of her life. No doubt she assumed Rutherford had been given instructions to spy on her as well. Once during our last case she had slipped away for a few days without anyone knowing where she'd gone, including me. Had

Rutherford been spying on us then, this might have been more difficult to accomplish.

"It has already started," her brother said. "I sent Rutherford over to the precinct a week ago, even before I learned that Zhu Wei had increased the number of agents he has watching Miss Barquist. Rutherford has spent time visiting the stables, getting to know Susie and the stableboys, as well as some of the officers. He has even met Miss Barquist already. No one will be surprised when she takes him on as another assistant."

Ruven. It could only be Ruven. Ruven was Sherlock Holmes's Rutherford.

Astraia waited for me to object, but of course I wouldn't. Sherlock Holmes knew too much about me. A slight smile played on his lips. Damn him.

"Anything else you need to tell me?" I asked him.

"You've been gallivanting around too much on your broken foot," he said. "I think you should rest it for a while, unless you want me to send the doctor back to see to you again."

"I understand," I snapped. Per his insistence, I had rested my foot for over two weeks after the last case, but I had certainly been on my feet a great deal in recent days. "Anything else?" I fully expected him to begin berating me over letting myself get stabbed. He was determined that if his sister was going to gallivant around the city investigating crimes, I was going to accompany her.

"No," he said. "That is all."

We left, both silent until we got back into the carriage and John started the horses heading down the road back toward Whitechapel and the Leman Street station of the Metropolitan Police.

"Why did you let him do that to you, Maddie?" my friend asked finally. "I have to let him boss me around because he controls my financial affairs. But you don't owe him anything."

"If I had told him no, do you think that would have been the end of it?" I asked.

She sighed. "Of course not. You're right—if you had refused this Rutherford kid, he would have been ordered to sneak around watching us anyway. At least this way we'll be able to observe what he's up to." She patted my shoulder. "That was a good idea, Maddie. You've really learned how to manage things with my brother."

I smiled wanly. The truth was, her brother knew very well how to manage me. For example: that intrusive comment about my foot. Sherlock Holmes was concerned that I would damage myself permanently and become unable to accompany his delicate-seeming sister on her adventures, thus putting him in the untenable position of having to find someone to replace me as her confidante now that she was committed to her new career as a detective. I would do as he instructed and rest my foot for the next few days. And allow my sutures to heal.

John stopped off at a costermonger so that I could procure a few comestibles before going home. Thus it was that Susie and I were sitting down to a nice tea of boiled corned beef and turnips when Rutherford the bodyguard came by that evening to formally ask me for a job.

He knocked before he came in, which I approved of, and straight away took off his cap in respect when he saw me, which felt disingenuous.

"Ruven!" Susie said, jumping out of her chair and running over to greet him. "I'm so glad you could join us tonight! I haven't had a chance to ask Miss Maddie yet though."

"Ask me what?" I said.

"I was wondering if you might need another person to help you here with the horses, Miss," the boy said diffidently. "I would work ever so hard."

I tried not to frown as I looked at him. I did not want to distress Susie. "Ruven is an unusual name," I commented.

"My real name is Rutherford, miss," he said. "But my friends call me Ruven."

I nodded, giving in to the inevitable. "Would you like to join us for dinner, Rutherford?"

"I would like that very much, Miss," he said, almost shyly. Very disingenuous, I thought.

At my prodding he washed his hands at the pump and came over to join us at table. I set a plate of food and a cup of tea in front of him, which he quickly scoffed up. Then I began my interrogation. "Susie says she taught you poultice-making today," I remarked.

"He's as good as I am now, Miss Maddie," Susie said. I smiled. Susie had learned how to make simple poultices less than twelve hours ago.

"I saw Georgina in the middle box when I came in," I said. "She no doubt has a sprained fetlock; that's what usually lames her. You can both demonstrate your poultice skills on her after we've eaten. Have you ever worked with animals before, Rutherford?"

"My friend John is a coachman," he said. "He lets me groom his horse sometimes."

Now, there was no reason for me to assume that Astraia's coachman John was Rutherford's friend; most coachmen are called 'John', after all. But Astraia's coachman spied on her for Sherlock Holmes. I felt confident this would be the same man.

"So you'll let Ruven work here with us, Miss Maddie?" Susie squealed. "He'd be such a big help to us."

"I'd be ever so grateful," the boy said solemnly as he finished his second helping of corned beef.

So disingenuous. As if I had a choice. "We'll see," I said. "I need to see how well you work with the animals, Rutherford."

"Old Vic adores him," Susie said. I had already noticed the obnoxious cur licking the boy's hand. And Juno, my traitorous cat, sat purring on his lap.

"I'd be happy just to keep the boxes clean and groom the animals and keep their water fresh," Rutherford said.

"We'll see," I said again. Normally I would have had to say no even if I'd desperately needed additional help, because I wouldn't have had the money in my budget to hire assistance. But just as Mycroft Holmes had ensured money was made available to support Susie, I knew Sherlock Holmes would make arrangements for Rutherford's wages. And I expected I would find additional money provided for myself each month to cover the cost of having an additional mouth to feed.

"Where do you expect to sleep?" I asked. "With the stableboys?" The regular horse stable was located near by to the veterinary stable.

"Couldn't I just sleep in here?" he asked. "In that corner by the stove, where Old Vic sleeps?"

Susie and I slept in the back room, where I used to do small animal surgeries before I moved in here to live full time in order to reduce the strain on my foot from constantly walking from home to work. Old Vic's bed was next to the stove, but in fact he usually slept with us. I suspected, however, that if Rutherford moved in Old Vic would be switching bed partners.

I shouldn't feel so betrayed, I thought. It's not as if I actually liked the wretched cur.

"Let's see how you do with Georgina," I said.

He did splendidly. Examining the mare's foot, I saw that in additional to the fetlock sprain she showed indication of incipient thrush. I instructed the two children on signs of thrush, and then taught them how to pick the horse's feet twice a day, and how to make a foot packing with clean water and borax. I did the first fetlock poultice and thrush treatment myself, then watched them repeat the regimen on the other three feet. Of course Georgina did not need a poultice or even the thrush treatment on all four feet, but it was good practise for the children and I think the horse liked the attention. Susie was good, but I could see that Rutherford might even be better. He was gentle and thorough. It occurred to me that one of these days I might see about getting him an apprenticeship with a farrier, because he showed a true talent with horse feet.

I told him that I'd give him a week's trial, and went through my pile of horse blankets to find the cleanest and least moth-eaten for him to use in making up his bed. Tomorrow I would send a message to Astraia's Letty to ask her to procure a pallet, a pillow, and some human blankets for him. I would also give him money to pick up some less threadbare clothes, as well as a pair of shoes. And a coat. It was winter, for God's sake. Everyone needed to wear shoes and a coat in the winter, even spies.

This reminded me of Chan, Zhu Wei's spy. "Susie, can you check to see if Chan is out there this evening?" I asked. "If he is, can you and Rutherford take him the leftover food, and make sure he has enough warm clothes on?"

"He's been gone the last few days," she said.

"I was gone," I said. "So he didn't need to be here. But I'm back now. He might be back too."

She went outside for just a minute, then returned to say "Yes Miss—that blue scarf of his is out there again." She loaded a plate with the last of the leftovers (more turnip than corned beef now, but Chan wouldn't complain), and as she and Rutherford left the stable I heard her trying to explain to my newest child spy the unusual relationship I had with a child from the Limehouse underworld.

While they were gone, I thought about the other spies Mr Holmes had said were watching me, the foreign sailors. Were they also out there tonight? I assumed Rutherford knew about them. He probably knew more about them than I did. I considered the fact that neither he nor I had told Susie what his real purpose was in being here. For the time being, I would continue to keep this secret. I did not want to worry her unduly. In fact, I probably should have never told her about Chan.

***

"The subservient demeanor of your boy bodyguard reminds me of someone," Astraia said the next night as we rode in her carriage to the home of Lady Isabella

Somerset to attend the joint meeting of the Central Committee of the National Society for Women's Suffrage and the Central National Society for Women's Suffrage.

"Uriah Heep," I said.

"That's the one."

"That's unfair," her housekeeper and companion Letty said. Letty almost never interrupted our conversation, and we both stared at her.

"Why do you say that, Letty?" I asked.

"The boy is dependent on you for his food and shelter, Miss Maddie," she said. "Of course he wants to please you."

"You're dependent on me for your food and shelter," Astraia pointed out. "I've never noticed you trying to please me."

Letty turned her head to look out the window, but I thought about what she had said. Maybe what I had been reproving as obsequiousness was just simple human desperation. I'd try to give the boy a fair chance to win me over.

The meeting tonight would take place at one of the London mansions of Lady Isabella Somerset, who had inherited the place and numerous others after the death of her father, Lord Somers. Astraia had learned that she preferred to be called Lady Isabella, as her father's daughter, not Lady Henry as her husband's wife—she was estranged from her husband, Lord Henry Somerset, due to his abusive behaviour. Society more or less shunned her because she was quite open about why she left her husband, which was very awkward for him—and he was of higher rank than she was, though she was much richer so the whole thing was a great scandal.

"The temperance issue appears to be more important to her than suffrage," Astraia said. "But Mycroft said she also seems to be interested in the Fabian Society, so you could talk with her about that."

"Fabians are socialists," I pointed out. "She's rich."

"So maybe you could convince her to give all her money away to the poor," Astraia said. "That might be entertaining." She pulled a folded paper out of her reticule. "Speaking of Fabians and entertainment, I received this letter from Nora today," she said, handing it to me.

I perused the short document. "I don't believe it!" I said. "Dr Dryson and Mrs Tillis can't have got married so soon! They only just met a few days ago. It takes longer than that to publish the banns!"

Astraia shrugged. "They don't need to publish banns if they're not married in an Anglican or a Roman Catholic Church. It sounds like they were married by a local registrar in Cambridge. Like any common atheist or Baptist."

"I think there's a Spiritualist church," I said. I'd heard mention of it among the Psychical Research people.

"There you are, then. They probably had a ceremony with a local Spiritualist priest or whatever such clergy are called. Held a séance to get blessings from their ancestors, perhaps. Nora says Valerie Tillis even wore the same green robe she wore when she performed the séance that night. Hopefully she washed the vomit off first. Nora says there was a photographer present, at Dr Dryson's insistence. I'd love to see the photographs."

"At least they got married," Letty sniffed. "That's more than either of you have done."

"Letty, are you well?" I asked. It was unheard of for her to be this contrary. Normally the most emotion she showed to Astraia's pronouncements was the occasional eye-roll.

"She's just annoyed because I didn't get her a birthday present," Astraia said.

"You've never gotten me a birthday present," Letty said. "Why should this year bother me in particular?"

"Letty, is today your birthday?" I asked in dismay. "I'm so sorry I didn't wish you many happy returns of the day."

"I did," Astraia said. "I said it first thing this morning."

"You didn't mean it," Letty said.

The carriage slowed and I hoped that meant we were nearing our destination so we could get out. Letty would not be accompanying us to the suffrage meeting, which would probably be a good thing given her current disposition.

"How do you know what I meant?" Astraia asked her companion.

"You've never meant a single nice thing you've ever said to me in your life," Letty said.

John stopped the horses in front of a large house on a fashionable street, and came around to assist us out. After I stepped out and got my cane situated I turned back to Letty and said, "Letty, I wish you many happy returns of the day. I hope you know I mean it."

"Of course I do, Miss Maddie," she said.

"Enjoy your birthday dinner," Astraia said sweetly to her, then added, thankfully under her breath, "I hope you choke on it."

"We won't be too long, Miss Astraia," John said. John was Letty's brother. I assumed he was taking his sister out for a celebratory meal.

Astraia waved him away and we walked to the door.

"What in the world is wrong with Letty?" I asked.

"She's going through the change of life," Astraia said. "Once in a while she becomes real tetchy about it. But now that she's reached fifty years of age she needs to get over it. I'm fed up to the eyeballs with her."

"Maybe she's sad that she never married. And maybe that she'll never have children," I said. Letty had always been good to me, and I was sorry that she was feeling sad on her birthday.

"Well, neither one of those things is my fault," Astraia said. "She needs to stop punishing me for her own missed opportunities."

The front door opened. A butler showed us to a drawing room where a maid took our wraps and hats and helped us to repair our hair, before a footman showed us to a reception room where several dozen women mingled together. Most of them wore mourning, and the tenor was much more subdued than would be normal with a group of ladies who all knew each other. Then I remembered that besides Lady Deborah's death almost a month ago there had also been the death this week of temperance leader Margaret B. Lucas. Many of these women no doubt felt bereft at the loss of two such important women.

Florence Balgarnie, dressed in black, left the group she was with to hurry over and welcome us as her guests.

"I'm so glad you could join us, Miss Holmes, Miss Barquist. Let me introduce you to our hostess, Lady Isabella."

"Astraia and Maddie, please, Miss Balgarnie."

"And I'm Florence," she reminded us. She took our hands and lead us to a group of ladies, stopping in front of a stately woman wearing a simply-cut dress in rich dark fabric. "Lady Isabella, these are Eleanor Sidgwick's friends that I mentioned earlier, Miss Astraia Holmes and Miss Madeleine Barquist."

Astraia took the letter of introduction from Nora and handed it to Lady Isabella. Lady Isabella glanced at it for a moment, put it into her bag for closer study later, and smiled at us. "I am so glad to welcome you both to this evening's meeting," she said. "Thank you for coming to my home. We usually meet in one of the temperance halls, but since this is a joint meeting and not everyone in the Central National Society for Women's Suffrage is a proponent of temperance, we felt it would be injudicious to our mutual effort to meet there."

"Is temperance the only issue that divides the two groups?" Astraia asked.

"Not at all," Lady Isabella said. "We in the Central Committee of the National Society for Women's Suffrage are Liberal Unionists. Those in the Central National Society for Women's Suffrage are members of the Women's Liberal Federation. So you see, we have very different ideals. But what unites us is our passion for suffrage, and I am determined that all other topics will remain forbidden tonight, lest we lose our focus."

"May we offer our condolences on the recent deaths of your friends Lady Deborah Peacham and Mrs. Margaret Bright Lucas?" Astraia asked. "They were both warriors in the fight for temperance, and we are very sorry we never had the opportunity to meet either one."

When Astraia wanted to sound sincere no one could top her. Lady Isabella's eyes filled with tears.

"Thank you, my dear," she said. "I will miss them both, very much."

I was taken aback that Astraia broached the subject of Lady Isabella's two late friends; my Mummy had always taught me to not allude to another's sorrow unless they brought up the subject first. But Lady Isabella seemed to not be offended by Astraia's forwardness.

"I hope someday you will feel open to sharing your memories about them with us," Astraia said.

Lady Isabella actually gave us a bright smile. "I would love to do so," she said. "Please send me a note and we can make arrangements to visit soon."

She left us to greet other guests, and Florence reclaimed our arms. "Isn't she wonderful?" she gushed.

"Indeed," Astraia said. "Is Rebecca Ravenwood Thornapple here as well? We also have a letter of introduction to her."

Florence looked around. "Yes she is," she said, in a flat tone. I glanced over in the direction she was looking and saw a slender, laughing woman in a robin's egg blue dress. Her demeanour and bright colours were the very antithesis of bereavement. Clearly, this woman was not in mourning over the deaths of temperance leaders Lady Deborah Peacham and Margaret Bright Lucas.

But Florence knew how to be gracious, and walked us over to the woman in blue. "Rebecca, I'd like you to meet two new friends of mine, Astraia Holmes and

Madeleine Barquist. Astraia and Maddie, this is Rebecca Ravenwood Thornapple, an officer in the Central National Society for Women's Suffrage."

Astraia gave Rebecca the letter of introduction from Nora. Rebecca spent a little more time studying her letter than Lady Isabella had. While she did, I admired her abundant chestnut hair, beautifully coiffed and held up with several tortoiseshell hair combs. "It's been a long time since I saw Nora," Rebecca said finally. "How is she doing?"

"She's about to publish her report, *Health Statistics of Women Students of Cambridge and Oxford and of their Sisters*," Astraia said, apparently deciding to not share gossip about the digitalis death at Nora's house during a séance only a few days ago.

We spoke about Cambridge for a while. I contributed little, as I'd hardly spent 24 hours in the place. Rebecca introduced us to a few of her friends, and I tried my best to memorise their names since Astraia would expect me to make notes on our way home. Finally Lady Isabella Somerset opened the meeting and introduced tonight's speaker, who to my surprise was our new friend Florence. The women cheered loudly when Florence took the dais, and I quickly realised why.

Florence Balgarnie was the most powerful and compelling speaker I've ever heard. And I regularly attend Fabian Society speeches by gifted orators such as Annie Besant and George Bernard Shaw.

She began calmly, with a history lesson. "In education, social freedom, and opportunity, there has been most satisfactory progress made by women during this century. One need only examine the life and extraordinary accomplishments of our dear friend Margaret Bright Lucas to see a shining example of what women can aspire to today." Burst of tears and applause resounded through the room, and Florence paused before she went on.

"But our political standing is still as it was in 1790, one hundred years ago, when one learned writer explained that people unfit for the local franchise were those who 'lie under natural incapacities, and therefore cannot exercise a sound discretion, or who are so much under the influence of others that they cannot have a will of their own in the choice of candidates. Of the former description are women, infants, idiots, lunatics; of the latter, persons receiving alms and revenue offices.'"

Florence then walked us through some of the highs and lows of the fight for women's equality during the last hundred years, becoming more and more dramatic in her pronouncements, and finally ended with these stirring words: "On the one side are the hosts of the mighty entrenched behind the ancient fortifications of sex domination, prejudice and self-satisfaction; on the other is the gradually growing force of sex equality, democracy, justice, and common-sense. That is why we are here tonight, sisters: we are the heart, the lungs, the sinews of this growing force, working to promote just legislation for women and to protect the interests of children. Women must attain the same measure of enfranchisement as men now enjoy. We must burst the sex barrier which has so long held us in thrall. We owe it to our sister Margaret Bright Lucas. She would want us to fight on."

The women cheered and hooted and clapped, even the most elegant and upper class of them. The collective emotion connecting us all together was extraordinary; I had never experienced the level of fervour and elation I felt in that room that night; and looking at Astraia I was confident she felt the same way. But even as she was exalted by the passion of the moment, she searched the room, analyzing the attendees, making an assessment of who among us might be a murderer.

Not that she actually thought anyone here was a murderer, of course. She felt confident that Sir Peter Peacham had killed his wife. But she had made a promise to her brother Mycroft to thoroughly investigate the crime, and she was determined to do as she had promised.

After Florence's speech, Lady Isabella spoke about the plans for another march on the House of Commons. It seemed clear to me that every woman in this room planned to attend, whether they were aligned with the Central Committee of the National Society for Women's Suffrage or its antagonist, the Central National Society for Women's Suffrage.

We congratulated Florence on her excellent speech and made arrangements to get together soon. As we were leaving, Astraia handed her card to Lady Isabella, with her address penciled on the front. "Tonight was life-changing, Lady Isabella," she gushed. "I hope you will add us to your membership rolls."

Lady Isabella nodded with pleasure, and we left.

We were standing at the street waiting for John, chatting with other women from the meeting, when Astraia suddenly nudged me, tilting her head toward a couple across the street who had just got out of a cab. The man was of middle years, well dressed and well fed.

I gasped, then lowered my head before any of our new friends could notice what had alerted my attention. The laughing blonde lady clinging to the man's arm with great familiarity as they walked into the mansion across the street was Mrs Richard Dryson, the medium we had met last week in Cambridge when she was still Mrs Tillis. Her hair had been dark then, and her manner not remotely so lively. But this was unquestionably the same woman.

"Can you believe that?" hissed Miss Maria Norton, one of Rebecca's friends. "Look at the Peacham house! Lady Deborah has only been dead a month, and that lecher is already carrying on."

"That bastard!" her companion Miss Lydia Percival said in disgust.

Both women stared angrily at the couple who had entered the stately home across the street, the charlatan medium and the man who was apparently the leading suspect in our murder case.

Chapter Five

"So Sir Peter Peacham is trysting with Mrs Dryson," Astraia said when we were back in the carriage. "Nora mentioned that the Drysons were moving straight away to Dr Dryson's home in the city. Apparently they've already arrived. I think we must plan to visit them soon to give our best wishes. You should find out their address."

I glanced at Letty, whose snores indicated she was sleeping off a large birthday meal. "Is there any chance we are mistaking that woman's identity?" I whispered. "Mrs Dryson is a brunette, not a blonde."

Astraia rolled her eyes but whispered back. "You recognised her as well as I did."

I nodded. "I'll check the Fabian Society membership book for Dr Dryson's address," I whispered. We discussed everyone we met tonight, considering whom to contact next. I took notes.

I was careful to not wake up Rutherford when I entered the stable, though it was difficult to avoid making noise while maneuvering my cast and cane. As I'd anticipated, Old Vic slept on the new pallet beside him, the dying stove still offering remnants of heat in an otherwise cold night. The boy looked warm and cosy. All in all, given the rags he wore when he'd shown up here, he probably had it better here than he did in his former life. I made a mental note to find out if he had family to support. If so, I would find out what their needs were, and see if I could provide any assistance. He really was proving to be of substantial help with the animals.

According to Susie, Rutherford and Chan were becoming friends, which I could only take as a good thing as long as Chan didn't get in trouble for befriending someone who worked with me. Both being boys of the streets, I supposed they had much in common. And if Chan could spend his time spying on Rutherford while Rutherford spent his time spying on Chan, I would not complain. It would take time away from them both spying on me.

The next morning as I worked in the regular stable, showing my two young assistants how to scrutinise for an impending birth in a pregnant mare (a lecture and demonstration which seemed to embarrass both Susie and Rutherford, strangely, even though he'd grown up on the streets and she on a farm), we received a visit from my gentleman friend and Astraia's nemesis, Detective Inspector Samuel Rankin.

He said hello to Susie, I introduced him to Rutherford, and then he said, "Miss Maddie, would you like to take a walk to the pub with me for a while? I need to consult with you about a few things." He did not seem overly happy about this consultation, which told me he had probably been told that Astraia and I were investigating the Peacham case. DI Rankin was with Scotland Yard. They did not like working with amateurs.

"Let me wash up," I said. I instructed the children to groom the poor pregnant horse whose vulva and belly had been on display for the past half-hour, and went to my veterinary stable to clean up with plenty of hot water and soap. I was, to be blunt, disgusting. I felt glad we weren't going anywhere nice, since I would need an actual bath before I could pass muster in any society but the pub.

Happily Samuel was a police officer and fairly inured to such things as the smell of a few dribbles of horse faeces splattered on a lady's frock. I did the best I could with a clothes brush, pinned a hat to my head, grabbed my coat and cane, and met him outside the stable door for the short walk to a neighbourhood pub where we often spent an afternoon hour or so.

***

"We have verified Sir Peter Peacham's alibi," Samuel said. He took a long sip of his ale. "He was with his sister at his country estate in Kent when Lady Peacham died.

"Lady Deborah," I corrected absently, sipping my own half-pint.

He glared at me. He really did hate this, having to share details about a case with non-police interlopers. But he had his orders from Mr Mycroft. "Yes. Her."

"Why did it take so long for you to verify his story?" I asked hastily.

"His sister was on the continent for the last month," he said. "She came back to town yesterday and he immediately brought her into the station to confirm his statement. And really, it doesn't matter even if he had been in London when his wife died. The murder act was committed several days before Lady Whoever succumbed to her wound."

This surprised me. "Why?" I asked. "We were told she had been stabbed." In truth, Astraia and I had been picturing the lady stabbed in her own bedchamber with some sort of knife or carving implement as yet undiscovered.

"Yes, that's true," he said. "She was stabbed. However, it's unlikely that Sir Peter would have chosen the particular murder weapon used. It appears likely that a long hatpin was forced up through the lady's ribs and pierced her heart. It may have taken several days for the damage to that organ to result in death."

I thought about this for a moment. The suffragists' rush on the House of Commons had occurred a few days before Lady Deborah Peacham died. Incredibly, it seemed possible that Mycroft Holmes could have been right all along and Astraia and I were not wasting our time: a sister suffragist might have been the murderer after all.

And then something else occurred to me. "When was a hatpin identified as the murder weapon?" I asked. "Was it during the necropsy?"

"Well, yes," he admitted, dipping his head and taking another sip of his drink.

The post-mortem examination had been completed weeks ago, within days of the lady's death.

I didn't say anything.

He looked up.

"We were still working our investigation and needed to keep such details quiet," he defended. "We were still convinced that Sir Peter was the villain."

"Let me guess," I said. "You didn't find any hatpins dripping with blood in his home or on his person."

"No."

"And then his sister confirmed that he was far from London when his wife died."

"Yes."

"Which didn't matter anyway, since Lady Deborah had been pierced with a hatpin some unknown days prior to her death."

"Correct."

"You don't really know when or where the attack on her took place."

He sighed and ordered another drink for himself. "That's right."

"But she had been with a large crowd of women just a few days before, most of whom were probably wearing hats secured with hatpins, some no doubt long enough to be potential murder weapons."

"We presume so, yes."

"And you don't have any mode for infiltrating that particular group of suspects."

"Not really."

"And Mr Mycroft Holmes told you over a week ago that he had assigned this case to his sister, for exactly that reason."

"He did."

We both sat in silence for several minutes. "Is there any other information you have not yet shared with me about this case?" I asked finally, in quiet rage. Had Astraia been here, her rage would not have been so quiet. Which was probably why the detective inspector had arranged to meet with me alone to contribute this clue.

"No," he said.

"Do you have any suspects, for instance?"

"I still think Sir Peter did it," he said.

"But you have not one shred of proof," I said.

"No," he admitted. "We know he is a philanderer. We know he inherited a great deal of money from his wife's estate. We've interviewed all of his lady friends we could find, but none of them were able to provide any leads."

I knew the name of the lady friend Sir Peter had been laughing with just last night, at his own house. But I would be damned before I would share such a nugget of intelligence with this pompous policeman.

I stood. He stood too, helping me with my coat even as he objected to my decision to leave. "You haven't finished your refreshment yet," he said.

"I'm no longer thirsty," I said. "And I need to contact Astraia straight away about the case. How the victim died, which you've known for weeks, was information we should have the day we were assigned this case. I hope the delay doesn't harm our ability to uncover the truth and capture a killer." I knew it would have made no difference to our investigation, but I was angry. The police should have shared this information with Astraia long before now. I was confident Mr Mycroft had expected them to do so.

I picked up my cane and started away before he could pay the tab and escort me.

"Wait, Miss Maddie—I wanted to talk with you about our day trip to the Shoreditch music hall this next Sunday."

"I'm afraid I will be too busy to accompany you to any entertainment this week."

I left the pub with as much dignity as an angry woman with a faeces-bedraggled dress can demonstrate.

***

"He's not good enough for you, Maddie," Astraia said. Astraia and Samuel Rankin had grown up in the same village. She held him in the same low regard as she did all those who had been telling her what to do all her life.

I poured the tea I had begun preparing when Rutherford left on his errand to the Whitechapel Library, Astraia's place of employment, to tell her that I had important news for her. A plate of Feinman's gingerbread was in the middle of the table, along with sugar and milk for Astraia's tea (I did not require such adulterants).

I did not answer her slur against Samuel. He was handsome and kind. I believed he cared for me. My heart fluttered whenever he was near. Whether or not he was good enough for me seemed irrelevant. But the way he always tried to keep Astraia and me from our work was certainly very annoying. I would avoid him for the time being at least, until I got past my anger.

"So Lady Deborah bled out slowly," Astraia said. "From her heart into her chest, one assumes."

"Yes. I wonder if she was in pain?" I said.

"She probably felt discomfort without knowing exactly what was wrong," Astraia said. She sipped her tea thoughtfully.

I touched my side, which had recently been pierced with a less effective weapon than a hat pin. It was healing well, so I thought it unlikely that any of my organs had suffered damage. "Why do you suppose your brother Mr Mycroft Holmes never told us that she had been killed with a hatpin?"

Astraia gave an unladylike growl. "He probably thought we knew. He no doubt expected the police to give us the details when he informed Samuel that he had assigned us to the case. He's probably been wondering why we haven't got further on this investigation before now."

"So what do you want to do next?" I asked.

She slipped a note out of her reticule. "We have received a very interesting invitation," she said, handing the card to me. "Lady Isabella has invited you and me to accompany her to tomorrow's funeral for Margaret Bright Lucas, the late president of the British Women's Temperance Union. Do you have anything in black?"

Happily one of the new dresses Letty had made up for me was of a dark grey, adequate for the funeral of someone I had never met. "I'll need to buy another hat," I said, after thinking about it. "And some black gloves."

***

I sent Susie to Jenny's Rag Shop that afternoon to see what used clothes she could find. I gave her a little extra money to buy something for herself, since it seemed unfair that Rutherford should receive new clothes, I should get a new hat and gloves, but she was still wearing the two old dresses of mine that Letty had altered for her use when she'd first come to work for me. She returned with a pile of colourful fabric in her arms.

I did not see a funeral hat nor gloves, but did notice a red taffeta corner sticking out from under a folded dress in blue chintz.

"What did you buy, Susie?" I asked.

She blushed. "Jenny didn't have any nice black hats or gloves, Miss Maddie. So I'll go over to the library and see if Miss Letty will help me shop for you." Letty usually accompanied Astraia to her place of work, and filled in for her when she had detectivist errands to perform.

I nodded. "That seems like a good solution," I said. "What did you get for yourself?" I reached for the clothes in her arms. She tried to pull back, but I was much larger and it was a simple thing for me to grab them.

"This chintz dress looks fine," I said. "You should take it with you to Miss Letty to alter. You can wear it when you go out somewhere nice, not when you're working here in the stables. But I don't think Miss Letty would approve of the other dress, do you?" The frayed red taffeta dress looked like exactly the sort of apparel Madam DuBarry would have dressed Susie in if the girl had not been rescued from DuBarry's pimp by the police the morning she'd arrived in London. Luckily for her, Archie brought her to the stables to work for me when they realized she was a country girl and probably knew something about horses.

She hung her head. "I suppose not, Miss Maddie. But it's just so pretty. I like pretty colours."

I studied the dress. A few beads and feathers still clung hopefully here and there to the skirt and tiny bodice. I was surprised that such a dress should have lasted more than a few hours at Jenny's, but supposed the small size was the reason it had not yet sold. It would be tight on Susie, and she was still a child. I mentally sorrowed for the girl who had last worn it, and damned the man who'd originally bought it.

"I have an idea, Susie. Take this red dress with you to Letty too. Tell her I would like her to teach you how to sew a doll, and the two of you could use this material for the doll's dress." Letty was very fond of Susie, and I knew it would make her happy to sew a doll for her, and probably to teach Susie to sew, which was something I did not know how to do with any expertise. I'd noticed all the cloth dolls in Astraia's old bedroom when I'd stayed there during a recent indisposition, and felt sure it had been Letty who'd made them.

Susie's face lit up. "A doll? I can have a doll? I've never had a doll, Miss Maddie."

I felt ashamed that I'd never thought of it before. I'd had dolls when I was Susie's age. My Mummy had made them for me.

I hugged Susie, something I rarely did. I felt ashamed about that as well. She was a dear girl, and such a help to me. "Of course you can have a doll, Susie. And I'll bet Letty will be glad to help you make lots of clothes for it. Run along to the library now. Just don't forget my hat and gloves."

"Oh, I won't, Miss Maddie!" she said, and quickly folded up the dresses again before she hurried off to find Letty.

Rutherford noticed her leaving as he entered the veterinary stable. "Where is Susie going?" he asked me. Except for a few hours when I'd sent him to the library to deliver my note to Astraia and then to Frank Podmore's home to get the address of the Dryson newlyweds, he'd spent all day with the expectant mare. He found the foal moving around in the horse's flank fascinating.

"She's gone to ask Miss Letty to help her shop for a hat and gloves for me, and also teach her to sew a few things," I said.

He nodded. "Do you want to come check on the mare now? She's acting sort of restless and swishing her tail a lot."

"Sounds like we'll have a new foal before too long," I said, following him into the regular stable. I hoped I was right about that. Horse labour can last for many hours, sometimes days. If I had to leave the labouring Bluebell in the barely competent hands of Harry the stablemaster in order to attend Margaret Lucas's funeral, Susie and Rutherford might be left out of the delivery which I knew would disappoint them.

***

Happily the stars aligned in my favour for a change: Letty provided both hat and gloves and was delighted to have a pupil to whom she could tutor sewing; and Bluebell foaled that night, a lovely roan colt. Rutherford immediately fell blissfully in love, and even convinced Chan to enter the stables to see the beautiful foal. Susie begged to cut down a horse blanket to fit the small thin frame of little Charlie the colt. Watching these three young people, I could see that Rutherford might have a future as a farrier or a veterinarian, and Susie as a vet or a seamstress, but I remained undecided about what kind of career Chan might be able to follow. He had certainly persevered in his spying vocation—even during the coldest of nights he stood out in the street as directed by his fiendish employer, watching the stable where I lived.

I suddenly realised he'd make a splendid night watchman. I wondered if the Metropolitan Police ever considered hiring a Chinese police officer. Surely someday they'd open a police station in the Limehouse neighbourhood, and a Chinese officer would be invaluable there. I decided to discuss the situation with Mr Sherlock Holmes the next time I saw him.

When John collected me at the stable soon after dawn the next morning I learned from Astraia that the reason we were leaving so early was because instead of taking us directly to Margaret Bright Lucas's funeral service he was returning us to Lady Isabella Somerset's house. Apparently we would be riding to the Lucas family home with Lady Isabella and Florence Balgarnie in Lady Isabella's own carriage.

"That's quite an honour," I said, confused. "I would have thought there'd be a dozen women she'd invite before us. People who'd actually known the deceased, perhaps."

Astraia shrugged. "I received a note from my brother Mykie," she said. "He and Lady Isabella have been in communication. In fact, I surmise that Lady Isabella may have been the person who first requested that he look into the death of Lady Deborah."

"So she knows that we are investigating that death?"

"I believe so. I think she invited us to the funeral so that we can have another opportunity to consider potential suspects."

"So should we remove her from our suspect list?"

"Not yet," my friend said thoughtfully. "If she's the murderer, it would only be to her benefit to expand the list as broadly as possible. But I do think it's unlikely that she did the deed."

"Do you still suspect the widower?"

"I don't know if I suspect him so much as I wish it to be him. Such a cad. And certainly he is as competent as anyone else to wield a hatpin, even if it seems an improbable choice of weapon for him to select. We'll need to interview him soon. But you should mark his name in the unlikely column as well."

This was our third trip to the West End of London in only four days, which seemed extraordinary to me but was as nothing to Astraia, who often travelled there to visit her brothers. I had had virtually no sleep. I'd been up all night delivering Charlie and then straight away bathed and dressed in preparation for this early excursion. Astraia was also quite tired, since she'd had to get up very early to drop Letty off at the Whitechapel Library to cover her shift before driving to the Leman Street police station to collect me before we headed to Lady Isabella's.

Letty had prepared black mourning cockades for both of us. We helped each other attach the ribbons to the arms of our coats with pins, then both of us took the opportunity to nap during the long carriage ride to our first destination.

**

We—Astraia, Lady Isabella, Florence Balgarnie and I--arrived in Lady Isabella's luxurious coach at the Bloomsbury home of the late Margaret Bright Lucas shortly before ten-thirty o'clock, in good time to join the dark sea of mourning entering the deceased lady's house. I had enjoyed the coach ride very much, revelling in the supreme luxury of soft seats held in a suspension that bounced just slightly as the horses—four of them, my first time in such an equipage—gently trod the roads in alignment.

When we arrived, I quickly discovered there are other benefits to being with the highest ranked person at an event such as this. I did not have to be careful with my cane, because the crowd separated before us, allowing us freedom to enter the domicile. I did not have to search out a place for us to sit, because an usher escorted us into the parlour to the reserved chairs for Lady Isabella's party which were clearly identified by cards on the seats (after the service, I slipped my seat card into my bag as a keepsake--it's a black-bordered memorial card with the words "In Memoriam: Margaret Bright Lucas Died 4 February 1890" printed underneath a funereal cross-and-lilies image; below these words someone had hand-written "Lady Henry Somerset party"). And since our seats were in the second row, I would not have to strain my neck trying to see around or above the hats of women sitting in front of us once the service started.

There are also disadvantages to being in the party of the highest-ranked person at a funeral service. We were the first persons to be seated, directly behind the family, who would be the last seated. My chair was the closest of us all to the open head of the casket; I am very tall; the casket had been placed on a low bench. Therefore I sat in silence for at least half an hour as mourners slowly entered the room, my only entertainment a close and unobstructed view of the dead woman's face, occasionally interrupted by mourners who came over to pay their respects to the honoured doyenne, a few even bending over to lay a light kiss on a cold waxen cheek.

I wondered what kind of person Margaret Bright Lucas had been. On the drive over, Lady Isabella had mentioned that she was a Quaker, and in the coffin I could see her white hair was covered with a white Quaker cap. She was seventy-one years of age, and had already been widowed for twenty-five years when she died of tuberculosis. I frowned, questioning the wisdom of holding a crowded funeral displaying the open coffin of a tuberculosis victim, and as the person physically closest to the late individual I tried to modify my air intake to short, shallow breaths.

This made me more conscious than usual of the breathing sounds of Astraia, sitting beside me. I elbowed her awake, an action I would find myself taking three times more before someone finally closed the lid of the casket and the seats in front of us filled with mourning family members.

I fancied I could hear the collective sighs of gratitude from the entire room when the casket lid was closed. No amount of camphor or lilac stuffed into the coffin could disguise the fact that Mrs Lucas had now been dead for five days, and in accordance with her religious beliefs, she had not been embalmed. Thankfully this was winter and no doubt while awaiting today's service her body had been resting somewhere frigid.

Many of the day's rituals were in keeping with Church of England customs that would be familiar and therefore comforting to most of Mrs Lucas's friends, such as the wearing of mourning, the use of memorial cards, the decision to give seats of honour to Lady Isabella's party, and the physical presence of the deceased herself in the room. However, the funeral service would be conducted according to the Quaker tradition. A Quaker gentleman came to the front and explained to us that this was a meeting in thanksgiving to the grace of God for the life of our friend, and said that we would all sit in silent meditation except for those who felt moved by God to give words to their thoughts.

After a long period of silence Lady Isabella rose to speak about Mrs Lucas's dedication to the cause of temperance. Then Florence stood and told about the lady's work for peace, and for suffrage. Soon others rose to talk about her work on moral causes such as Sunday closures and ending prostitution. Many people spoke about how much they admired Mrs Lucas, who had accomplished an astonishing number of things in a long life well lived, and their impassioned paeans to a beloved woman, often accompanied by loud sobs, were enough to keep Astraia awake for well over an hour.

Lady Isabella's carriage was of course one of those invited to participate in the funeral cortège to the internment, ranking first in order of carriages after the family. As we rode in comfort to the Highgate Cemetery where Mrs Lucas would be buried with her husband, Florence and Lady Isabella, still overcome with sorrow, spoke for a time about their friend until Astraia, now refreshed and reinvigorated from her pre-funeral naps, interrupted their sad reminiscences to broach another topic. "Did Mrs Lucas participate in the rush on the House of Commons last month?"

Florence looked horrified, and Lady Isabella choked out a laugh. "Heavens no. Margaret was the most ladylike of ladies, the epitome of feminine sanctity. She believed in the moral superiority of women, and often preached that women's virtue alone keeps the base nature of man from fully manifesting its heinous degradation upon the earth."

I began to smile at her words, but upon seeing the expressions on the faces of Florence and Isabella I realised she had not been joking.

Astraia responded. "That's an exaggeration, surely."

Lady Isabella shrugged. "A little, perhaps. But the only reason Margaret joined the suffrage movement at all was because she saw women's votes as the best way to pass temperance laws. I don't think she ever believed in suffrage as a goal in and of itself like Florence and I do. I admit I was at the House of Commons last month, along with Lady Deborah and others—I think you were on a speaking tour, Florence. But certainly Margaret was not there. She believed in petitioning the House of Commons to further her causes—and did so more than once. But she would never have done something so unladylike as actually interrupt a session."

"So who was there that day, interrupting the House of Commons?" Astraia asked.

"Let me see," Isabella said, and began listing the names of about two-dozen women. Knowing it would look very strange if I started writing this information down, I memorised the names as best as I could, knowing that any I forgot would be remembered by Astraia when we finally took notes together on our way home. Astraia had a prodigious memory for such things.

Florence might have been surprised at the conversation, at the way Lady Isabella listed name after name for Astraia and me, but if she was she didn't say anything. I do not know if she was aware at that time that Astraia and I had reason to meet these women beyond our devotion to the cause of suffrage. Perhaps she did. At any rate, this most talkative of women listened in silence while Lady Isabella gave us the names of all the potential suspects and then spoke about the order in which women entered Westminster Palace and then the corridors to the Commons

Chamber, describing times when women were crowded together so closely that one could hardly see where one feathered hat ended and another began, or distinguish between whose gloved and fluttering hands belonged to whom.

"Many of those women will be gathered at my home after the internment for a light luncheon, a very informal gathering of friends to commiserate over our mutual loss," Lady Isabella said. "I shall be happy to introduce you."

"What was the impetus for the rush on Parliament last month, Lady Isabella?" I asked.

"There will be many important decisions made in Parliament this session," she said. "We intend to witness them. We were inspired by our foremothers. Did you know that in 1739 the Duchess of Queensberry, the Duchess of Ancaster, Lady Huntingdon, and Lady Westmorland were denied access into the House of Lords because men wanted to sit in the gallery instead? But they refused to leave—they rushed in and sat in the front rows of the gallery where members of Parliament had wanted to sit. That extraordinary demonstration by those brave women occurred over a hundred-and-fifty years ago—yet we are still denied entry to Parliament, either the House of Lords or the House of Commons. Instead, they built that damned Ladies' Gallery cage where we're supposed to sit, that you can't even see out of. It's disgraceful."

"Appalling," Florence said.

Astraia and I nodded in agreement, though certainly neither of us had ever tried to watch a session of Parliament.

After a short service at the cemetery with the few invited guests, we returned to Lady Isabella's home for the informal gathering—and that was when I realised why she had invited Astraia and me today as her personal guests to the funeral. Attending the funeral with Lady Isabella had given us cachet, as we learned when we joined the group of mourners, women and a few men, who milled around a large parlour drinking tea, eating titbits, talking about the funeral and their sorrow over the death of Mrs Lucas, waiting for their hostess to arrive. Not all of the women on the suspect list were there—Rebecca Ravenwood Thornapple, for example, was missing—but that was to be expected since these people were mourning the loss of a temperance leader and not all suffrags were temperance proponents. But most of the women who had stormed the House of Commons were there. And it seemed they were all now close friends of Astraia's and mine.

Lady Isabella told us that she was leaving the next day for Eastnor Castle, her home in Herefordshire, but that we could write to her if we needed anything; and then she and Florence left us to our own devices as our new dear friends began to clamour for our attention. The first to make it through the throng were Maria Norton and Lydia Percival, the ladies who had been so outraged the other night when they saw Sir Peter Peacham escort Mrs Dryson into his house. As soon as Lady Isabella and Florence left us on our own these ladies swooped in, cutting off the rest, putting their arms through ours, expressing their gratitude that we were able to join them today, and sympathising with us on our great loss although I knew for a fact the greater loss had to be theirs since we had never even met the late Mrs Lucas. But I decided not to mention that fact, since I felt our lack of a relationship with the deceased could only be awkward and cause gossip, which we certainly did not want. Astraia took it even farther, agreeing with the others that "dear Margaret could never be replaced" and wondering "whatever will we do without her?"

Miss Norton invited us to her home. "I would be honoured to hear your advice as to whom we should support as the next president of the British Women's Temperance Union. The BWTU will be holding a meeting in a couple of weeks, but a few of us should meet before that to plan our strategies."

"Oh, I agree completely," gushed Astraia, and I wrote down Miss Norton's address and a date a few days hence in my notebook.

Miss Percival asked us to counsel her on a few financial investments she was considering. Of course neither of us had the remotest clue about finances.

"We would be happy to advise you," Astraia intoned. I took down Miss Percival's specifics and appended this meeting to our calendar.

Mrs Howard ("call me Clara") Finchley, whom I had seen at the occasional Fabian gathering but never spoken with, invited us to attend an upcoming Fellowship of the New Life discussion panel with her, on Ethics and the Biological Urge; panelists to include Herbert George Wells, Havelock Ellis, and Edward Carpenter. I had already decided to forgo this particular event, since I'm never comfortable attending a lecture by men talking about sex, and I could imagine few things of less interest to Astraia.

"We look forward to it," Astraia assured her, and I included this event on the list, along with Mrs Finchley's address. "We should plan to go out for a late supper afterwards, so we can get to know one another better," Astraia added with her most sincere fake smile.

And so it went, for over an hour—murder suspect after murder suspect approached us to beg us to spend time with them. Our calendar filled and a few times we had to demur on the first invitation because we had already made an obligation—but that was no impediment since the women were more than happy to suggest an alternate date or event, and we were glad to accept whenever we had free time available.

***

"I don't see how I can possibly attend all of these activities," I said when we were back in Astraia's carriage mid-afternoon. "Or you either. We both have other employment, remember?"

Astraia brushed that off. "We will have solved this case long before most of these events occur. Next week, perhaps. Then we can simply cancel the rest of the appointments. Or did you really want to attend that tedious lecture in two weeks? Or that excursion the following week to Mrs Williford's country estate for the winter shooting?"

"You think we will have this case solved by next week?"

She shrugged. "I shouldn't be surprised, now that we know the key piece of information---the hatpin murder weapon. It's obvious Lady Isabella believes the murder attack must have occurred when the women crowded together in Westminster Palace, packed so tightly that no one would notice what was happening below their shoulders. I am inclined to agree with her, but there are a few other possibilities that need to be eliminated first. Which reminds me—do you have Dr Dryson's address with you?"

I told her I did, and she pounded on the roof of the conveyance to let John know she had a new direction for him. "Since we're out and about anyway, I think it's time we visited the newlyweds, don't you? At the very least, we should be able to determine whether or not

Mrs Dryson was the blonde woman we saw with Sir Peter Peacham the other night."

I expressed willingness to make one more visit today. I wasn't hungry, since Lady Isabella had provided plenty of food, of much finer quality than my standard stable fare, so trying to find out more about Valerie Dryson—including whether she was actually blonde or brunette—seemed as reasonable a way to spend the afternoon as any other.

I mentioned the concern I had felt during the funeral about sitting so close to the dead tuberculosis victim.

"Well, it's not like she was able to breathe on anyone," Astraia said reasonably. I had to agree this made sense, and we spent the rest of the trip to the Drysons listing all of the suspects in my notebook and discussing the best ways to contact those few who had not attended today's funeral luncheon.

Chapter Six

The new Mrs Dryson was surprised to see us, but graciously invited us to enter her home and sit down with her for tea. Her hair was styled in the same mousy brown bun we had seen at the séance.

"Actually, it's nice to have company," she said.

Astraia and I glanced at each other. The woman had got married just days ago. We both assumed most newlyweds disliked receiving company, or having any other distraction from the bliss of love.

"Dear Richard has been sick ever since we arrived in London," Mrs Dryson explained. "He's developed a dreadful cough, and has most strictly forbidden me entrance to his sickroom for my own protection." She delicately tapped at her chest. "I have weak lungs," she said. "And of course he is unable to receive visitors at this time, though I know he will be terrible sorry to have missed you."

"Oh, how unfortunate," Astraia said. "But fortuitously that means we can get to know you better." She slipped an arm into Mrs Dryson's as we entered the parlour, an affectionate act that first surprised me until I realised that since Astraia was quite short and Mrs Dryson very tall, being pressed next to her required Astraia to stare up at her when they spoke. Such close proximity allowed Astraia a better opportunity to examine the genuineness of the woman's hair. Mrs Dryson excused herself to leave us alone in the parlour for a minute while she instructed the housekeeper to prepare tea. This parlour was clearly Dr Dryson's hideaway for psychical research pursuits. I walked around, noticing the accoutrements of an occultist—a spiritualist talking board and wooden planchette set up on a small round table; supernatural charts and symbology hanging on the walls; and many, many books on spiritualism piled hither and thither, including both volumes of Madame Blavatsky's *Isis Unveiled* as well as her new two-volume Theosophical behemoth, *The Secret Doctrine,* their combined weight testing the capacity of a fragile Georgian end table. I picked up a Freemasonry ritual manual—forbidden to me as a woman to read—and started poring through it, curious to discover what the fuss was all about.

But before I had a chance to learn how to blow up the world, Astraia called to me from an alcove room.

"Mrs Dryson is a talented sculptress," she said, pointing to a clay head positioned on a cloth-covered table.

I walked over to examine the work. "My God," I said. "It's Richard Dryson." The modelling of the bust was uncompleted—the receding hair was as yet only traced in, and the shoulders rough—but the face of the man was perfect, down to the jowls below the cleft in his chin and the eyelashes framing the slightly-asymmetrical bulgy orbs.

"Why do you think Mrs Dryson is the artist?" I asked.

"Maddie, you're a better observer than that," my friend chided me. "For one thing, the clay on this bust is still wet. For another, Mrs Dryson still had remnants of clay on her hands when she greeted us."

"For which I must apologise, ladies," Mrs Dryson said, entering the room. She walked over to the bust and re-covered it with the wet cloth. "I don't want this to dry out before it's finished," she said. "It's a surprise for dear Richard, for when he recovers." She walked back to the door, indicating for us to exit her workroom.

As we walked out, she noticed that I still had the prohibited book of Freemason rituals in my hand, and laughed. It was the first time I ever heard her laugh, and quite enlivened her normally mousy features. I felt even more convinced that she was the woman we had seen the other night with Sir Peter Peacham. "Please feel free to take that book with you, Miss Barquist," she said. "I don't think my husband will have much time to focus on Freemasonry in the future." She leant over to me and whispered, "If he notices it missing, I'll contact you to send it back." She gave me a wink and a little smile, like two girls plotting a schoolroom trick.

She led us to a tea table, moving books off of chairs so that we could sit, similar to our visit with Florence Balgarnie a few days before except that she wasn't nearly as careful with the books as Florence had been. When Florence moved her books, it had been as though they were beloved members of her family, much as she would have moved a revered elderly cat from a pillow. As Mrs Dryson pushed tomes off chairs, I felt that she was annoyed by her husband's clutter and would have been just as happy tossing them into the refuse bin. I saw other books scattered on the floor and realised these were probably volumes that had been hastily dispatched from the table when the tea cart was rolled in.

Which seemed odd, since she was a spiritualist medium and occultist herself. I would have thought she would be glad to be surrounded by a library dedicated to her vocation.

Before Mrs Dryson could pour the tea, Astraia stood. "I'm so sorry, Mrs Dryson, but would you mind if I used your water closet?" she asked.

Brief annoyance crossed over Mrs Dryson's face, but she could hardly refuse the request. She gave Astraia directions, and my friend quickly left the room.

"While we're waiting for Miss Holmes to return, would you like to see more of my ceramic work?" Mrs Dryson asked me.

"Indeed I would!" I said, and followed her back into her workroom.

This time I noticed more of the small room than I had before when I had been admiring the bust of her husband. This had probably been a ladies' retiring room when the house was built, back in the early days of the century. Such a room was seldom used in a bachelor establishment—and not even necessary after a modern water closet was added to the indoor premises.

"My husband used this room for storage," Mrs Dryson said. "He has a large collection of occult memorabilia, much of it not worthy of display. I had everything in here boxed up and moved to the attic. I doubt he will ever notice anything missing."

"Like the Freemason book?"

"Just so." She led me over to an old display case. "But this was a nice piece, so I kept it in here after I crated up the stuff he had piled on the shelves. I'm using it to array my own work."

I stared in awe at the six ceramic busts now exhibited in the case. "Did you really make these?" I asked in amazement.

She preened, and lit several display lamps so that I could better appreciate the pieces. "I did," she said.

I stared at the busts, each in turn. Six different men, all precisely captured in clay and brown-gold glaze. I had never seen such perfect examples of the art. Young, old, handsome, plain, ugly—all very different. All certainly, clearly male. Somehow, the cold clay exuded warmth and masculinity.

"Would you like to hold one?" she asked. I nodded as she took one down from the shelf and handed it to me.

It was heavy, weighing several pounds. I held it up into the light, admiring the laughing mouth, piercing eyes, and flip of hair. I felt that if I saw this man in the street, I would immediately recognise him from this bust. I could almost fall in love with the man, just from this face.

"Who are they?"

"Oh, just men I've encountered here and there. No one important. I liked their faces."

I caressed the smooth cheek. "The colour of the glaze is extraordinary," I said. "It changes in the light."

"You should see it in the sunlight, or when the dawn rays hit it," she said with pride. "I make the glaze myself, to my own special recipe."

I looked over to the table where Dr Dryson's bust was covered in wet cloth. "Will you give that bust a glaze like these?"

She shrugged. "Probably. I'm still waiting for one or two of the ingredients. And I haven't found a kiln yet here in London."

I handed her back the precious piece of art. She returned it to the shelf with its brothers and we left the room. "I might be able to help you with that," I said. "There's a potter in my neighbourhood, George Woodward. I'll give you his name and direction. Tell him my name and I expect he'll let you use his kiln for free." I had once cared for his son when he'd fractured his arm, and knew he'd be glad to do a favour for a friend of mine.

She smiled at me, a big smile that completely changed her face, and I knew in that moment that she absolutely was the exuberant woman we'd seen with Sir Peter. "Why, thank you, Miss Barquist. You're very kind," she said.

I had just finished writing down the potter's information when Astraia returned. We settled down to a nice tea while I extolled the beauty of the ceramics in the other room to my friend. Astraia begged to see them before we left, and Mrs Dryson agreed gladly.

"Your work should be in a museum," I said.

She shrugged. "It's just my little hobby," she said self-deprecatingly. But I knew she was pleased with my enthusiasm.

Eventually we talked about the funeral that Astraia and I had attended that morning, speaking about Margaret Bright Lucas as though we'd actually known her.

"I confess I am not a proponent of temperance," Mrs Dryson said, "although I do not drink myself. But my dear Richard enjoys his post-prandial brandy, and I would not deny him that little pleasure." She added that she had never thought about women's suffrage but that she would be interested in learning more about it if we thought it worthwhile.

Astraia mentioned that we had gone to Lady Henry Somerset's home after the funeral, and used that as a transition to the awkward issue that had brought us here today.

"Are you familiar with Lady Henry's home, Mrs Dryson?" she asked.

"No, I don't believe so," Mrs Dryson said. "You see, I am an American, and not very familiar with the London area."

"Of course not. Well, you'll be interested to know that her home is across the street from that of Sir Peter Peacham, where you visited the other night."

"Who?" Mrs Dryson asked innocently.

"Sir Peter Peacham. Maddie and I saw you there two nights ago, as you and he entered his residence together."

"Miss Holmes, I don't find that amusing," Mrs Dryson said, scowling. Her hand trembled for a brief moment but she quickly brought herself together. "I have only been in London for a couple of days, and I have spent all of that time caring for my sick husband."

"And modelling his bust," Astraia said.

"As you say. Which I have been doing to keep my worries about dear Richard's health at bay. I assure you, I certainly have not been visiting other men while my husband has been indisposed." She stood. "And now I think it's time for me to check on my sick spouse's welfare. I appreciate that you came to visit, and will let him know you were enquiring after him."

She started walking toward the door, leaving Astraia and me to hurriedly grab our things and scramble after her.

"Don't forget the Freemason book, Miss Barquist," Mrs Dryson said as she left the room. I snatched the book on my way out of the door and slipped it into my bag.

"I'm sorry I didn't get a chance to view your ceramics, Mrs Dryson," Astraia said.

"Perhaps next time," our erstwhile hostess said, holding the front door open for us.

Less than three minutes after the name "Sir Peter Peacham" left Astraia's lips, we were standing alone outside on the top step of the house, a light icy drizzle falling on our heads. I noticed a brilliantly coloured bird house to the side of the front steps, its bright reds and yellows incongruous in the grey of the day.

"I'm glad I never took my hat off," Astraia observed. "We're lucky to have got our coats on before she hustled us out. Let's go see if we can find John."

After trawling in the cold for ten minutes we discovered John in a pub down the road, his cab and horse settled out front. Astraia damped down her temper when he told her he had hot tea and whisky waiting for us inside the cab, as well as a couple of warm rugs.

We settled back into the rugs and warm libation as John began the long trip back to my home at the Leman Street police stables.

"This has been quite the day," Astraia said.

"She was the woman with Sir Peter," I said. "I'm sure of it."

"I concur. That brown hair she wears is a wig."

I thought about that for a minute. It was very unusual for a blonde woman to pretend to be a brunette.

"What do you think is going on?" I asked.

"I'm not sure," Astraia said. "But there's something very wrong in that house."

"I'm sorry you didn't get to see her other ceramics," I said. "As you noted, she has extraordinary talent."

"I didn't see the ones you saw," Astraia said. "But I did see some others." She reached into her reticule and pulled out two small exquisite ceramic statues. "Dozens of others. Just like these."

I took one of the tiny statues from her. "You stole these?"

"I did."

There wasn't much to say to that, so I simply examined the thing. About half the height of my hand, it was a statue of a naked woman with a mass of curly hair. She stood on a flat base, wide hips, narrow waist, delicate ankles and feet, defined and rounded buttocks.

Her arms were bent at the elbows, her hands resting on her rib cage just below jutting breasts. Her face was every bit as cleverly delineated as the faces on the male busts in Mrs Dryson's workroom, despite being less than three inches high. I compared this statue to the other one Astraia had stolen. Both were identical in appearance except for the faces and hair styles, which differed dramatically. One had the face of a woman from the Orient; the other the face of a woman from Africa. One had short curly hair; the other a complicated up-do. Both had been fired in the same exquisite brown-gold glaze as the busts.

"Most of them have European faces," Astraia said. "I just found these particularly interesting."

"They all have different faces?"

"Yes. Identical bodies. Unique hair and faces. Dozens of them."

"And you found these in the water closet?" I asked.

She laughed. "Of course not. I sleuthed. I am a detective. It's part of the job, you know."

I ignored this. I had sleuthed today too. "So where did you find these?"

"In the lady's bedroom, down the hall from Dr Dryson's. I stole a look at him. He was sweating profusely, his limbs were spasming, and the stench in the room bore testimony that he is suffering an indisposition of the bowels. There was no one in the room with the poor man, not a servant nor a nurse.

Which makes the Fowler's Solution I found in Mrs Dryson's room of particular concern to me."

"Fowler's Solution? Lots of women use Fowler's Solution to treat their skin," I said.

"Lots of women use Fowler's Solution to poison their husbands," Astraia said. "It contains arsenic."

"Oh dear. What should we do?"

"I think we should tell the police," Astraia said. "Don't you?"

I was not sure what the police could do. Fowler's Solution was a common household item. You couldn't arrest someone for having it in their home, even if their husband was sick. "I'll mention it to Archie Froest," I said. "But I doubt that he'll do anything." In all probability, he'd say Astraia was giving in to female hysteria. Except for the fact that she wore a wig and we were sure she had visited another man the other night, there was no reason to doubt Mrs Dryson's devotion to her husband.

Astraia shrugged. "We can at least try."

I agreed. "So what else did you find?"

"I found a shrine," Astraia said. "A goddess shrine, with candles and flowers and incense. And dozens of these statues, in a variety of sizes. I took these two because they're small enough that I don't think she'll notice their absence.

I had never seen a goddess shrine. Had never even heard of such a thing, outside of horror stories or tales of our barbarian past. "Who do you think this goddess is?"

"I have no idea," Astraia said. "But it shouldn't be too hard to find out. I'll check the library. You can look in the British Museum."

I nodded. Perhaps I could take Susie with me. She could wear her new dress.

"I discovered something odd too," I said. "Her workroom was the place where Dr Dryson stored his occult memorabilia overflow. She boxed up all of his treasures and banished them to the attic."

"They've only been in London for what, two days?" Astraia said. "She must have started boxing up his possessions first thing when she moved in."

"Seems like a strange thing for someone to do on the first day of their honeymoon," I said.

"Not a very promising beginning to wedded bliss," she agreed.

***

John told us Letty had closed the library early to spend the afternoon in the stable with Susie, teaching her to sew. Astraia decided to go to my office with me to let her servant know it was time to leave. This decision was fortuitous, because my friend PC Archie Froest hurried there as soon as we arrived, with news of interest to both of us.

"Maddie, thank God you're here. We need you to do us a favour," he said.

"Of course, Archie," I said. I had been admiring the wobbly stitches in the hem of Susie's newly-altered dress. I had also been admiring the now-clean stable office. I loved it when Letty came to visit. The woman was a gem. Astraia did not deserve her.

"We need you to house a woman prisoner here with you for a few days," Archie said.

I had housed the occasional prisoner before, but not since I'd moved into the stables to live. "I don't think I have the room, Archie," I said. "Susie is here with me now. And Rutherford. Where would this prisoner sleep? And why can't you just put her in the usual cell you use for women in the gaol—is the gaol full again?"

"No, the gaol isn't full. But this is a special prisoner—a socialite."

Astraia perked up at this. "A socialite? What on earth did she do to merit gaol?" Most of the time when women were arrested in this part of town, they were poor women prostituting themselves in order to feed their families. I didn't think we even had any socialites living around here.

"She was arrested for harassing a member of Parliament," Archie said. "Her third such arrest in a month, apparently. This time, the judge sentenced her to gaol time. Unfortunately, the West End gaols refused to accept her because they don't want the political fallout. DI Rankin suggested that you might be willing to hold her here." The annoyance in his voice made it clear what he thought of Samuel's idea to move this hot potato into the Leman Street police station. Archie and Samuel did not share a collegial relationship.

"DI Rankin is not in charge of this station," I said. I knew why he had made this suggestion. He thought if I was busy being a gaol matron, I wouldn't have time to be a detectivist.

"No, he's not," Archie said. "But Sergeant Wilson thinks it's an excellent idea. He is trying to get funding for expansion, and thinks cooperating with the big boys will help us. He asked me to tell you to view this as a personal favour for him."

"Archie, I'm not sure where the prisoner could sleep," I said, looking around. I could move Rutherford in with the stableboys; that was no problem. But when I had housed prisoners in the past, they had slept in the back room where now Susie and I slept. "I suppose I could put her in the bedroom and Susie and I could sleep here on the floor by the stove," I said unhappily. Getting up and down from the floor was very awkward with my broken foot. I much preferred sleeping in a bed.

It seemed I had become quite pernickety since knowing Astraia. Where once I would settle down in a damp bed roll to watch over a sick horse through the night without a second thought, now I expected to sleep every night in a bed.

"Letty and John could bring over some more bedding," said Astraia helpfully. Over in the corner of the room, Letty rolled her eyes then leaned down to whisper to Susie.

Her comment to Susie had an immediate result. "Oh, Miss Letty, could I?" Susie squealed in excitement. She ran over to me. "Miss Maddie, could I stay at Miss Astraia's house while the prisoner is here?" she asked.

I looked over at Astraia, who shrugged. "Why not?" she said.

"We could bring a camp bed in here for you, Maddie," Archie said. "It won't be as comfortable as your regular bed, but it will be better than sleeping on the floor."

It seemed the decision was made. I would be sure to mention this example of my assistance to women prisoners the next time I met Florence Balgarnie. "When will she arrive?" I asked, giving up to the inevitable.

"We can have her here this evening," Archie said, relief in his voice.

"In time for a late supper, I presume," Astraia said. "Do you need us to bring in food?"

That was too much for me. Astraia Holmes, a private citizen, should not have to provide both food for criminals and bedding for gaolers. That was the responsibility of the government.

"No, she can eat the regular prisoners' fare," I said. "Right, Archie?"

"Actually, the prisoners are having stir about tonight," Archie said. Stir about was a nasty-tasting cornmeal and oatmeal mush. "If Miss Astraia could bring in something more palatable for our special prisoner, I think Sergeant Wilson would be grateful."

"Letty, you could bring in something better than cornmeal mush for Miss Maddie and her prisoner to eat tonight, couldn't you?" asked Astraia.

Letty gave a short, uninformative nod.

I sighed, tossing my hands up. "Fine," I said ungraciously. "I'll get the prisoner's room ready while the rest of you get everything else in place." Everyone started leaving the office, Archie to give the good news to Sergeant Wilson and find a camp bed for me, Rutherford to move into the stables for the night, and Astraia, Letty, and Susie to go to Astraia's house to gather up food and bedding for the prisoner.

I stopped Archie before he left.

"Who is this socialite anyway, Archie?"

"Oh, she has a whopper of a name," Archie said. "In fact, she's one of those three-name ladies. Miss Rebecca Ravenwood Thornapple." He left, and Astraia and I froze, staring at each other.

"Letty, you and John will have to prepare everything by yourselves," Astraia said. "I will be staying here with Miss Maddie for the next few hours, and will join her in tonight's meal with the prisoner. John can take me home afterward."

While I made the back room fit for a detainee, Astraia and I discussed how we would use this opportunity to gain information from the murder suspect. We decided we wouldn't enquire into specifics about the events that had brought her into captivity unless she brought up the topic first, because it seemed rude to ask someone why they had been arrested. We didn't want to antagonise her. We wanted her to feel comfortable with us, so that she would share her thoughts about the events that had resulted in Lady Deborah's death.

***

Three hours later, Astraia, I, and our new prisoner Rebecca Ravenwood Thornapple sat down to what was without question the fanciest meal ever provided to any prisoner at the Leman Street police station in all its history. We had fish soup, hot roast ham, cold roast beef, glazed carrots, game pie, salad, cheese, and wine, with tea and biscuits available to nibble on afterward in case we remained esurient. Letty had prepared and packed everything, but stayed at home with Susie while John in his butler garb served the courses to the three of us on what I later learned was Astraia's best silver and bone china dishware. The place settings included satin and lace table linens and three forks each, all crowded together on a gauzy pristine tablecloth covering the battered and rickety old table in my office where I did my accounts and operated on small animals. I was glad I was still in my funeral dress, because my normal faeces-bedewed work rags would hardly have done the silver settings justice.

With Letty's permission, Susie had sent food over to Rutherford to share with the other stableboys, which I hoped would encourage them to be kind to him tonight.

I had wondered if Rebecca would be shackled. She was not. Nor was she expected to wear prisoners' garb. She wore a handsome blue day dress with a stunning fox collar and patent leather ankle boots, the shiny shoes hardly glossier than the thick chestnut hair held in place with two elaborate tortoiseshell combs. She removed her hat when she entered, a saucy thing decorated with peacock feathers, perhaps better suited to spring than to winter, and set it and the coat she carried on top of the portmanteau that apparently her guarders were allowing her to keep with her as well. John carried her things into the bedroom where she would spend the night; I wondered if she would expect me to lay out her nightclothes in the absence of a maid, and decided that in this at least she would be treated as a prisoner. It was enough that I would have to empty her chamber pot. She could set out her own nightgown, by damn.

She made no comment about the rustic environs. I did notice her wrinkle her nose once in distaste, which I could hardly find fault with since after all this was a stable for sick horses and not a French parfumerie. Thank God Letty had cleaned in here today and had removed some rags I'd thrown into a bucket in the corner, sopping with horse placenta from last night's birth.

Astraia and Rebecca both behaved as though this was just a normal social evening at a friend's house.

"This ham is quite delectable," Rebecca said after her first dainty nibble at the slender slice she'd allowed John to place on her plate.

Astraia and I looked at each other, wondering who should accept the compliment. She had provided the food, but the palatial abode and title of "warder" were mine; which of us was the hostess?

John resolved the crisis of etiquette. "Thank you, miss," he said.

"I quite adore that hat you wore tonight," Astraia said in admiration.

"Madame Bouvier just released her spring line," Rebecca said. "It's not quite the season for peacock feathers yet, but I just can't help myself. I have an especial weakness for hats."

"I certainly understand that, but it seems a shame to cover your glorious hair," Astraia fawned.

"Well, that's a problem all of us ladies must live with," Rebecca said. "Your own hair is magnificent. I always wished I had red curls."

She said nothing about the sparse brown strings I had pulled back into a sloppy knot at my nape. I took my own bite of food, eating quietly while the other two flattered each other over apparel incidentals and discussed the latest fashion nonsense.

Rebecca was right. The ham was delicious. I let John give me a second piece, and listened to twenty minutes of disingenuous toadying. I say this because, knowing Astraia, I was confident not one word in ten she uttered was sincere and I assumed that the same dubious intent applied to our incarcerated guest. After I finished my last bite of cheese and sip of wine, I injected a moment of sincerity into the conversation in a way that also brought up the topic du jour.

"Rebecca, those tortoiseshell combs you wear are so beautiful. I first admired them when we met at Lady Isabella's home the other day."

She patted her hair, pleased at what she recognised was a genuine compliment. "Why, thank you, Maddie. Actually, they're not real tortoiseshell—they're celluloid. I don't wear real tortoiseshell because I worry about the decimation of the hawksbill turtle simply to suit the whims of fashion. That's the same reason I prefer peacock feathers to egret plumes, because I opt to support farmers and industrialists rather than hunters. I have dozens of combs like these, mostly coloured as tortoiseshell because I think they look more true to the original material. For example, the carnelian coloured ones look so cheap, don't you think?"

I frowned, wondering if she had seen my little jewellery box, where my one precious celluloid hair comb awaited my next special outing, probably to the Shoreditch music hall with a certain gentleman with whom I was currently at odds. I liked the bright orange-red colour, myself.

Astraia decided to take advantage of my mention of Lady Isabella before we started another half-hour talking about hair decoration.

"You can tidy up here now, John," she said. We had not thought to prepare an empty horse box to retire to while the servants whisked away dirty plates, so she just pushed her chair back a foot to indicate a symbolic separation from the dinner remains. Rebecca and I followed her example, and John moved in quickly to perform his duty and set out tea and biscuits for afters.

"That meeting at Lady Isabella's home was so fascinating," Astraia said. "Maddie and I are quite thrilled to join one of the suffrage groups, and as you can see by this evening's wine intake, we plan to join yours, not the temperance assembly."

"I'm so glad to hear that," Rebecca said. "Tying suffrage to temperance is a terrible strategy. No man is going to give women the vote if they're only going to use it to take away his drink. Which the temperance suffragists openly advocate for."

"I couldn't agree more," Astraia said, perhaps her first truly honest statement of the evening. "Do you plan to attend the next rush on the House of Commons, Rebecca?"

"If I'm free from gaol by then," Rebecca said, giving me an audacious wink.

"Were you at the last one?" I asked.

"I was," she said proudly.

"What was it like?"

She told us much the same story of that day as we had heard from Lady Isabella, but with more drama. "There was so much energy in the place, filled as it was with the colours and sounds of two-dozen women acting as a single united force trampling the halls of Mammon with holy feet, intent upon ensuring justice for the female race."

"That sounds very exciting!" Astraia gushed, and indeed it did. I found myself wishing we were actually planning to attend the next suffrage protest at Parliament.

"Did you know Lady Deborah Peacham? I understand she may have sustained an injury that day that resulted in her death," I said.

Astraia frowned at me. We had discussed several times the pros and cons of letting the suspects know we were investigating the murder, and had decided against it. It would certainly allow us to ask much more focused questions if they knew what we were doing—but it would also put them on guard against us. We had decided that being free to inveigle ourselves into their society was much more likely to result in an opportunity to canvas a wider range of suspects. However I was feeling impatient—the woman had been dead almost a month already—and I did not think this question gave us away. And besides, the hatpin clue was bound to hit the newspapers soon. Samuel Rankin probably wouldn't have told me if he hadn't thought the news was about to made public anyway.

But Rebecca frowned at me too. "Where did you hear that?" she asked. "I hadn't heard any such thing."

"Maddie works for the police," Astraia said. "She often hears things before the public have any knowledge. But please keep it quiet for now." She moved her head around to make sure John was out of earshot, which in fact he was.

"Oh yes, please," I said. "Please do keep it quiet. I shouldn't have said anything." I thought that this strategy of letting-her-in-on-the-secret should make Rebecca feel more at her ease—and perhaps even encourage her to share her own thoughts about what might have happened, since ladies often bond over gossip.

This approach worked. "But I thought she had been stabbed," Rebecca said.

"She was," Astraia said. "But it seems likely she was stabbed with a slender implement some days before she actually died. Perhaps even during the rush on Parliament."

"Oh, how awful," Rebecca said. "But it still seems to me that Sir Peter is the most likely culprit. He is a truly dreadful man."

"Oh, we agree," Astraia said.

"But if it wasn't Sir Peter, if something happened that day at Westminster instead, I can think of a couple of people the police might want to question," Rebecca said. "Almost no one in the Central National Society for Women's Suffrage supports temperance—I say almost no one because there are a few temperance suffragists who broke away with us over the home rule question rather than the temperance issue—but there are two particularly hypocritical ladies who are especially vociferous against the anti-drinkers, Maria Norton and Lydia Percival. I can get you their addresses. They fawn on Lady Isabella and pretend to be on the side of temperance when they're with her society friends, but drink like pub brawlers when they're with those of us in the Central National Society. They're actually rather amusing to have around, but neither of them has ever had a kind word to say about Lady Deborah. You might mention them to your friends here on the force, Maddie. I didn't like Lady Deborah myself—but she didn't deserve to be murdered."

"No one does," I said solemnly, if a tad hypocritically; I myself had killed three men in the past; oh wait, it was four now, wasn't it? I was surprised that Rebecca was so willing to put her friends forward as suspects, even to the extent of telling us where to find them, but was grateful that she was proving to be such a responsible citizen, albeit one under arrest at the moment.

Astraia and John left a half-hour later, and Rebecca and I spent a while talking over the last of the tea and biscuits. I wondered what she had done that had got her arrested. Perhaps there was a particular member of Parliament with whom she was having hostilities. I hoped she would bring it up herself, to assuage my curiosity.

But she didn't. Instead she asked me questions about my life as a police veterinarian, and I joined easily into the new subject, telling her what it was like to be a female horse doctor working in the city. I even invited her to visit the new colt with me the following morning, an invitation she accepted gladly.

"This is an interesting place you have," she said, and stood up to tour the tiny office. "Do you do animal surgeries in here?"

I admitted I did but did not confess that those surgeries were often practised on the very table upon which we had just enjoyed our dinner.

She glanced over the office shelves, mostly empty now that I had removed the last of my father's equipment and belongings that did not pertain to the practise of veterinary arts, an action I had taken after Astraia and Sherlock Holmes had both used the display of rusted implements and jars of God-knows-what to make conclusions about certain uncomplimentary attributes of my father's character. Rebecca froze in front of the little goddess statue, which I had taken out of my bag when I'd come home a few hours ago and set on a shelf for later examination.

"You have an Asherah statue," she said, wonderingly.

"Um, yes," I said with hesitation.

"She's quite beautiful."

"Yes. She is." I walked over to join her in contemplation of the small sculpture.

"Have you been a practitioner for long?" she asked.

I'd had the thing for less than five hours. "No," I said. "Not long."

She lifted the fox collar on her dress to show me a pin she wore hidden underneath. It too was this same goddess figure but as an enamelled piece of jewellery, a naked woman with bent elbows and hands placed underneath her breasts.

"Ah," I said. "Lovely." Was this some secret cult, like a female version of the Freemasons? Was there was some secret sign or handshake I was supposed to make now?

If there was, I didn't know it, and after a moment she moved away. "I think I'm going to go to bed now," she said. "Good night, Maddie."

"Good night, Rebecca."

She repaired to the back bedroom and I made up the camp bed for myself. Old Vic was nowhere to be found, and I assumed he had moved into the other stable with Rutherford for the time being. I conscientiously locked the door to the outside, turned down the lamps and blew out all of the candles, and went to sleep in my new bed by the stove.

Although the camp bed was not as comfortable as my normal berth, this had been a very long day and I had not slept at all the previous night, having spent my time in horse labour and preparing for the early trip to Margaret Bright Lucas's funeral. I fell into a deep sleep, from which nothing could arouse me.

Which was unfortunate, because sometime during the night my prisoner escaped from her stable bedroom cell.

Chapter Seven

DI Samuel Rankin blamed me, which really wasn't fair. "There isn't a lock on the outside of my bedroom door to keep prisoners from escaping," I pointed out with asperity.

"Then how did you keep that opium dealer from escaping last month?" he asked.

"I stayed awake all night watching the door that time," I said. Which wasn't entirely true—he had been under the influence of his drug, and sleeping heavily, so, well... But mostly I'd stayed awake. "Did you expect me to stay alert all night and every night while Miss Ravenwood Thornapple was here? Am I to get no sleep at all, ever? Didn't you think to put an officer on guard outside the door, since she was such an important prisoner?"

He growled and turned away, which was his acknowledgement that the police had failed in their duty. There should have been a guard outside my stable door all night.

It occurred to me to tell him to ask Chan if he'd seen anything, since the boy had no doubt spent the night out on the street as usual, spying on me for his villainous master. Then I thought the better idea would be to have Rutherford ask Chan; I could provide that information to the DI if there were any details worthy of sharing. Let him know I had my own resources.

Astraia came in, followed by John who was laden with a large basket of breakfast foods and tableware, and Susie who carried a sewing basket I presume Letty had gifted to her.

"Our pretty pigeon has flown the coop," I told Astraia.

A delicate eyebrow rose. "When?"

"Sometime during the night," Samuel said. "Miss Maddie slept right through it."

I scowled. That trip to the Shoreditch music hall stretched farther into the future.

"Didn't you stand a guard outside the door?" my dear friend asked her childhood foe, incredulity dripping from her voice.

Samuel stormed out without another word to us; on his way, no doubt, to ring a peal over the officer on duty last night who had not thought to place a guard outside the temporary gaol.

John set the basket down and began to prepare the scarred old table for the morning meal. "More breakfast for us, then," Astraia said. I usually had just a light tea in the morning. Astraia had brought breakfast here today in order to further interrogate Rebecca. Which meant there was enough food for at least three people, probably more.

"Just a moment," I said, and walked outside to the other stable. I quickly found Rutherford with the new foal, happily petting the dear little creature as it suckled at its own breakfast, and instructed him to come into the veterinarian stable for a minute as I had an errand for him.

The blight of a table was in disguise again, covered with a lovely yellow daisy tablecloth. John was setting it with ham, eggs, and sausages, plus rolls and preserves. I went over to the stove to start the tea.

"Rutherford, you can have breakfast, and then I want you to take some to Chan and ask him if he saw a lady running away from here in the middle of the night. If he did, see if he remembers what time it was, which direction she went, and whether or not she met up with someone or escaped all alone."

"Will do, Miss," he said. "Are there enough buns for the other chaps in the stable, Miss Astraia? They've been jolly kind to me."

Astraia handed a bun to Susie, then responded to Rutherford. "If you and Chan share one, and Maddie and I share one, you can take the rest to them," she said, nodding to John who began wrapping buns into a large napkin. "Be sure to bring the napkin back to me, mind."

"Oh, of course!" he said. "Thank you ever so much, Miss Astraia." He took the bundle of rolls and a jar of preserves from John. "I'll just deliver these to the boys, then I'll come back and get the food for Chan, Miss," he said to me.

"That was nice of you," I said to Astraia as we watched Rutherford leave. "I know you don't especially care for those boys." Truthfully, I didn't care for Jamie and Little Teddy either. They were very disrespectful toward me.

"They're rotten cretins who would be robbing old ladies on the streets if they didn't have such a rewarding and undemanding job here working for the police," she said. "But I'm not that fond of bread at breakfast anyway, so it's not such a sacrifice."

After Susie polished off a plate of ham, I sent her to check on the horse in the infirmary box. Astraia and I prepared our breakfast plates and tea, and sat down to discuss the escape in the night and plan the next stage of our investigation.

I told her that the name of our little goddess was Asherah, and that she might be the focus of devotion for others, including Rebecca.

Astraia was thrilled with this news. "Fascinating," she said. "Good work, Maddie. This information actually inspires me to go in to work today, so that I can use the library resources to find out more about this Asherah. Excellent." She dug into her eggs and ham with gusto.

I sipped at my tea. I was not so enthusiastic as she about consuming meat in the morning. I preferred bread.

John cleared his throat. "Asherah was the name of the wife of God," he said.

Astraia's fork clattered onto her plate then fell to the floor. "What are you talking about, John? I never heard that God was married."

John picked up her fork then handed her a clean one from the basket. "You may recall that I have always been interested in religion, Miss Astraia," he said. "I have studied quite a bit. Asherah was the wife of Jehovah, the God of the Israelites, but was also associated with Baal, the God of the Caananites. We don't know very much about her. When she's mentioned in the Bible, it's usually in an inflammatory manner, because the people have put up an Asherah pole as an idol."

"So, if she's God's wife does that mean she was Jesus's mother?" my friend asked. "I thought her name was Mary."

I was taken aback by all the blasphemy in these sentences, but John took it in stride. He was more used to Astraia than I was. Astraia and her brothers were not religious people.

"Asherah was from the early days of the Old Testament," he said. "She had nothing whatsoever to do with Jesus."

I had read the Bible many times but had never thought about who Asherah might have been though I had certainly seen the name. I found this whole idea of God having a wife very troubling, for some reason I couldn't explain even though logically I could see no reason why God couldn't have a consort. All the false gods were married, weren't they? Like Zeus and Odin and Osiris? Still, just the thought of it disturbed me.

"Well, we shall have to think about what this means," Astraia said. "Why would people like Valerie Dryson and Rebecca Ravenwood Thornapple worship the wife of God? Do you have any ideas, Maddie?"

"Might it be related to the suffrage movement?" I asked.

She shook her head. "No, I don't think so. Remember that Mrs Dryson told us she didn't have any opinion about suffrage one way or the other. But the next time I write Nora I'll ask her if she knows anything about Asherah worship. I received a new letter from her in the last post yesterday. She deprecates all the militancy being shown by some London suffragists—I assume she means Rebecca; have we heard yet what she was arrested for?—and she also said that she's heard Dr Dryson has been very sick. Which we already knew, of course."

"True. So what shall we do next with the case?" I asked. I hoped she would say there was nothing to do for the time being, because I needed to catch up with work in the office.

She said that I could focus on my actual job for a day or two, but not to forget that we had an engagement at Miss Maria Norton's house in two days' time to give our advice about whom they should support as the next president of the British Women's Temperance Union.

"Oh, that's right," I said morosely. I could not have cared less who governed the BWTU.

"Miss Lydia Percival will no doubt be there too," Astraia said. "So perhaps we will learn enough from them that we won't need to follow up the day after with our appointment at Miss Percival's home to help her with investments."

"That would be best," I said. "I'd look quite the fool, offering someone financial advice."

"Although if Rebecca is right and these two ladies look suspicious, we will need to spend more time with them," she reminded me.

"Let's hope they're innocent, then," I said.

Rutherford ran in, with information from Chan. The child was very grateful for the breakfast, and sorry he would not assist with our inquiry. He had not seen anyone leaving the stables last night.

I was not surprised that he had not seen Rebecca's escape. The poor boy had to sleep sometime.

***

It became obvious that day that Susie preferred sewing dolls and doll clothes to caring for sick horses. I offered to let her spend two hours a day at her sewing, during daylight hours. I did not want the girl to ruin her eyes as so many other girls and women did, sewing in

139

the dim light of candles or paraffin lamps. She hugged me in gratitude, and sang as she worked on the horses, counting the minutes until three o'clock when she would be able to sew once more.

Rutherford came in soon thereafter, bringing me a note from Sherlock Holmes. This note said that Zhu Wei had increased his Ya Zi dragon terrorism activities in the Limehouse district, and that I needed to be on my guard.

As I was drafting my response for Rutherford to deliver to his master, he spoke up. "Miss Maddie, Chan has offered to show Susie and me around Limehouse. I thought it might be a good idea to get a sense of what the area is like. If you don't mind, of course, Miss."

"Rutherford, I don't think that's wise. Mr Holmes said in this letter that the villains are increasing their criminal activities."

"But we'd go during the day, Miss," he said. "Today we could go. And no one's going to hurt us, because we're just street kids, Miss. And we'll be with Chan."

Susie ran over. "Oh, please, Miss Maddie, please can we go?"

"I don't think it would be safe for you, Susie," I said. I noticed that if her choice was between spending time today with her beloved sewing or with Rutherford, she gladly chose the boy.

"I'll take care of her, Miss," Rutherford said. "And so will Chan. You don't have to worry about her, Miss."

"Please, Miss Maddie? Please?"

I sighed. Things were unusually quiet in the veterinary stable just now; I was at the table bringing my accounts up to date. I really didn't have much work for them to do anyway.

"You have to be back before dark," I said.

"Oh, we will!" Susie said.

"I promise, Miss," Rutherford said.

I even thought of a task they could take on for me, something I'd been planning for a while. "I would like to find a laundry," I said. "I understand there are many to chose from in Limehouse. You might see if there's a laundry that would trade services with me—they could clean our clothes, and I would take care of their delivery horses when they're sick."

Rutherford nodded. "Chan should be able to help us with that, Miss," he said. "Thank you, Miss." The two children hurried out.

I sat staring at my accounting ledger, thinking about other things. I wasn't troubled about Rutherford, who'd spent his whole life on the streets. I wasn't very worried about Susie either, who'd be with both boys and would return before dark. And then I smiled. Two of my spies were out of the way for a few hours, leaving only the two foreign spies I hadn't identified yet. It was too bad I didn't have anywhere very important to go.

I decided to walk over to the Whitechapel Library to see how Astraia's research was going and to tell her about the note I had received from her brother.

During my walk, I had the good fortune of noticing a couple of men following behind me. One, the shorter, wore a sailor's cap and a dark cloak; the other a battered brown hat and brown coat. From time to time I stopped for a moment to shift my cane between my hands, glancing around as I balanced from one foot to the other. In this way I was able to memorise the faces of my two followers. It was not hard. They were not being cautious. I suppose it did not occur to them that I knew they were watching me, and I was very careful to never stare at either of them but rather to allow my eyes to just pass over their faces as I took in everything else around me.

They both had dark skin, but I could not tell if that was due to nature or sun exposure. They wore beards, but Sailor Cap's beard was much scragglier than that of his colleague, whom I mentally designated Pale Eyes in reference to the most noteworthy element of his physiognomy.

They did not follow me into the library. Unfortunately, one of the patrons did.

"Miss Barquist! What a pleasure seeing you again!" A man of middle years dressed in a respectable brown suit with a jarring orange-coloured waistcoat rushed over to me as I cautiously climbed the stairs to the building.

"Hello Dr Inskip," I said with much less enthusiasm. Dr Martin Inskip was a phrenologist with a peculiar predilection for the shape of the bumps on my head.

He tried to grab at my hand, but I pulled it back. "I'm sorry, Dr Inskip—I find climbing stairs very difficult, and must cling to the banister, as you can see." Indeed, the new Whitechapel Library—with steep stairs both outside and inside the building—was an exhausting climb for someone wearing a plaster cast.

Dr Inskip held onto my arm to help me up the stairs, which in all honesty I must confess was of great assistance. When we reached the top of the stairs inside and he still grasped my arm, I tried to dislodge him.

"Dr Inskip, it was lovely to see you again but I need to visit with the librarian on a private matter now," I said briskly. I saw Letty sitting at the front desk and nodded at her, so she would go find Astraia. She saw me but did not move from her location.

"Just give me a minute, Miss Barquist. I have thought of you so many times since we met. Would you allow me to take you out sometime, perhaps to a musicale or to the opera?"

I did not intend to spend any time in an enclosed or dark space with this man, where he would no doubt find some excuse to rub my head again.

"No, Dr Inskip—I do not care for music," I lied.

"Then perhaps I could take you to dinner," he said.

"I don't think so, Dr Inskip." Letty continued to watch us, a slight smile on her face, damn her. I looked around for Astraia. "I really do need to find Miss Holmes."

"I won't take no for an answer, Miss Barquist," he said earnestly. "I must see you again. Where shall we go?"

As he stared at me, I realised the way his eyes were set reminded me of a camel I had seen once on a trip with my Mummy. "The zoo?" I blurted.

"The zoo would be splendid, Miss Barquist!" he said. "Tomorrow?"

Tomorrow would be Saturday. My half-day was Sunday. I had hoped to spend it at Shoreditch...

"I cannot go tomorrow," I said. "But Sunday would be fine." If I made plans to go out on Sunday with Dr Inskip, I would be unable to change my resolve and go to the music hall with Samuel, should he ask me again.

"Where shall I collect you?" he asked.

"I'll meet you there," I said. I did not want him to know where I lived.

We made the arrangements and the phrenologist finally let go of me so that I could find Astraia and he could attend to his own library business.

Astraia sat at a table in the back, poring over books on mythology and ancient religions. "Have you found anything?" I asked.

"Not much," she said. "John told us pretty much all there is to know." She opened a book to show me some engravings of Asherah and Asherah poles. The old statues were much cruder than Mrs Dryson's, but I could see that they probably represented the same deity. "I haven't read anything yet to indicate there might be an Asherah secret society or anything of that nature," she said. "But that means nothing. A secret society is hardly secret if you can find out about it from a library book."

I told her about the new warning from her brother of an increase in villainy in Limehouse, and said that I had seen Zhu Wei's two foreign spies on my way here, detailing the features of Sailor Cap and Pale Eyes so she might be able to recognise them herself.

"That's wonderful," she said. "You can describe their appearance to Shirlie."

I had not thought about that. I might not like it, but she was right. I'd revise the message I'd prepared for Rutherford to deliver to Sherlock Holmes.

"I'm going to the zoo on Sunday with Dr Inskip," I said morosely.

She stared at me. "Why on earth would you want to do something like that?" she asked.

I did not discuss the ups and downs of my relationship with Samuel with my friend. "I like the zoo," I said.

She shrugged. "Well, don't forget that we have plans to see Miss Norton that evening," she said.

I had completely forgotten that, but was glad of the reminder. It would give me a good excuse to make an early end to my day with the phrenologist.

***

It had been years since I had visited that most wondrous site, the gardens of the Zoological Society of London in Regent's Park. As I told the children good-bye late on Sunday morning, I promised them both that if they were very good today, I would take them both to the zoo the following week. That way, I would accomplish three things: it would alleviate the guilt I was feeling by not taking them with me today (bringing my wards along seemed an overly unkind thing to do to Dr Inskip—plus if I had them with me he'd certainly learn where I lived); it would assure one more week when I could not accept an outing with Samuel Rankin; and it would allow me to enjoy the place in a way I did not anticipate experiencing today in Dr Inskip's company.

The best way to get to Regent's Park if you have a broken foot is via omnibus. As I made my second bus change, it occurred to me that I could have met Dr Inskip at some other place closer to my home and ridden with him in his carriage. But no, that would have given him more time with my head bumps. Dr Inskip found my head bumps stimulating to his area of study. Apparently my lobe of "conjugal love" is very pronounced.

I missed the timing to catch the third bus, and decided to view this trip as research for the visit next week with the children. Next week, I would do better.

When I reached the zoo, I was surprised by the paucity of visitors. Dr Inskip stood out, wearing a royal blue waistcoat today, a limp nosegay in his buttonhole. He practically ran toward me and latched himself to my side.

"On Sundays, the zoo is only open to Fellows of the Zoological Society and to those of us to whom they provide tickets," he explained. "Fortuitously, one of these Fellows attends my church, and he gave me tickets this morning after mass."

I frowned. This would complicate my plans to bring the children to the zoo on my half-day next week. I did not know anyone who was a Fellow of the Zoological Society, and I would not ask Dr Inskip to get tickets for me. He'd want to join us.

As we entered we discussed the order in which we should visit the collections. I wanted to start with the parrot walk; he was happy with whatever route I wished to take, as long as we spent some time at the giraffe house and the monkey house. He came to the zoo often, and was a font of information.

I was surprised there were so few people here today, even with special tickets. "It is much busier in the summer. But in the winter many of the more interesting animals, like the elephants, are not allowed to leave their cages," Dr Inskip explained. "All tropical animals are kept indoors, so that they can survive the winters. Even if they were to be allowed out into their little enclosures, the pools they usually enjoy are frozen over."

"Are the houses for the attractions heated?" I asked. It wasn't a fiercely cold day, but there was a wind, and it would get uncomfortable standing for long in front of cages full of shivering animals.

"The Society has always provided heat to the animals in the winters, because they knew the creatures needed that in order to live comfortably in the English cold. But it took them years to determine how best to heat the cages and enclosures, and many animals died as a result—for example, in the early days usually lions and tigers would only last a year or two before dying. Now there is ventilation as well as heat, and many animals survive for many years in peace and contentment."

"How many animals are there?" I asked as we entered the parrot walk.

On our way to the wonderful blast of colour these exotic birds and their tropical trees provided on a dreary winter day, I had noticed that most of the visitors at the zoo today were well-dressed and respectable, no doubt a reflexion of their association with the Fellows of the Zoological Society, the group that funded the zoological research. But I also noticed a few furtive types of the sort of person who lived in my part of town, whom I assumed had either climbed a fence or shimmied open a door to get into the place.

These individuals were not admiring the animals. They were watching the humans. Searching out their prey.

The parrot walk was hot, humid, colourful, and overwhelmingly loud, as alien to my daily experience as could possibly be imagined. Extraordinarily beautiful parrots, toucans, parrakeets, cockatoos, and macaws screamed at us and at each other in their unintelligible bird languages. Dr Inskip had to lean close to me to answer my question. "There are over 2,000 animals here in the zoo—about half of them are birds."

"And how many of the animals die each year?" I asked, watching a pathetic limp-feathered cockatoo who was clearly not long for this world.

"Unfortunately, the annual mortality of these creatures is almost half," he said sadly, then smiled at the antics of a bright macaw cleaning its feathers just a foot away from his face.

"Half!" I said, horror-struck.

"Yes," he said, "but you have to remember that animals do not live as long as humans do. And happily the zoo continues to grow, because although almost a thousand animals might die in a year, that number is somewhat exceeded by the number that are purchased by or presented to the Society, or that might be born here in the gardens."

"Somewhat exceeded?"

He nodded. "A bit. Not enough that they have to build new cages or enclosures very often. But enough that visitors don't feel cheated. And as I said, it used to be worse."

"Before they understood that animals need ventilation as well as heat."

"Yes. It was worse then."

We stopped for a long while to enjoy the huge beasts in the elephant and rhino house. When I was a child, my Mummy had brought me here to see the magnificent Jumbo. One of the greatest thrills of my life was riding on his back. Although Jumbo was no longer here, having been sold some years ago to a circus in America where he soon died, I was happy to see there were other elephants in his place, and Dr Inskip assured me that these animals also gave children rides. I knew Susie and Rutherford would find the experience as exciting as I had. I looked forward to bringing them here later on in the year, when the great beasts would be allowed once more to leave their cages and indulge in exercise.

I had begun the day excited to see this place that in my childhood had brought me such joy, and it wasn't until we got to the lion house that the tragic aspect of the zoo began to fill my heart. We walked through the exhibit, where the majestic creatures were all confined to cages of concrete, wood and steel; the lions, leopards, and tigers, each in their own cage, the lucky ones sharing their small area with a female of their same species; unable to run and hunt as I knew they must have done in Africa and India. Here, all they seemed to do—all they had space to do—was sleep. It was far more quiet and peaceful than any place full of wild animals should be. One old man sat on a bench in front of the king of the beasts, snoring along in lethargic companionship.

"I am sorry we're still too early to witness feeding time," Dr Inskip said. He was eyeing my head, something I'd caught him doing more than once today. I knew he wanted to touch it, to rub my lobes. I was glad I wore a hat. "At 4 o'clock feeding begins, and that's when the crowds come because that's the only time there's activity. The big cats only become energised and entertaining when food arrives, bounding and running around chasing their tails in small circles in anticipation of their daily joint of beef."

He stared into my face, and grasped my hands in his. "We could have tea, then return when it's time to feed the lions," he suggested.

I pulled my hands back and started walking toward the exit. "I'm sorry, Dr Inskip," I said. "I can't stay out that long." I thought of something that might change his mind about wanting to pursue a relationship with me. "Miss Holmes and I are visiting some other suffragist friends of ours this evening," I said.

"Oh," he said. He followed me out and we walked toward the monkey house. Few men think fondly of women's suffrage, and I congratulated myself on having identified something to deter him in his attentions toward me without having to actually tell him who I was or what I did. Which interestingly enough, he hadn't even asked any questions about yet.

The creatures at the monkey house were the first animals we'd seen today who seemed to be actually enjoying their lives. There must have been a dozen different types of monkey, lemurs, capuchins, and so many others; most of them quite jolly except for the barbary ape and the orangutan who were kept segregated from their fellows. Dr Inskip, an old hand at the zoo, had brought some nuts with him to feed to these dear little creatures, and while he was tossing nuts into a group of them a green monkey reached its little hand out through the cage to grab Dr Inskip's flower from his buttonhole, and promptly stuck the flower into its mouth and ate it. I started laughing at that, and after a moment Dr Inskip began laughing too. This was the highlight of the afternoon.

Next we visited Sally, the most famous animal at the zoo now that Jumbo the elephant was gone. Sally was a bald-headed chimpanzee who was very smart. Dr Inskip told me that a researcher worked regularly with Sally, and she could understand human language and count to six, using straws. But while we were there she simply lay on her side, slapping at other animals whenever they came near to her. Dr Inskip threw her a nut, which she observed listlessly then ate, without giving him the least bit of attention. He started calling to her, since she supposedly knew her name and recognised human words, and his attention was so focused on the female in the cage that he didn't notice the human female who moved to his other side and slipped her hand into his pocket.

I did notice, however, and I yelled "Thief!" The girl began running away, the monkeys cheering her on, but she was a tired and malnourished creature and my long legs quickly caught up to her, even with one foot in a cast. I was able to catch her, and I held onto her arms while Dr Inskip took his wallet back from her hand and checked to make sure the contents were still in place.

Other men and women around us began checking their own pockets for their possessions, and one who found his watch missing began yelling for someone to get the police. I frowned at this, but continued to hold onto the girl (who could not have been more than a year or two older than Susie) until the forces of the law appeared to remove her from my custody.

The police constable who took possession of the girl needed my name and address for the record. I sighed, then gave it to him as Dr Inskip listened avidly.

The young officer looked impressed. "I know you!" he said. "You're one of those detectivist ladies who solved that dragon ripper crime last month!"

I admitted I was, and all around me the people oohed and aahed, happy to be in the presence of such a celebrated lady detective. The old man from the lion house cupped his palsied hand over his mouth in surprise. Even the young pickpocket seemed in awe.

Unfortunately, another of the people who was impressed to learn of my achievement was Dr Inskip.

He insisted that we needed to go to tea so that I could tell him about the case; I reiterated that I had another engagement and couldn't be late; he said that he would take me home himself so that I could be back home in time. I finally agreed. I was taller than he was, and almost certainly stronger. I could take care of myself if he became too amatory.

I had my cane with me.

In Dr Inskip's hurry to whisk me away we skipped the stork and ostrich house, the grand aviary, the reptile house and even the giraffe house that he had particularly wanted to visit today. We passed by the bear pit and I thought: the children will want to see that.

We stopped at a tea house on the outskirts of the zoological gardens, where Dr Inskip ordered tea and sandwiches for us. This was unusual for me, I thought; when I went out with Samuel Rankin we always stopped at a pub. And then I scolded myself for thinking about him.

Although if there had ever been a time I could use a drink, that time was now.

"Tell me all about the dragon ripper case," Dr Inskip insisted. "I myself witnessed one of the killings, you know."

"I know," I said. "You told us about it the day I met you. In fact, what you told us helped us quite a bit in determining the solution."

I shared details I thought he might find interesting, and for a while he actually seemed attentive as I spoke. But that didn't last too long. Eventually he began talking about his own work as a phrenologist, learning about the characteristics of individuals by studying the shapes of their heads and the bumps that brain muscles exert upon the skull.

"I am fascinated to hear that you work for the police, Miss Barquist," he said. "You know, I have a deep interest in anthropological criminology. I believe very strongly that criminals and deviants are born that way. The country could save a great deal of money and heartache if we simply identified criminals when they were children by studying their physiology and locking them up before their baser urges overcome them."

"You don't think training them to behave properly before they begin to act on their bumps might be a more Christian approach?" I asked. "A sort of pre-reform, if you will?"

"Ah, the kind heart of a good woman," he said, smiling at me with the 'pat-the-good-dog' look I've received so many times from men. "No, I think pre-emptive punishment is the best plan for society. I would love to speak with your supervisors about my ideas."

"I'll see what I can do." Naturally I would do no such thing.

He leaned closer toward me. "You have a most splendid head, Miss Barquist," he told me softly. "Very sensual."

"So you mentioned before," I said, leaning away. "Tell me about your church." I wanted to change the subject from the topic of my voluptuous head bumps and the head bumps of criminally-minded toddlers, but the only other things I really knew about him from the first time we met were that he was Catholic and seemed to dislike Chinese people, and I was uninterested in hearing him expound on the latter topic.

He was happy to tell me about his church, St Mary of Perpetual Help, where he served on the council and sometimes as a lector. He was very proud of his knowledge of Latin. He had considered becoming a deacon but did not do so because he still had hopes of marrying and raising a family.

"You should come to mass with me next week," he urged.

"I work on Sunday mornings," I said. "I only have a half-day off each week."

"It's appalling that they make you work on Sundays!" he huffed. "I shall speak with someone about it."

Actually, if I wanted to go to church on Sundays, no one would have said a thing about it. And my "half-day off" had become much of a joke ever since Astraia's brother Mycroft Holmes had told the police force that my assistance to her had to take precedence over my work in the stable. So far this hadn't caused any difficulties—he had also been responsible for them hiring Susie to help me—but I could imagine a time in the future when I would be expected to choose between examining a corpse with Astraia and performing an emergency horse operation. I did not look forward to that day.

I convinced the phrenologist to return me in plenty of time to prepare for my visit with Astraia that evening to discuss the future of the British Women's Temperance Union with Miss Norton and Miss Percival. He tried to persuade me to take off my hat during the hackney trip back to the Leman Street police station ("It looks so uncomfortable!") but I resisted his entreaties. Just sharing such a small cab with him was bad enough; it seemed as though there wasn't enough room in the thing for both of us to have arms of our own.

I also resisted making any additional plans to see him. He assured me he wouldn't give up, and grabbed my hand at the door of the stable to kiss my knuckles. I couldn't get inside to my office fast enough.

Once inside, leaning against the door, eyes closed, I experienced my first surprise of what would be an evening full of them.

"Hello, Miss Barquist. Let me congratulate you on your quick response at the monkey house today," Sherlock Holmes said.

Chapter Eight

"Oh God. What do you want?" I said rudely. Luckily there seemed to be no one else around to hear me speak so disrespectfully to the great man.

He grinned. "You sent a message to me."

I frowned, then remembered he was correct. I'd had Rutherford take him a message. "I can recognise the foreign spies now," I said. "In case you need me to identify them."

"That won't be necessary," he said. "I can recognise them myself."

"You can?"

"Certainly. I've been following you myself these last few days, and have obtained for myself a good idea of their habits."

Following me?...and then I noticed his apparel.

"You were the old man at the zoo!" I said. "The one sleeping in the lion house."

"I wasn't really asleep," he confided.

159

"Why were you following me?"

"I told you. I've been learning the habits of Zhu Wei's spies."

"But they didn't follow me into the zoo," I said. "At least, I didn't see them."

"No, they didn't follow you into the zoo," he said. "I presume they didn't have tickets. I had one, though; Mycroft is a Fellow of the Society. They followed you and your head bump friend to the tea shop afterwards, however."

"Astraia and I are going out this evening," I said. "Will they follow us tonight?" It might be useful for Astraia to be able to recognise Sailor Cap and Pale Eyes for herself, in case their criminal boss instructed them to shift their focus from me to her.

"I doubt it," he said. "From what I've observed, Zhu Wei does not appear to have given them enough funds for evening cab fare. But I'll make sure John stays close by, just in case."

He stood to leave, and I remembered something else I wanted to speak with him about.

"I've been thinking about young Chan," I said, walking him to the door.

"Who?"

"The boy in the blue head scarf."

"Oh yes. What about him?"

"I've been thinking he would make a good night watchman, once he gets older. What do you think? Will the police ever hire Chinese police constables?"

He studied my face. "I'll look into it," he said. He opened the door.

"Wait," I said. "I just thought of something else. Since you're here anyway, are you able to tell me why the police arrested Rebecca Ravenwood Thornapple?"

He barked out a laugh. "Yes, I can tell you that. I watched her leave here the other night. I didn't stop her. She shouldn't have been placed under arrest, and she certainly shouldn't have been gaoled, just because she won't stop sending threatening letters to the wife of her former fiancé. If you don't like the mail the postman hands you, just don't read it."

"Her former fiancé?"

"Well, she says he was her fiancé. He says he never was. And she hasn't been able to provide any billet-doux or witnesses or anything else to substantiate her story. I understand the threats she sent are fairly benign, like implying she would say vicious things about the wife to her hairdresser, a source of society gossip."

"They gaoled her for sending letters? Why would she send them to his wife, anyway, instead of to the lover who betrayed her?"

"Miss Ravenwood Thornapple says that it's the wife's fault that he broke their engagement. He decided to go into politics—he's now an MP—and his wife's father is the person who funded his campaign. I'm surprised that the scandal hasn't hit the newssheets yet, and can only suppose that the father has also paid them off. Similar to the way he paid off the judge and the police to arrest Miss Ravenwood Thornapple and put her behind bars. Good night, Miss Barquist."

Smiling, I closed the door behind him. I no longer felt bad that Rebecca had escaped my custody.

***

I refreshed my hair and clothing for the visit to Miss Norton's home, and allowed myself a few bites of day-old gingerbread even though I'd had tea with Dr Inskip a short time ago and would no doubt be offered additional refreshment by Miss Norton. Sometimes you just have to treat yourself.

Susie and Rutherford arrived home, excited as always by the ride through London in John's carriage despite having to spend the trip in the company of Astraia, who was never a child's most pleasant companion. They'd spent the day at her home, where Susie had sewn with Letty and Rutherford had demonstrated on John's horses what he'd been learning here under my tutelage. Letty had filled them with food before they left, so I felt at ease leaving them at home and following John to the carriage where Astraia awaited me.

Astraia handed me a letter as soon as I sat down, which I squinted to read in the dying light. She took it back. "Never mind—I'll tell you what it says. Dr Dryson has died."

"He's died?"

"Yes. Nora wrote to me as soon as she heard. I received this yesterday."

"How awful! When did he die?"

"I'm not sure, but I think possibly the very day we met with his wife," she said.

I was so horror struck by this I did not know what to say. "Was it our fault, Astraia?"

She did not try to sugar-coat the feasibility of our responsibility in his death. "Possibly. He may have lasted a few more days if we had not confronted his wife about seeing her at Sir Peter Peacham's home. But I think he was doomed to die either way."

"What are we going to do about it?"

"At the least we should tell PC Froest," she said gloomily. She had mentioned to Archie her concerns about Mrs Dryson on the evening when Rebecca came to horse gaol, and as we'd anticipated he had dismissed our worries. Of course, given what we now knew, Dr Dryson was probably already dead when we spoke with Archie.

"We need to solve this case as well," I said decidedly.

"Yes," she said. "We will."

I told her the reason Rebecca had been arrested and sentenced to gaol, which somewhat lightened the mood. "If the wife doesn't like the mail she receives, she should just refuse to open it," she said.

"That's what your brother Sherlock said."

"Did he say anything else useful?"

"Not really. He's been spying on me himself and following the two foreign sailors in Zhu Wei's employ."

"I thought that was why he sent Rutherford to you."

"Apparently he doesn't think Rutherford's talents are sufficient to obtain the information he desires."

"So you have, what, five spies watching you now?"

"At least they're not all following us right this minute," I said. "Your brother said that Zhu Wei doesn't pay the foreign sailors enough to hire cabs to follow us in the evenings when we go out."

"No, in the evenings when we go out we have John spying on us," Astraia pointed out.

"Ah, yes. There's that."

I described Mr Holmes's masquerade as an old man in the zoo, and told her of my adventures in the monkey house with Dr Inskip, the pickpocket, and the policeman who had blabbered everything that I had been trying to keep secret from the phrenologist. She laughed, as I'd hoped she would.

"Letty wants to know if you have any clothes you need her to wash," she said casually. I had gotten in the habit of acquiescing when Letty took my laundry back with her to Astraia's house. She did such a splendid job of caring for my clothes, which she thoughtfully patched and darned as well as washed.

But I always felt guilty about burdening her with my things, so I was happy to be able to tell Astraia I was hoping to make other arrangements, with a laundry in

Limehouse. And I had every expectation that Susie would be happy to take up patching and darning duties for me.

I had learned a lot about life in Limehouse from Rutherford, after he and Susie had accompanied Chan into the district. Apparently Chan's mother was a white woman, a former prostitute who had settled down with a Chinese sailor. This was the normal situation whenever one saw Chinese children on the streets—there were no Chinese women in London, and all of the Chinese families in Limehouse were made up of sailors from China who had married English women and settled here in this new country with their new families. Often they opened laundries or restaurants to cater to other Chinese sailors—and this occurred now more than ever, due to the women's motivation to get off the dangerous streets of Whitechapel.

As Rutherford had explained this to me, I realised that my monstrous father had been an impetus to a new type of family dynamic—women of the streets afraid of encountering Jack the Ripper were roused to leave prostitution and find a safer new life with foreign men who wouldn't judge them but would instead rely on them for success in England. The women possessed something their foreign husbands didn't have: fluency in the local language and an ability to function in the larger community. They could do business with the locals, which was difficult for their husbands. This ability made them precious to their husbands and therefore gave them a modicum of safety they lacked when they married English sailors or local English businessmen.

The children had suggested I use a laundry at the edge of the district, an easy walk away. The owners had a delivery horse, and might be interested in trading services with me if I asked. I planned to meet them when I had time. The wife was English, so I'd be able to explain my proposal.

"Please tell Letty she does not have to wash my clothes any more," I said. "And let her know how grateful I am to her for asking." I doubted that Astraia would forward this second part of my message to her servant. I would need to remember to mention my thanks to Letty myself, the next time I saw her.

We spent the rest of the trip discussing the best ways to inveigle information about the death of Lady Deborah from Miss Norton and Miss Percival.

In the end, we hadn't needed to strategise our conversation in advance after all. There was nothing Maria Norton and Lydia Percival loved more than sharing gossip and intrigue.

We sat down to refreshments of wine and biscuits, after Maria Norton had hesitantly asked us if we wouldn't enjoy something stronger than china tea to drink. She was looking longingly toward the sideboard when she spoke, where a decanter of wine held prominence. "We love wine and biscuits," Astraia assured her.

"Well, don't let Lady Isabella know that," Maria giggled. "We're here tonight to talk about the British Women's Temperance Union, after all." She poured us each a small glass of wine.

Astraia brushed her comment aside. "There is a world of difference between respectable ladies such as ourselves spending an occasional social evening enjoying a glass or two of wine with friends, and men drinking up the family funds in the pub night after night," she said, and made a great show of downing her entire glass in one big gulp.

Lydia hugged Astraia, and I realised the social evening of wine drinking had probably started before we'd even arrived. "That's what we always say!" she said. "But it is important that the laws are changed to protect us from those drunkards on the streets."

"Oh, absolutely," Astraia said adamantly, holding out her glass for a refill.

As the evening progressed I noticed she never actually drank any more, but her early enthusiasm completely charmed the other two. The four of us decided that Lady Isabella Somerset should be elected the next president of the BWTU, and swore we would do everything in our power to encourage other temperance suffragists to vote this same way.

The evening's official business over in the first five minutes, I brought up the real reason for our presence here this evening. "How well did you two know Lady

Deborah Peacham? Were you there with her at the House of Commons last month?"

They did not question why I had conflated the death of Lady Deborah with the rush on Parliament. They were just thrilled to have the opportunity to gossip about both.

"Oh, we loathed Lady Deborah, didn't we, Maria?" Lydia Percival said with a giggle.

Maria Norton laughed too, but decried the sentiment. "I wouldn't say we actually loathed the woman," she said. "We didn't celebrate when she died. Let's say, rather, that we don't miss her now that she's gone."

"No," Lydia agreed, "we don't miss her."

"Why not?" Astraia asked.

"Well, she was such a prig," Maria said. "Always so judgemental about people."

"Judgy, judgy, judgy," Lydia said, helping herself to a refill from the decanter, then giving a moue. "Maria, this bottle is gone. Is there another?"

"I'll have Mrs Peterwick bring us more," Maria said. "I told her to decant several bottles, just in case, you know..." She looked at us, and I realised they had hoped we would be willing to drink with them this evening but couldn't be certain that would be the case, given that we had originally met one another in the home of a prominent temperance leader and were presumably here tonight to discuss temperance issues.

Astraia gave me a nudging look, and I drank the rest of my own glass. "I too would like another glass," I said heartily. In truth, I wasn't much of a wine drinker, preferring harder spirits. I considered asking them if they had any whisky, but remembered that the point of the evening wasn't to imbibe alcohol, at least not so far as Astraia and I were concerned. We were here on an investigation.

"Who do you think killed her?" I asked.

"What, wasn't it her husband?" Maria asked in surprise. "I thought everyone knew it was her husband."

Astraia looked around the room, as though worried there might be someone else listening, and whispered in a dramatic sotto voce, "Actually, we have information that her husband didn't do it," she said.

"Really?" the two ladies said, both shocked and thrilled at this news.

"Yes. The police think that she was stabbed a few days earlier, but it took her a while to die. But don't tell anyone." She put her fingers to her lips. "It's still a secret."

"We won't tell a soul," they vowed. I knew that by tomorrow evening every lady in their social circle would know everything they swore tonight to keep secret, and wondered why Astraia was telling them. She probably assumed it would make the newspapers soon anyway, and we might as well benefit from seeming to bring Maria and Lydia into our confidence.

"Oh, my goodness," Maria said. "Then who did kill her?"

"It could have been anyone," Astraia said. She leaned closer. "Even one of her dearest friends."

Lydia threw her hands up in horror, and the last splashes from the glass she held spilt out and plopped on the sofa. Neither she nor Maria noticed. Astraia took the fresh decanter and refilled Lydia's glass.

"Who were Lady Deborah's dearest friends, anyway?" I asked.

Maria and Lydia both looked at each other in bemusement. "Do you know, I'm not sure she had any real friends," Maria said finally. "Not anyone close, at any rate."

"Judgy, judgy, judgy," Lydia repeated, taking a sip from her refreshed glass.

"So who were her enemies?" Astraia asked.

"Besides us?" Lydia asked, giggling.

Maria, the more sober of the two, realised the conversation might be getting too frank. "I think there were many people who disliked the woman," she said.

"Judgy, judgy, judgy."

Astraia decided to steer the discussion into deeper waters. "Tell us what it was like to storm Parliament," she said breathlessly. "It must have been so exciting! We do wish we had been there."

Maria Norton and Lydia Percival then told us much the same tale as we had heard from Lady Isabella and

Rebecca Ravenwood Thornapple, albeit in a more entertaining manner.

"Well," Isabella said. "For one thing, it started much too early in the morning."

"Much too early," Maria agreed dramatically.

"When we have the vote, there will be none of that holding meetings at 10 o'clock in the morning business."

"None of that."

They sat for a moment in silence, remembering the horror of having to arise early in the morning.

"So what happened?" I asked finally.

"Well, we all gathered together at the front gates of the Palace of Westminster at this ungodly hour of the morning," Maria said.

"Ungodly."

"We told them we were all going to the Ladies' Gallery," Maria said.

"That's what we said."

"Of course we had no intention of that."

"No indeed."

"The brass grille work you have to look through to see the floor—it gives you such a headache!" Maria said.

"At least that's what everyone says," Lydia said. "I've never actually been in the cage myself."

"We've never actually tried to watch a session," Maria admitted.

Astraia nodded. "Too early in the morning," she said. "So you didn't go into the Ladies' Gallery. Where did you go? And how many of you were there?"

"There were hundreds of us," Lydia said.

I frowned. According to Lady Isabella, there had been around two-dozen suffragists in Parliament that day.

"Oh, I don't think there were that many," Maria said, contradicting her friend. "But there were a lot."

"Women everywhere."

"Squeezed in tightly."

"I could hardly breathe."

"It was so hot."

"I actually took off my hat. Maria removed her coat, I think."

"So I did. I actually removed my coat."

"Lots of women did."

They were silent for a moment, remembering the discomfort of too many women squeezed into too tight a space, in the heat.

"Why was it hot?" I asked. "The rush on Parliament happened during the coldest part of winter."

"That's why we all had our coats on! And our best woollen hats! We thought we'd be freezing!"

"Huh!" said Lydia. "We wished we were freezing. When we finally left the building, I actually put my hand out into the snow and rubbed my face with it."

"So did I. Quite ruined my new kid gloves."

"I believe the Palace of Westminster is renowned for heating certain of its chambers in the winter," Astraia said to me. "There have been members who passed out from the heat in January."

I thought back to the lions in the zoo in previous years, before zookeepers realised that ventilation was necessary as well as warmth.

"So, when did it get so uncomfortable for you?" Astraia asked our hostess. "You entered through the public entrance. Was that too hot?"

"Oh, not at all. That was fine."

"Except there were too many people," Lydia said.

"Well, yes. But we were still moving then."

"We were fine as long as we kept moving."

"But then we got into the corridors leading to the House of Commons," Maria said.

"Which were fine. As long as we were moving."

"But they had the doors closed to the Commons Chamber!" Maria said, affronted.

"They wouldn't let us in!"

"And we waited and waited, and it was so hot, and they still wouldn't let us in."

"How did the Duchess of Queensbury and her associates get in back in 1739?" I asked.

"Well, they were quiet as a mouse that time, and eventually the Lords thought they had left," Maria said. "So they opened the doors to the House of Lords— because, you understand, it gets very hot in those rooms—and then the ladies rushed in."

"But we weren't able to fool them that same way," Lydia said sadly. "We couldn't be that quiet. The Duchess only had a few friends with her. We had hundreds. There were just too many of us. And it was too hot. Eventually the ladies nearest to the exit were persuaded to leave so that those of us near the door, who were suffering the most, could get out of there."

"I believe one or two ladies actually fainted," Maria said.

"I believe they did," Lydia agreed. "I almost did."

"And I really don't think there were hundreds."

"It certainly felt like it."

"Actually, I think Lady Deborah might have been one of those who fainted," Maria said after a moment's pause. "I believe she was assisted out of the corridor, at any rate."

"You know, I believe you are right, Maria."

"Do you remember who assisted her?" Astraia asked.

They looked at each other.

"I don't remember," Lydia admitted.

"Neither do I," Maria said.

We could tell they were fairly intoxicated by this time, and decided to bring the evening to a close.

"Well, I'm glad we've resolved who should be the next president of the British Women's Temperance Union," Astraia said, standing to leave. "Please let us know when the election meeting is to be held. We'll certainly want to be there to cast our votes for Lady

Isabella." She set her glass on a side table, and I stood to join her.

"Oh, we will," Maria said.

We collected our coats and hats, and Astraia turned to Lydia. "I believe we have an engagement to visit with you at your home tomorrow, Lydia, isn't that correct?"

She looked at us in some befuddlement, then said "I believe so, yes. You are going to give me advice on investments, I think."

"Unfortunately, there's another matter we must attend to tomorrow evening," Astraia said sadly.

"Oh, no!"

"But we can give you all the financial advice you need right now."

"Well, thank you!"

Astraia looked at the two ladies solemnly, then proclaimed, "You should only invest in those stocks that are rising on the exchange."

"Really?"

"Absolutely. If you invest in stocks that are going down, you will lose money."

"That is so amazing!"

"Yes. I like railroads, myself. As society grows people need a way to get places quickly, and there will never be a faster way to travel than by train. And ice companies are another good stock. People will always need ice delivered to their homes."

"That's brilliant!" Lydia said in awe, and then we all hugged and Astraia and I left. "I'll have my stockbroker contact you," my friend said as we waved goodbye.

"Have him contact me too," Maria said, her voice much louder than it should be on such a quiet street this late at night.

John was waiting for us at the other side of Maria's gate. He helped me into the coach, which was a blessing. Once again I had overworked my broken foot, walking through the zoological gardens today. The blasted thing was aching once more. Letty had not accompanied her brother so there was plenty of room inside. Astraia helped me set my foot up on the opposite seat to rest.

"Are you really going to have your stockbroker contact them?" I asked.

"You must be joking. I don't have a stockbroker."

I nodded and we sat in companionable silence for a time. "I like them," I said finally.

"I think I do too," Astraia said.

"So do we remove them from the suspect list?"

"Not yet. I don't believe either of them stabbed a hatpin into Lady Deborah deliberately. But I can easily imagine, in the crowd and the excitement and confusion and heat, a scenario in which one of them could have stabbed her by accident and never even realised what she had done."

"Especially if they had been enjoying a bottle or two of social conviviality prior to going to Westminster."

"Exactly so."

"What did you think about us drinking bottle after bottle of wine while we planned the future of the British Women's Temperance Union?" I asked.

"That was illuminating, and possibly tells us a great deal about the temperance ladies, at least those in society. It's all right if they drink alcohol, but it should be kept away from the lower orders."

"So you think the temperance movement might be another indicator of class conflict?" I asked.

"I think it's worth considering," she said.

"I may turn you into a socialist yet," I said.

She laughed, and for the rest of the trip we discussed the best way to find out from our suspects who had been the persons who had assisted Lady Deborah out of the corridors of the House of Commons.

The next day, all of the London newspapers featured the same story: Lady Deborah Peacham had been stabbed with a hatpin at the Palace of Westminster.

Several of them also provided more troubling information. They said that Miss Astraia Holmes and Miss Madeleine Barquist, the lady detectivists who had solved the dragon ripper killings, were investigating the case that was now being called *The Suffragist Murder*.

Chapter Nine

"I'll kill that Samuel Rankin!" Astraia said that morning when she stormed into my office, a pile of newssheets in her arms.

"Why do you blame him?" I asked, scanning through the headlines. I was just grateful not to see a repeat of the inflammatory images they'd printed during our last case, drawings of a swooning lady in a torn nightgown with my name printed underneath.

"Don't you see—he must have been the one who told the reporters that we were on the case. He thinks that if that fact is publicised, none of the suspects will talk to us and the police will get another chance to solve it."

I had to admit this sounded plausible.

At this rate I would never see the inside of the music hall in Shoreditch again.

"I received another letter from Nora this morning," Astraia said, handing an envelope to me. I opened it, then my mouth fell open as I perused the first page.

"Oh my God. Already cremated?"

"Already cremated. And no funeral."

"She didn't even know where to go in London to get her pottery fired, but she knew where to get her husband cremated?"

"So it seems."

"I wouldn't know where to go to get someone cremated—would you?"

"I would not."

"I have never known of anyone being cremated before." I was flabbergasted at the idea.

"Neither have I."

"Why would anyone want to do that?"

"You mean besides in order to cover up having poisoned her husband?"

"Well, yes. It would be illegal if that was the only reason it was done."

"I understand that some people believe cremation is more sanitary—it cuts down on the spread of disease. Also people worry about anatomists digging them up after they're dead and dissecting them. But it's people who worry about being buried alive who are the most likely to request cremation," Astraia said.

I could understand this. It seemed like every week there was another scare story in the newspapers about someone being buried alive. The only way to ensure that didn't happen was to wait until the body began to decay before it was buried (like Margaret Bright Lucas). But no one wanted to keep checking their loved one's corpse to make sure they had started rotting.

"It is possible that Dr Dryson did make that request," I said slowly. "He was the sort of person to worry about being buried alive."

She dismissed this. "That's irrelevant, Maddie. We both know that woman killed him."

My friend PC Archibald Froest made the unfortunate decision to enter the stable at that moment. "Who killed whom?" he asked, frowning.

Astraia turned on him. "Valerie Dryson. Remember her? The one who was feeding her husband Fowler's Solution? I told you about it just days ago. And now he's dead."

"The one you alleged was feeding her husband Fowler's Solution," Archie corrected. "But if he has indeed died, I will investigate the situation to see if we need to examine his remains for arsenic."

"Good luck with that," Astraia snapped. "His wife had him cremated."

Archie blinked. "Cremated? When did he die?"

"Three days ago," Astraia said. "But she must have had him cremated quite quickly afterward—perhaps even the following day."

"You'd better give me the details," Archie said, and he sat down to take notes while Astraia gave him the pertinent information about the newlyweds.

"We will look into this," Archie said. "I promise you."

Astraia just shook her head and stalked away. I smiled at Archie. "Thank you. I know you'll find the truth." I wasn't actually confident of this, but knew Archie felt dismayed at Astraia's clear disappointment in him. I accompanied him to the door.

"Oh, Maddie—I forgot," he said. "You received a letter." He handed it to me, and left.

This was such an unusual event that I stared at the thing for a moment before opening it. Once I did open and read it, I started to laugh. Somewhat hysterically.

"What?" Astraia said, rushing over. "What is it?"

For the first time in our acquaintance, I handed a letter of mine to her.

"Damn," she hissed, reading it.

The letter was from our friend from the Fabian Society, Frank Podmore, who had also attended the séance at Nora Sidgwick's home at which Dr Dryson and Mrs Tillis had become affianced. Mr Podmore was greatly disturbed by Dr Dryson's death, which he had learned about when Dr Dryson's widow had written him a letter telling him that his friend had died, that there would be no funeral, and that she had had him cremated *"as he had so often wished"*.

But in Mr Podmore's letter to me, he insisted that *'at no time in all the years I've known Richard Dryson did he ever expressed any desire for cremation. And more troubling still, I have just learned that Richard's widow is a FRAUD—she is not the real American spiritualist Valerie Tillis, the person with whom my dear friend corresponded for so many years. The real Mrs Tillis arrived in England yesterday, and straight away reached out to the Society for Psychical Research. She is of course horrified to discover that someone has been impersonating her and married her old letter-writing friend by trickery!'*

Mr Podmore, who knew about our work on the dragon ripper case, pleaded with Astraia and me to investigate the spurious widow. He had gone to Dr Dryson's house several times since his friend's death, but the widow was never around to answer his questions.

'*You know her*," the letter read. '*You've met her. Even if she disappears from society, you will remember what she looks like. Find her and bring her to justice.*'

The children ran in, the dog Old Vic at their feet. "Miss Maddie, the animals are fed and watered," Susie said. We only had two horses in the veterinary stable just now, so this hadn't been a difficult feat.

"Did you clean out the boxes?"

"Yes, Miss," Rutherford said.

"How is Georgina's thrush?" I knew Georgina's thrush was on the mend; I had checked her myself just a short while ago. But I wanted to hear the children's report.

"It looks much better," Susie said. "But I gave her another borax packing anyway, just to be safe."

"And how are Bluebell and Charlie doing this morning?"

Rutherford beamed. "They're both doing very well. I brushed both of them earlier, Miss."

"Very good." They stood looking at me expectantly, awaiting my next set of instructions. This was the problem with having assistants. Sometimes you ran out of work for them to assist with.

"Has anyone seen Juno today?" I asked. Juno was the queen of the barn cats, my particular favorite. Back when I lived and worked here by myself, she and I were inseparable. But I didn't see her very often now that there were always so many people around.

"I saw her last night, Miss Maddie," Rutherford said. "She was chasing mice in the other stable."

Astraia bent down to pet Old Vic, who adored her. "We need to talk about Mr Podmore's concerns, Maddie," she reminded me, somewhat impatiently.

I decided to ask the children what they wanted to do today. "You've both been working so hard lately, and I'm very pleased. You can have a free day today if you'd like," I said to them. I turned to Astraia, but she knew what I wanted to ask and turned me down before I said a word.

"Letty is working for me at the library today," she said. "She doesn't have time to give sewing lessons."

"Can we go back into Limehouse, Miss?" Rutherford said. "Chan showed us how to buy food there, and I'd like to procure lunch for us all."

This surprised me. "Do you have money to buy lunch?"

"No, Miss. You would have to give me the money," he said, his head hanging in embarrassment.

I took some coins from my purse. "Astraia, would you like lunch from Limehouse?" I felt a moment's gratitude that for the first time in my life I possessed enough money to buy food for other people. I had Mr Mycroft Holmes to thank for this, since he had pressured the police administration to be more generous with my wages.

"What is it?" Astraia asked.

"Seafood, Miss," Rutherford said.

"Maddie doesn't have time to prepare seafood today," she said.

"No, Miss. It comes already prepared."

She came to a decision. "You can bring me some," she said. "If I don't like it, Old Vic can have it," she said, giving the cur another scratch under his chin.

The children ran off and we settled down to discuss what to do about our two cases, Old Vic snoring contentedly on Astraia's feet.

"Will any of our suspects talk to us now?" I asked.

"I think they'll want to talk to us now more than ever," she said. "People always want to talk with famous people, and this newspaper attention has made us famous. The real question is: can we trust anyone to be honest with us now, since they'll know we're investigating the murder. Now the murderer will be on her guard. Mykie must be furious. He worked very hard to keep our names out of the papers last time."

Although Mr Mycroft Holmes supported his sister in her detectival pursuits, he detested the idea of her being the focus of common gossip. All of the public acclaim for the success of the last case had been awarded to the police. Which had annoyed Astraia and me, because the police had mostly been barriers to our solving the murders. Well, not all of the police. DI Rankin, mostly.

Since I was thinking about him anyway, I wasn't too surprised when the tall Detective Inspector knocked on the door of the stable a few minutes later. He did not just enter, as PC Froest had done earlier. He waited, as always, for me to answer the door, just as though this was a normal residence where normal people lived a normal life. Which was one of the things I liked about him.

"Good morning, Miss Maddie," he said with his rich deep voice, a big smile on his handsome face. Then he noticed my other visitor. "Oh, hullo Astraia."

"Congratulations on your success getting Maddie's and my names trumpeted through the streets of London," she said with an angry sniff.

He reddened. "I don't know what you mean," he said, then turned back to me. "Miss Maddie, we've arrested someone who's admitted he's Zhu Wei, but I need you to come identify him for confirmation."

I nodded. In truth, I was surprised it had taken so long to round him up. "Is he in gaol here or has he been moved to prison?"

"He's here."

"All right. Astraia, I shouldn't be long."

"I'm coming too," she said, putting her coat back on.

"No, you are not," Samuel said.

"And why not?"

He hadn't even considered her statement about coming with us before he'd turned her down. I looked at him, giving him my version of one of Astraia's sugary sweet inauthentic smiles. I knew what he wanted to say was: the gaol is not a place for a lady. But then he'd have to explain why it was all right for me to enter one, but not his childhood friend.

Astraia and I left the veterinary stable together to accompany DI Rankin into the bowels of the Leman Street gaol.

I didn't go into the gaol very often. A dozen small cells in a low-ceilinged basement, the stairs at one end connected the gaol to the police station while the stairs at the other end directed prisoners up into the police court to face judgement. All light was provided by flittering gas lamps, since there were no windows down there. It reeked of basement damp and human desperation.

Both Samuel Rankin and I had to stoop while walking down the gaol corridor, a problem we did not share with the petite Astraia.

He stopped at the steel door of cell 3 and pushed open the spy hole. I looked in, seeing the small cold room with the customary mattress on a brick bedframe, the open privy closet with a wooden seat over a steel bucket, and the single small gas lamp high on the wall that lit the figure of a pathetic human laden with chains and handcuffs. I stared at the captive for a minute or two, then backed away so that Astraia could see.

"No," I said. "That's not Zhu Wei."

"How do you know?" Astraia asked, backing away from the door in disgust. "His face is so swollen from being beaten up that it could be one of my brothers in there and I'd hardly recognise him."

DI Rankin glared at her but chose to ignore her words. "How do you know it's not him, Miss Maddie? The light is flickering badly and you can hardly see. I'll have him come closer." He barked orders at the prisoner, who obediently moved closer to the door.

I looked again. "No," I said. "That's not him."

"Look again," the detective inspector said. "Really study him."

"I can study him all day if you like," I said. "That's not going to make him miraculously turn into someone he isn't."

Samuel let the spy hole cover fall shut. "He said he is Zhu Wei," he said with careful articulation.

"I don't care," I said equally carefully.

"Why would he say he's Zhu Wei if he isn't?" he insisted.

"Can we continue this fascinating conversation somewhere else?" Astraia asked. "Somewhere with a stove? And fewer moaning and crying people?"

We climbed the stairs back into the police station and then traipsed back to the veterinary stable, not saying another word until we reached my much warmer office.

"I can see why you didn't want Rebecca Ravenwood Thornapple kept in one of those cells," Astraia said to Samuel while I started the tea. "Have you found her yet, by the way?"

He growled but stayed on the present topic. "Miss Maddie, that has to be Zhu Wei," he demanded. "Why would he say he is if he's not?"

"Let me make a list of possible reasons," Astraia said. Astraia loved to make lists. "Possibility one: Zhu Wei is his actual name. There are probably a hundred Chinese sailors named Zhu Wei in London. I expect it's a fairly common name. Possibility two: he's done something so bad that the real Zhu Wei wants to kill him, and he thinks that as awful as British jurisprudence might be it won't be as bad as whatever Zhu Wei will do to him if he gets his hands on him. And possibility three—my favorite, actually, the one I think is most likely—he got tired of being beaten up by the police and finally agreed to whatever you said to him, just so you'd quit hitting him. I can think of at least five other possibilities, but I think those three provide enough options for you to start with."

The Detective Inspector left in disgust a few minutes later, and Astraia and I sat down to drink our tea. "So how do you know he isn't Zhu Wei?" Astraia asked me. "I meant it when I said I wouldn't have recognised one of my own brothers after the way that poor man was brutalised."

"The prisoner is at least a half-foot shorter than Zhu Wei," I said. "I've told them over and over that Zhu Wei is almost as tall as I am, unusually tall for a Chinese person. They would have better results if they'd remember that crucial fact."

"Ah. Well, that's that, then. Are all prisoners treated that way?"

I wished I could give her a different answer. "Usually," I said.

"Even the women?"

I thought back to the women I'd been called in to search over the years. "Sometimes," I said.

"I may have to join Florence Balgarnie's campaign for prison reform," she said.

"I think that's just for women prisoners."

"So we'll start with them."

We returned to our discussion of our two cases. We decided that although finding the killer of Lady Deborah was our official case, finding Mrs Dryson was now a more immediate concern. The obvious first step was to return to her home.

I went into my bedroom to clean up a bit, since I was wearing my usual horse-faeces-flecked work ensemble. When I came back into the office, clean and tidy, the children were there, today including Chan.

"Look what we brought, Miss Maddie," Rutherford said proudly. He pointed out three small wooden pails sitting on the old table, steam rising from the edges of the closed lids.

I opened one to peer inside, and the smell of hot spiced seafood stew rolled out, filling the room, overwhelming the normal horse aroma. "This smells wonderful!" I said, and instructed Susie to find bowls and spoons for all five of us. Over time, Astraia had left so many dishes in the place that there wasn't any difficulty finding enough eating implements for everyone.

"Chan doesn't need a spoon," Susie said, gathering the dishes together and helping Rutherford to ladle bowls for everyone. "He uses those sticks he carries."

"These small buckets are oyster pails," Rutherford explained. "Chan got them for us, to get fish stew at the restaurant like the sailors do. He said we can keep them for the next time we want some. And if we take fresh oysters with us to the restaurant first, like the sailors do, the stew will cost us less money," he said excitedly. "I know a costermonger who'll sell me oysters real cheap."

Astraia and I sat at the table while the children huddled over their food on a bench. I watched as Chan indeed used sticks to pick out the fish, then drank the broth straight from the bowl. His method resulted in much less mess than the other two children made; admittedly he had more experience consuming this type of cuisine.

I thought it was delicious; and Astraia also finished her entire bowl before saying, "Maddie, we really should be going."

"Rutherford, Susie, can you keep an eye on things for the rest of the afternoon?" I asked. "I know I said you could have the day free, but something came up."

"Are you investigating, Miss Maddie?" one of my spies asked.

"I am," I said, and turned to the other. "Chan, thank you for helping us to procure lunch. I enjoyed it very much. Miss Astraia and I are leaving now for several hours. In case you need to report my whereabouts to anyone, we are going to the other side of London, in Miss Astraia's coach."

A small smile touched his mouth. He nodded, the blue scarf on his head bobbing a bit. He did not look at me. He did not say anything. He had never spoken a word to me directly, though I knew he could talk in Chinese because I had once heard him speak with his master Zhu Wei, and it was clear he spoke often in English with Rutherford and Susie. I remembered

191

Rutherford had told me Chan's mother was an English woman.

I wondered if anyone had ever taught him to read...for that matter, I wasn't sure if Rutherford knew how to read either...Susie was literate, but just barely...

So much to think about...

Astraia pulled me to the door, and soon we were in her coach on our way back to the Dryson home. But before we stepped into the coach, I handed an oyster pail with the rest of the seafood stew to John, to enjoy while his mistress and I were busy detecting at the widow's house.

***

Every orifice of the Dryson house sank swathed in mourning crepe, windows, doors, front yard gate, even the entry to the cellar. The building seemed to sag under the weight of sullen black. The trees and bushes were wrapped in black cloth, and the colourful bird house I had appreciated on our first visit had now been painted black as well. To the casual passer-by, there was no question but that someone who lived here had died, and the impression given from the amount of effort and expense spent on mourning was that this someone had been deeply loved and would be greatly missed.

"Her servants must have worked on this display for days," I said as we stood on the sidewalk outside the gate, staring at the pageant of black veil and ribbon.

"Interesting, isn't it?" Astraia said. "I agree—quite the difference from when we were here just four days ago. Dr Dryson must have just barely drawn his last breath when this demonstration went into production. If that. One might almost think, considering the amount of materials we see here, that the bereaved widow had planned this exhibit in advance."

"She certainly was a busy person for someone who only moved here a week or so ago," I said. "She cleaned out his storeroom, sculpted that bust, set up her shrine, killed her husband, found and utilised a crematorium, and managed the construction of this amazing panorama of grief. I think she might have almost as much energy as Florence Balgarnie." I had always been envious of energetic people. Some mornings it was all I could do just to crawl out of bed to check that none of the horses in my care had expired during the night before I collapsed in exhaustion for the remainder of the day.

"I don't believe she expected to have to set this exhibition up quite so soon," Astraia said. "She would never have bothered to clean out the storeroom if she expected to only live here a week. I think her original plans were to be here for some time, maybe even stay here after Dr Dryson died. With arsenic, you can keep someone alive but poorly for a long while, you know."

"Do you think she's gone then?"

"Oh, I think she must be," Astraia said. "Either we pushed her into taking action with her husband when we let her know she'd been seen with Sir Peter Peacham, or she learned that the real Mrs Tillis is now here in England. Either way, she knew her masquerade was over. I expect she's long gone. But let's go see."

We walked to the door and stood in front of the crepe-covered door knocker. People covered their knockers with black crepe to avoid being disturbed in times of deep mourning. An overblown display such as the one at this house was intended to emphasise the fact that visitors were not welcome. Knocking on this door would be rude in the extreme.

I used all my strength to heavily pound the door knocker, tearing some of the crepe in my insistent fist.

No one answered my query. We got the same response the second and third time. And we heard no noise to indicate anyone was inside the house ignoring us.

"Let's go check the windows," Astraia said. "Perhaps somewhere there's a corner they missed covering with black."

We peeked in all the windows we could reach. There were a few edges and corners that had avoided being covered with black material, but all we could tell from those small views was that none of the lamps were lit and no one was moving around in those rooms.

The outbuildings in back of the house were empty of all but yard and garden maintenance tools. Dr Dryson's carriage, presuming he had one (there was evidence of a horse normally in residence), was gone.

A single bicycle was propped against the back door porch.

All of the doors and windows of the main residence were locked. We stood at the back door, discussing next steps.

"We shall have to break in," Astraia announced.

I looked over toward the homes of the neighbours on either side. No one had come out to protest our activities. If we began breaking windows, they might.

"Someone might call the police," I said. "Neighbours usually object when miscreants break into the house next door."

She shrugged. "Try to break in quietly then. If we get thrown in gaol, Mykie will bail us out. Probably."

So I picked up a rock and broke the glass in the back door as quietly as I could (luckily all the crepe helped muffle the sound) and soon we were indoors. I made a mental note to remind Astraia that she had mentioned once that she would learn how to pick locks for just such an occasion as this.

"It's so dark!" I exclaimed. "Shall we try to find some candles to light? Just finding them will be its own challenge."

"Is anyone here?" Astraia yelled. When no one responded, she turned to the back door from which we had entered and yanked the crepe down from the broken window. Grey winter light streamed into the room.

"You can find candles now," she said.

I rummaged through the shelves that can usually be found in back entryways such as this one, and found a stack of candles, wicks still connected, and a box of matches.

We left this area to enter into the blacked-out kitchen. Once again, Astraia pulled the covers off a window, then she used this light to find a knife so that I could cut the candles apart while she searched out a couple of candle holders.

"Ah, better yet!" she said, bringing over two paraffin lamps. I set the candles down and lit the lamps, both of which appeared to have sufficient oil for several hours.

"What is your impression here?" she asked.

I felt the stove. It was ice cold, as was the fireplace. In fact, the entire kitchen—usually the warmest room in any house—was almost as cold as the outside. "No one has cooked in this room in at least a day," I said.

She looked into the scullery. "All of the food is gone," she said. "There are a few jars of pickled fruit left, but that's it."

"So no one is planning to return," I surmised.

"She must have dismissed the servants," she agreed.

"I seem to remember there was gas lighting in this house, at least in the two rooms I was in," I said.

"So there was," Astraia said, and we left the kitchen to learn what we could in the back parlour.

We tried to switch on the gas lights in the room and discovered the gas had been turned off. Astraia pulled down the coverings on one window and we saw immediately that this room had been where the black crepe shrouds for the house had been fashioned. Black material, crepe and bombazine, was piled and strewn over a large table in the centre of the room, and scissors, pins, and black scraps lay everywhere. In addition, there were enough bolts of black still left in here to cover another three homes in similar fashion.

"She did not buy all this material in just one day," I said decisively.

"I concur. She must have held it in storage," Astraia said.

"So does that indicate she intends to come back to retrieve the rest of it?"

"For next time she's widowed, you mean?" Astraia asked. I hadn't really been thinking that, but it was an interesting question.

We carried our paraffin lamps into the front parlour where we had sat for tea with the mysterious widow only days ago. This room looked much as it had before—in fact, I could identify nothing out of place but the black window coverings. All of Dr Dryson's occult memorability remained, abandoned.

"Let's see what she left in her workroom," Astraia said. I followed her into the room where Mrs Dryson had displayed her magnificent pieces of ceramic art after throwing out Dr Dryson's psychical bibs and bobs.

All of her work was gone now, including her newest piece, the bust of her now-deceased husband.

We looked at each other, sharing the same thought. "The Asherah shrine!" we said.

Astraia led the way upstairs, since she was the only one of us familiar with that floor plan. As I climbed the creaky steps, carefully dragging my plastered foot as I clung to the banister, I began to notice other vague sounds about the house though I couldn't say whether the source was a resident, or the normal nebulous pops and moans of a wood-built home, or another intruder such as ourselves.

"Hullo!" I yelled. "Is anyone here?"

No one answered, and Astraia and I continued our ascent up the dark stairs to the even darker area above.

"If Sherlie was here, he'd be making pronouncements based on footprints he'd pretend he saw in the dust on the floor," she said.

"Can't you do that?" I asked.

"Maddie, there is no dust on the floor," she said. "This house has barely been empty twenty-four hours. I'm just saying what my brother would do if he was here."

The upstairs hallway was very dark. I was grateful for our paraffin lamps. We passed by the first and second doors to enter the third room on the right. Astraia walked quickly across the floor to pull down the black window coverings.

"Someone is going to notice all these black curtains being removed," I said.

"I doubt it," Astraia said. "I've been careful to remove only coverings on windows facing the sides of the house, not the front. And since the inside of the house remains in pitch darkness, I expect no one will notice."

We stood in a lady's bedroom. I surmised this by the lacy coverlet, the pink floral wallpaper, and the delicate style of furniture. "Is this the widow's bedroom?" I asked

"It was." Astraia began opening the doors of the several armoires. All were devoid of clothing. "She doesn't appear to live here any more."

I opened the drawers in the bedside tables, chiffonier, and dressing table. A quick perusal verified that all were empty.

As in the other rooms we'd visited thus far, the ashes in the fireplace were cold.

"She has completely eradicated all evidence of her presence in here," Astraia said. "There's not so much as a hairbrush or a notebook left."

"Actually, there might be something left," I said. "I can see the corner of something pushed back on the top of the middle wardrobe."

Astraia smiled. "I'm so glad you're tall, Maddie."

I smiled back, then scowled. "I'm not sure how to retrieve it, though."

"Couldn't you stand on that chair?" my friend said, pointing to the delicate lady's cushioned chair placed in front of the dressing table.

"I'd try that if not for this blasted foot of mine," I said. "Could you ask John to come in to get the thing?"

"Do you really think John would enter a home we broke into unlawfully?"

I acknowledged the unlikelihood of this. "Well, if we can't find anything else, I'll try that little stick-and-plaster stool. But first let's see if there's something more sturdy in one of these other rooms for me to stand on." Even standing on a chair, Astraia wouldn't be able to reach the thing.

We moved into the dressing room attached to the bedroom. This room held a little more of Mrs Dryson's presence than we'd found in the other. There were a few hair combs and a hatpin, a delicate handkerchief and even an empty coin purse. But except for a few dribbles of wax and a couple of rose petals on the floor there was no evidence of the goddess shrine that Astraia said had been here before. Nor were there any bottles of Fowler's Solution, although a few other bottles of a feminine nature remained.

"She had to pack quickly," Astraia said. "I'm impressed at her thoroughness, given the pressure she was under. An extraordinary accomplishment when you think about it, especially since she was also busy making arrangements to burn up her husband's body."

"And cover up the house."

"Yes, and cover up the house. We should try and see if we can find any of the servants to question. I presume they were servants of Dr Dryson's, although the widow may have brought some of her own people into this unfortunate marital arrangement."

There was nothing in the dressing room for me to stand upon to reach the top of the armoire, so we next went into Dr Dryson's bedroom, the place where presumably the good man had breathed his last.

No attempt had been made to clean up anything in here. Even the bed remained unmade, unpleasant stains providing indication of the occultist's distress during his final hours.

"The real question for me is, why bother to kill her husband at all?" Astraia said in frustration. "She could have just run away in the middle of the night once she knew her ruse had been detected. Why was it so important to her that he die? It made things so much harder for her than it would have been if she'd just run away."

"Money?" I asked.

"That's usually the motive for spousal murder, either that or to end abuse. And I don't think Dr Dryson was beating her up, do you? We'll need to investigate that as well, of course." Astraia pulled down a black curtain and began to riffle through a secretary desk that stood directly underneath the window. I eyed the matching chair. It appeared somewhat more sturdy than the chair in the lady's boudoir. I lifted the chair and headed toward the door.

I dropped the chair and my lamp in surprise when I noticed the shadow of another person in the hall, tiptoeing stealthily toward the stairs.

Chapter Ten

"Hey, you! Stop!" I yelled, leaping toward the intruder. This startled the other person, who began to run the last few steps to the stairway.

I grabbed at shoulders in the dark, trying to pull them back away from the looming exit. But the anxious person twisted to escape from me, took an unanticipated step over the stairway, and began to topple down the stairs.

The box the intruder had been carrying fell, scattering papers all over the steps as the person stumbled down.

Astraia rushed out, still carrying her lamp. In the dim light, I could see that the interloper managed to find their feet again when they reached the landing. They ran the rest of the way downstairs, and Astraia rushed past me to follow them.

I listened as they ran through the building toward the back door. Two pairs of feet ran out of the house, the second pair several seconds later than the first.

There have been years in my life when I was an excellent runner. Such was not my forte now; perhaps it never would be again. I did not attempt to follow my friend. Instead, I found the paraffin lamp I had dropped, relit it, and began to gather together all of the papers the unknown intruder had dropped in the stairwell.

Back in Dr Dryson's room, I found a portmanteau in his wardrobe. Dumping the clothes out of it, which I recognised as those he had worn in Cambridge barely a week before, including a shirt, vest, and coat still besmirched with Mrs Tillis's (now the Widow Dryson's) vomit, I began to fill it with the papers that the stranger had been attempting to remove from the house. Most appeared to be letters, but I did not take the time to try to read any of them.

Once I had collected all of them together in the portmanteau, I tried to ascertain where the person had procured the box of documents. It became quickly obvious (since the door was still open) that they had brought it down from the attic.

I sighed. I did not have the physical capacity to climb steep and narrow attic stairs.

Astraia re-entered the house, slamming the door behind her. "Damn these skirts!" she swore as she pounded her way back upstairs.

I had noticed that the other intruder had worn trousers, but I hadn't thought about how that might give them an advantage in a foot race against a woman in a gown.

"They were a lot taller than you too," I said.

"What has that to do with anything?" she snarled.

"Longer legs."

She acquiesced. "True, but she was limping so that should have evened the score somewhat."

"It didn't?"

"No. It didn't. That bicycle out in the back was hers. She was halfway down the alley by the time I made it down the back porch steps."

I realised what she had said. "So, it was a woman?" I had wondered, but it just seemed so unlikely. I had never seen a woman wearing trousers outside of a music hall.

"Yes. She was a woman. A blonde woman, gathering from the hair blowing out from her cap that fell to the ground as she bicycled away. I did not see her face, unfortunately, since she was facing the other direction. But we can guess who she was."

I nodded. The widow had returned to the home where she'd murdered her husband in order to gather papers she either cherished or that would provide evidence against her.

"I put all the papers she dropped in a portmanteau," I said.

"Good idea," Astraia said. "Are there any other portmanteaux around? Or is there room for other papers in that one? I want to take Dr Dryson's personal and financial papers with us as well."

I assured her that there was plenty of room in the one we were already using, and pointed to where I'd placed the bag at the edge of the dead man's bed. She looked in to see the letters, wrinkled her nose at the stench that remained from holding filthy clothes for a week, and returned to her work gathering up documents from Dr Dryson's desk.

"I told John to try to catch her," she said. "I described her and told him the direction she'd taken, but I doubt that he'll find her. Bicycles are more adept at moving through alleys and narrow streets than horse-drawn carriages are."

I picked up the desk chair again and carried it into the widow's bedroom. A few scary minutes later, after almost falling down myself (you can't rely on a cane to assist you when you're standing on a chair with a broken foot trying to reach a box high above you that's shoved back on top of an armoire), I was swearing myself as I carried the large box into Dr Dryson's bedroom.

"Well, that was a worthless endeavour," I said in disgust.

By this time Astraia had completed emptying the desk and was shutting the portmanteau.

"What is it?"

Dramatically, I lifted the lid of the box. "A wedding dress," I said.

She removed the white silk and lace creation from the box. "Maddie, this is a wonderful clue," she said after only a few moments of study.

"It is?"

"Certainly. First of all, look at all of the stains and tears on this thing. I would say it's been worn many times."

I had to admit she was right.

"And you can tell by the size that it would be a perfect fit for Mrs Dryson. Or you, for that matter. But there aren't that many women around who are as tall and slender as the two of you are. So this wedding dress probably belongs to her."

This also seemed likely.

"But what's particularly intriguing to me about this is: she didn't wear this dress when she married Dr Dryson."

"She didn't?"

"No. Don't you remember the letter from Nora? She said the bride wore the same dress she'd worn during the séance, that flowing green robe thing. So there's some other significance to this dress unassociated with her marriage to Dr Dryson, some other reason she kept it on top of her wardrobe in her bedroom. I bet the letters weren't the only thing she returned to get. I'll bet she also planned to retrieve this dress."

"That seems unduly sentimental to me," I said.

"There's no reason to believe she's not a sentimental person," Astraia said.

"She didn't show any of the finer feelings in her treatment of Dr Dryson."

"No. That she didn't."

I carried the portmanteau back into the hallway, since it was too heavy for Astraia. I had already determined how to get it downstairs.

"You should probably check the attic to see if there's anything else she left up there," I said to my friend. "I'll take this outside, unless there are any other rooms you think we need to investigate."

"No, the attic is the only room left I'm interested in," Astraia said, and she climbed the steep stairs to the attic, a lamp in one hand, showing an agility I remembered possessing not that long ago myself.

I went down the stairs backwards on my hands and knees, pulling the portmanteau down with me. It wasn't very elegant, but it felt the safest way to traverse the stairway in the darkness.

Astraia did not find anything else of value to our case up in the attic, so we left the house. "If you write to Mr Podmore, you should tell him to get over to the house soon, to gather up any of Dr Dryson's psychical treasures his society might be interested in. Tell him the widow and servants have abandoned the place, someone has broken into the house, and there are precious items related to the occult in the attic as well as in the parlour."

"Why Astraia, what a nice thought!" I said. It hadn't occurred to me to rescue any of the occult items, but I was sure the Society for Psychical Research would consider many of Dr Dryson's things to be highly important.

"I'm just trying to cover our tracks," my friend said. "The more people who tramp through the place, the less likely anyone will find any evidence to connect us with the break-in. You might also mention to him that if he finds any books on the Asherah cult, we'd like to see them."

I looked across to where she sat on the seat of the coach, Dr Dryson's portmanteau and Mrs Dryson's wedding dress box nestled close beside her. I knew she was deeply focused on resolving this mystery, and wondered when we would return to the case of *The Suffragist Murder*.

"I won't go in with you," she said when we reached the Leman Street police station. "I'm going to have John take me to Mykie's club to drop off the financial papers for his review. I'm taking the widow's personal papers home with me to study. I'll contact you in a day or so when I have something to report."

In truth, I was happy to say good-bye. I looked forward to having a day or two to rest my foot. And all the twisting I'd been doing today, what with carrying chairs and climbing backwards down the stairway, had done my knife wound no good.

**

I realised the next day that I should have accepted Astraia's offer to have Letty do my laundry after all. My household had no clean clothes, and the horses no clean blankets.

So I decided to put off resting my foot and back for another day, and asked Rutherford to show me the laundry in Limehouse that Chan had recommended to him. We gathered up all of the dirty clothes we weren't currently wearing and tied everything up in two of the dirty horse blankets, one carried by Rutherford and the other by me. We left a protesting Susie at the stable in case a sick animal should be brought in for care.

Chan soon joined us and took my burden from me without saying a word. I would have protested but it was actually fairly difficult to carry the weight and also manage my cane and broken foot on the uneven roads and sidewalks, so I thanked him for his kindness and let him do as he offered.

The laundry where we took the clothes was situated at the end of Limehouse closest to Whitechapel so we didn't have to walk very far, for which I was grateful. We entered the first room of the building, where Chan set his bundle on a table. Rutherford followed suit. Chan opened a door and disappeared for a short while, returning soon afterward followed by an English woman carrying three small baskets, one filled with safety pins and the other two with bits of yellow and blue fabric scraps. Chan and Rutherford held a whispered confab, and then Rutherford said to me, "You and Mrs Ma can discuss your business, Miss. Chan and I will return soon to take you back home." The two boys left, and I faced the laundress.

"I'm Mrs Ma," the woman said. "I understand you're Miss Maddie and you work with horses." As she spoke, she unfolded our laundry and began pinning yellow and blue scraps to each item with a safety pin. After a moment I began to assist, quickly realising that these small coloured signals would be the way the laundry would differentiate my clothing and items from those of other people.

"Yes, Mrs Ma," I said. "The boys indicated to me that you might be willing to trade services with me. I would be happy to care for your horses if they are injured or sick, and in exchange you could do our laundry. What would you think of that?"

"Actually, one of our delivery horses is limping right now," she said. "Could you look at her today?"

I agreed to this. We finished pinning the clothes, and then she handed me a matching safety pin with two fabric scraps that I could take home with me in order to be able to claim my belongings if some confusion arose. She also wrote down each item in a ledger along with my name and the letters "B" and "Y".

"This is a very clever labelling system you use," I said.

She nodded. "It was my idea," she said. "I did not like writing the owner's name on a piece of paper pinned to the clothing, because paper gets wet in the wash and the ink sometimes runs or becomes illegible. This works well for us." She lifted a large basket from a pile in the corner, threw the items in, then hefted the whole thing in one arm and led the way to the back.

I was impressed to meet a woman apparently even stronger than myself, and followed her into the bowels of the laundry.

At least a dozen men were at work in the back, and as we walked through the rooms Mrs Ma explained to me what each were doing. "These men used to be sailors like my husband was," she said. "They decided they didn't like that type of work, for one reason or another; also, working in the laundry is better pay. They work hard, but not as hard as they had to work at sea." We dropped the basket off at the first work station, where a man would separate the clothes and blankets according to type of material and anticipated amount of cleaning needed.

"Sometimes the clothes people bring to us are utterly filthy," Mrs Ma said. "For example, some people will use their dirty clothes to wipe themselves after they go to the toilet, and then bring those clothes to us to clean. If you had brought me anything that foul, I would not have been interested in bartering business with you."

I was properly horrified. "Mrs Ma, I assure you I will never bring you any such thing!" I said. Then I remember my dresses dribbled with horse faeces. "Except, I'm sorry to say, sometimes there is horse excrement on my clothes. I'll brush it off as best as I can first before I bring them in. I'm so sorry—but it's part of my work." I thought for a moment. "Oh, and there's a great deal of blood on one dress and on a set of underclothes from when I was stabbed on the street last week."

She nodded. "I understand that. We won't mind that. That's not showing disrespect to us."

Mrs Ma asked if I needed her to also mend the clothes, but I said that my assistant Susie would be happy to take on that responsibility.

The laundress then took me to the wash area. Mrs Ma explained that here the clothes would be washed by hand once with a bit of starch in the water, and then a second time in clean water. Exceptionally filthy clothes might be washed a third or sometimes even a fourth time. She had me place my fingertip into the wash water. I was astonished that the man at the wash station could bear to put his hands into such hot water, almost boiling; and I saw that the skin of his hands was very thick and gnarled.

"Old sailors do best here," Mrs Ma said. "Their hands are already so scarred they hardly feel the hot water."

After the clothes were washed, they would be taken to the drying room where they would be hung up near coal stoves. Mrs Ma explained that the laundry was a very popular place to work in the winter, but that during the heat of the summer no one wanted to work in the drying room and she and her husband usually had to do that work themselves.

I was surprised to learn that after the clothes dried, they still weren't ready for the customer. The next step was ironing, an activity I never bothered with myself when washing my own clothes but which was an integral step in the Chinese laundry. Clothes and other items were set on a table, sprinkled with water, then pressed flat with hot irons. The irons were kept heated on a stove, and whenever one cooled too much to do its work it was replaced by another. Since the clothes had been washed in starch, ironing made them smooth and rigid.

The last step was the folding table where the clothes were folded and tied together in readiness for the customer, and the ribbon pins removed.

I told her I was extremely impressed. "You maintain a very well-run business, Mrs Ma," I said. She smiled, appreciating the compliment. As we walked out to see the horses she told me a little about herself and her family. She and her husband had a baby and lived in rooms above the laundry. They kept delivery horses in order to serve their English customers, who were primarily restaurants and hotels.

"They don't like to come out to Limehouse to pick up or deliver their laundry," she said. "But they appreciate the quality of our work. So we manage the pick-up and delivery for them."

Once we entered the small horse barn where two horses stood together by a trough of fresh water, I saw straight away the swollen front leg on the second horse. I gently pushed the other horse away and bent down to feel the injury. At first I worried a bone or tendon might be broken, so swollen was it, but I quickly found the place where the poor horse had been kicked or otherwise cut and realised the animal needed to have its injury lanced to release the discharge building up.

I instructed Mrs Ma on the need to keep the horses separated while the injured animal was treated and while it healed, and asked her to bring me clean rags, a large clean sewing needle or a sharp knife, and warm salt water. I would have preferred working on the horse in my own stable, but at least this was a clean barn; I did not want to move the horse while it was in this condition if such was unnecessary.

Several times while I worked on the horse Rutherford and Chan came by for a while to watch before running back out to prowl the neighbourhood. Each time I instructed Rutherford on what I was doing, this being a procedure he had not learned before.

An hour later the wound was clean and wrapped, and I thought the horse was probably feeling better. "Either I or one of my assistants will return every day for the next week or so to change the dressing," I told the laundress, "but until it is healed you should just let this animal rest."

This time it was Mrs Ma who slathered on the compliments. She was thrilled that I had been able to help her dear old Annie and assured me that she was delighted with the agreement we had made to share services.

I was smiling when I walked back out the front door of the laundry, and looked around to see if Rutherford or Chan were waiting to escort me back home.

I could see neither of them. But Sailor Cap and Pale Eyes both stood on the sidewalk leading back in the direction from which we had come. For a few moments we stared at each other.

Then they started moving toward me, and I realised I had made an error in letting them know that I had noticed them watching me.

Several thoughts entered my mind. I could stand here in the open and accuse them of spying on me. Or I could hurry back into Mrs Ma's laundry and wait for the boys. Or I could simply start yelling. But instead I chose what was possibly the stupidest of my options—I started walking down the road as quickly as I could manage, in a direction that seemed vaguely familiar to me from a trip I'd made to Limehouse a month ago, but which I soon realised led straight into the infamous Limehouse maze of crooked streets and alleys. And unfortunately, due to my various injuries, I lacked the capacity to walk very fast.

But I moved as rapidly as I could through the narrow roads, past curious onlookers and fascinating shops I would love to explore at some later date. The two men remained close on my heels, arguing with each other in a language I could not understand.

As I passed in front of an especially dark alley the men grabbed me and pulled me in, one putting his hand over my mouth to keep me from screaming. I pounded indiscriminately at them with my cane, landing a few successful blows, but eventually one of them wrenched the cane from my hand and walloped me with his fist. I managed to punch him back, but regrettably not as hard. I did feel his blood on my knuckles.

At some point I must have fainted, possibly from being pressed so close to the taller man that I couldn't breathe. I refuse to believe I simply fainted from the horror of the experience, since that's a thing I have never yet done nor do I intend to ever do in the future.

At any rate, I woke up some time later locked in a small room with whitewashed brick walls. It contained a small grubby window through which pale light streamed, which after my experience at the murder house the day before I felt grateful for. And the ceiling was tall enough that I could stand at full height, plus I was not chained up, so in that way it was at least better than the Leman Street gaol, though the bucket I saw in the corner implied that the two prisons had at least one thing in common.

The room was clean but I could smell a vague odour of opium, which reminded me of my old acquaintance Mr Wu, which reminded me of Mr Wu's master Zhu Wei, which reminded me of the men who had brought me here.

What did Mr Zhu hope to accomplish by kidnapping me and locking me up? And why now? Perhaps he thought this would put pressure on Sherlock Holmes, who seemed to have pitted himself against the Limehouse crime leader. Since Mr Holmes had never told Astraia and me anything whatsoever about his investigations into Mr Zhu's dealings, I could hardly begin to guess what might be gained by this manoeuvre.

I frowned. I had simply assumed I was locked in this room. I walked over to the door to try to open it, and discovered I had been correct in that assumption. The door handle with its locking mechanism appeared fairly new, and I promised myself that when the two cases were over both Astraia and I would learn how to use lockpicks, which we would then carry with us everywhere we went.

I wondered if I should be frightened. I had been through so many horrors in my life, I no longer trusted my instincts about that.

I sat for a time, thinking the situation over. After a while I heard a couple of men arguing outside of my door. Unfortunately I could not identify the language they were speaking. But the voices sounded like those of the men who had kidnapped me.

"Hey!" I yelled. "Let me out!"

They yelled back; I assumed they directed their comments toward me but because I couldn't understand the words I ignored the tone.

"Hey!" I yelled again. "Let me out of here now!" I kicked at the door. They yelled some more. I kicked again. They yelled louder. I hit the door hard with my bucket. Thus we continued for a time, until eventually their voices ceased berating me from the other side of the wall.

I sat for a while, a few hours maybe, waiting to see what they would do next. I might have slept. Eventually the boredom was too much; I needed to figure out my escape. I looked up at the window. It was too small and high to climb through. But maybe I could break it if I threw the bucket at it, and then I could start yelling again, and perhaps then someone from the outside would hear me and let me out.

I put this new plan into motion, and after several tries the glass broke and cold air began to seep into the room. Before I started yelling, though, I heard the sweetest sound I swear my ears ever heard.

Barking. A dog was barking.

My dog was barking.

"Old Vic! Old Vic!" I yelled. "It's me! I'm in here!"

The barking increased.

"Miss Maddie, are you all right?" Rutherford yelled with excitement a few minutes later.

"Yes, I'm fine!" I yelled. "But I'm locked in here."

"Don't you worry, Miss Maddie," Susie yelled. "We'll get you out of there!"

"Be careful!" I said. "Please, be careful! There are some bad men out there somewhere."

"Chan will deal with them," Susie said. "Just you wait a few minutes, and we'll get you out."

Once again I heard the male voices outside of my door, only this time a young boy responded to their rages, his voice even louder and more insistent than theirs, his demands punctuated by the fierce growls of my angry dog.

Finally the arguing voices quit and after a few minutes the door of my cell was unlocked. Rutherford entered, a set of lockpicks in his hand. I smiled to know I had found someone to teach this important skill to Astraia and me.

Old Vic ran in and jumped up on me, his tail wagging, something he had never done before. I reached down to pet him, something I did seldom (because he usually tried to bite me). This time, he licked my hand before running back to stand guard at the door with Susie.

Chan took one look at me, made a harsh sound in a language I did not know, said something to Rutherford, and ran out of the room.

"Where did Chan go?" I asked the two other children as we left my prison.

"He said he had to go do something, Miss," Rutherford said. "Those two men are gone now, but let's get out of here as quickly as we can."

"I'll do my best," I said, "but you'll have to help me. I seem to have lost my cane."

The children helped me walk as we hurried through the warrens of the Limehouse neighbourhood. As Rutherford confidently lead us through this twisty alley and that serpentine street, I was glad I had allowed him to spend so much time here with Chan learning the intricacies of the neighbourhood.

When we turned the corner onto Leman Street, we began to smell smoke. As quickly as we could, given our disadvantages, we rushed toward the police station. We stopped in horror as we saw that the veterinary stable was on fire.

Chapter Eleven

"No!" I screamed, stumbling toward the building where I both lived and worked. Smoke and flames poured out of the windows and doors, and ate through the rickety wood structure where I had spent most of the last fifteen years of my life.

"Maddie, thank God you're all right!" Samuel Rankin yelled, running toward me from the burning stable and grabbing me up in his arms. "Thank God, thank God you're all right!" He was hugging me with all of his might, and I swear I heard tears of joy and relief in his voice. His squeezing hurt the healing cut on my side.

"Samuel, let me go—I have to get the horses out!" I said.

"They're both out, Maddie, don't worry!" he said. "I was in there, I got them out; but I didn't see you, and I didn't know if you were lying on the ground somewhere, hidden in the smoke. I see the children are here with you too; thank God; thank God."

Now that I knew the horses were safe I could stop, breathe, and make a sensible assessment of the situation. I saw that Samuel's face was covered with soot. I saw numerous firefighters from the Metropolitan Fire Brigade, dousing the other stable and outbuildings of the police station with water as others worked to contain the fire in the veterinary stable. I saw police officers approaching me, all wearing expressions of relief and assessment as they saw that I was safe, and that I stood cocooned in DI Rankin's embrace.

I wriggled free. "Thank you for getting the horses out, Samuel," I said.

He shook his head, and his hands reached up to clasp my shoulders as he stared into my face. Then his expression of relief turned to concern. "What happened to your face, Maddie?"

Frowning, I reached up to explore my face. I quickly realised my nose hurt. My fingers came back bloody. "Oh, someone punched me," I said. "I'll be fine."

He pulled me back into his arms again. "I'm just so glad you're safe, Maddie," he said. "I thought you were in there."

I pulled away again. "I know, Samuel; it's all right. I'm fine." I'd tell him later that I had just been rescued from a kidnapping attempt, by children. Now was not the time.

"What happened here?" I asked.

"We don't know yet," he said. "It seem likely the stove was left unguarded and a spark started something on fire."

Susie had been crying over the loss of the new doll she'd been sewing, but spoke up at this. "That couldn't have happened, Miss Maddie," she said. "I was very careful to close up the stove before we left, just as you've taught me."

"Maybe someone did this on purpose, Miss Maddie," Rutherford said solemnly. "Someone who wants to hurt you."

"It couldn't have been the foreign spies," I said. "They couldn't have got back here in time."

"What foreign spies?" DI Rankin growled.

"Zhu Wei, maybe, Miss?" Rutherford said.

"Is that nefarious villain still bothering you, Maddie?" DI Rankin asked angrily.

"I'll talk with you about that later, Samuel," I said. "Right now I need to check on the horses. Their lungs could have been damaged from breathing smoke." I also needed to make sleeping arrangements for the two children and myself. I gave a half-smile, remembering I had taken virtually every piece of clothing we owned to the Chinese laundry today. At least we'd still have something to wear. I walked toward Harry, the stable master, standing nervously in front of his own building as he watched mine burn to the ground.

Samuel Rankin followed me, and the children and Old Vic followed us both.

"Are you concerned the fire will spread, Harry?" I said.

"Not any more," he said. "I'm glad to see you're not in there, Maddie. Your face looks awful; were you hurt in the accident? There was some panic around here for a while." He eyed the Detective Inspector quizzically.

"I'm sorry to have worried everyone," I said. We watched the firemen fighting the flames. Truly, the fire seemed to be burning itself out, and gave no indication of spreading to any of the other buildings. The rain-spitting weather worked in our favor.

Eventually I entered Harry's stable to check on the horses. All of them, including the mother and colt and the healthy horses and mules regularly stabled here, seemed nervous about the fire. The two who had been in the veterinary stable, Georgina and Old Toby, seemed particularly distressed. But I could see no indication they had experienced any undue injury from the conflagration and thought that a long night's sleep should bring them all back to their normal good-natured selves.

I told Rutherford and Susie to help the stable boys provide all the animals an extra helping of oats and water, give them a nice grooming, ensure their bedding was fresh, and assist them into their boxes to sleep. I instructed everyone to be as quiet as they could tonight, so as not to bother the poor things.

While the children worked together with the stable boys to care for the horses, I discussed the veterinary stable situation with Harry. We agreed that the east end of his stable could be remodelled as a temporary veterinary office and surgery, and the boxes closest to that space could be set aside for sick animals. We would work on the design tomorrow. I appreciated that he seemed so willing to share his space with me, and cynically wondered if part of the reason was because he thought that if I was in here watching over things, he would be able to spend more time in the pub.

There was really only one place for Susie and me to stay tonight. And although I could have insisted that Rutherford stay here in the stable with the other lads, I knew he would want to go with me as well. Sherlock Holmes would expect him to.

I limped back outside to find Samuel, almost falling several times on the uneven ground. Really, I needed a new cane. Or a crutch. Something. As I left the stable I was gratified to see the cat Juno run past me chasing prey only she could see, and I felt glad to know that all of my charges were safe.

The fire had practically died away. Samuel and a group of officers stood near by, talking quietly. The small old wooden shack had burned almost completely to the ground, and tears came to my eyes. I had not had many possessions in there to mourn. The most critical were my surgical implements, which had formerly belonged to my hated father. But there had also been a few things of my mother's. The furniture I had inherited from her was gone, of course. I wondered if Grace, her little china shepherdess, had survived the inferno. Perhaps it had. It had been created with fire, after all. I would dig through the ashes tomorrow, to look for her.

"DI Rankin, could I speak with you a moment, please?" I said as I neared the men. Normally I would have wanted to join their conversation—especially since I had no doubt they were discussing my building and the possibility of arson—but exhaustion had caught up with me in the last few minutes and I wanted nothing more than to fall into a clean bed and sleep the night away. Well, maybe a few bites of food first would be good. I was awfully hungry. And a rag to clean up my bloody nose would be nice.

He hurried over to me. "Of course, Maddie," he said gently, moving us away from the curious crowd. We walked back toward the other stable, he steadying my arm after I wobbled a few times.

"Could you take Susie, Rutherford, and me to Astraia's house tonight?" I asked. "Oh, and Old Vic too, I guess. I should probably take Old Vic." The dog had earned my gratitude today. The least I could do was keep him with me. Make sure he had a comfortable place to sleep and good food to eat. And Astraia seemed to like him, even if Letty didn't especially care for the animal.

"Of course, Maddie," he said. "Let me make arrangements."

He went into the stable with me and commandeered the old large coach which was almost never used by the police. Two of the horses who had thought they were about to get some rest for the night were harnessed up to pull humans across town instead. Then he went back out to the group of gossiping men to see if any of them wanted to drive the coach.

DI Rankin intended to sit inside with us, and I knew why. He wanted to hear more about the foreign spies, and why Rutherford had mentioned Zhu Wei as the possible arsonist. I imagined he'd have questions about how Astraia and I were doing on our investigation. If he knew I'd spent Sunday at the zoo with another man, I'd probably get questioned about that too. I knew how his mind worked.

As usual, the Detective Inspector had plans to interrogate me. But I had a different idea.

***

"And then Chan ran off, sir," Rutherford said.

"Ran off? Where?" Samuel asked. When we left in the police coach, I told the children to tell DI Rankin everything that had happened to us today. They were thrilled to do so; and still excited by the events of the day they had not stopped talking long enough for him to turn his attention to me. As I had planned.

"I think he ran to tell Zhu Wei what those spies of his had done to Miss Maddie," Rutherford said. "He said they weren't supposed to ever touch her, sir. They were only supposed to keep watch on her and report back to Zhu Wei. He said they would get into big trouble over this."

"You don't think Zhu Wei ordered them to kidnap her?" Samuel was very angry that I had been kidnapped and assaulted. I was too, of course...but my bigger concern right now was the loss of my home.

"Chan didn't think so, sir. Except—it occurred to me tonight that if Zhu Wei was the one who started the stable on fire, he might have ordered them to keep Miss Maddie safe so she wouldn't get hurt."

I startled at this. It had never occurred to me that the intent behind my kidnapping might have been to keep me safe.

"Why would Zhu Wei want to burn down the veterinary stable?" Samuel asked.

"I don't know, sir, but Chan says that he doesn't like that Miss Maddie works there."

"Why not?"

"I don't know, sir."

Old Vic gave a dreamy growl, and Samuel reached over to pet the dog sleeping on Rutherford's lap.

"I never knew this dog was a tracker," he said.

"We never would have found Miss Maddie if it weren't for him," Susie said. "Chan had no idea where those awful men took her."

"He's a great dog, sir," Rutherford said with fierce loyalty.

"And luckily Rutherford knows Limehouse so well," Susie said. "'Cause he was able to get us out of there quick as a flash after we got Miss Maddie out."

"How did you get Miss Maddie out of the locked room?" Samuel asked.

"Oh, I was able to jimmy the door open in a few minutes," the boy said. "It was an old lock, sir."

I smiled to myself. Rutherford knew there were some facts you just shouldn't share with the police.

I had my own question for the detective inspector. "Did no one see how the fire started?"

"Apparently someone did see a person wearing a greatcoat and big hat lurking near the building a short time before the fire started. He opened the door to the stable and may have thrown something in, which it now appears may have been a bomb. Then he ran off, no one knows where. Between the chaos of the explosion and then the fire, they were too overwhelmed to follow after the bomb thrower."

"You know, it's always been amazing to me how many people have been able to come and go from that building with no one on the police force ever asking a single question," I said.

"When the replacement is built, we'll make sure to include better security," Samuel said.

"Is there going to be a replacement built?" I asked, my heart lightening.

"Certainly there is," he said. "Actually, there have been plans for some time to replace the entire police station. This fire may be just the impetus needed to get that going."

"Will the new police station be built here?" I asked.

"It will still be on Leman Street," he said. "We're just moving it down the road a bit, to where the Royal Albert Theatre used to be. Expanding it."

The coach slowed down, and I realised with relief that we had reached Astraia's house without my being required to answer a single unwanted question.

Samuel escorted us to the door. John was surprised to see the delegation but let us all in, telling Rutherford and the dog to wait for him as he directed the rest of us down the hall where we found Astraia sitting in her parlour, writing in a notebook, piles of letters on the desk in front of her that were no doubt from Mrs Dryson's box.

I knew immediately she would not want Samuel to ask her questions about what she was working on, and I turned to him, my hand out.

"Thank you so much for bringing us here, Samuel," I said. "I'm very tired now, and I need to explain to Astraia why we're invading her home—ah, and I hear Letty now too. Susie, can you go see if she can find us something to eat?" I turned to Astraia. "If that's all right with you, of course."

"Of course," Astraia said, and she joined me in easing Samuel out of the room containing the murder house letters. Between us we edged him back toward the front door.

"But I have questions I need to ask you, Maddie," he said.

Astraia opened the door. "Tomorrow, Samuel," she said. "Can't you see how tired the poor girl is?"

I looked up at him, letting the tiredness show on my bloody face.

He relaxed. "Oh, all right. Tomorrow."

And then he did something he'd never done before. He bent his head to gently kiss my cheek, before quietly leaving the house without another word.

I stared at the closed door for a moment before turning to face my friend.

"Can we stay here for the night? Please?"

"Of course you can. But who hit you? And why do you smell like smoke?" She handed me a handkerchief for my bloody nose, and I followed her into the kitchen to get something to eat.

***

We agreed that I would tell her about today's events over tonight's dinner, and she would explain what she'd learned about the widow tomorrow morning at breakfast. Astraia was kind enough to offer us rooms to stay in her home for as long as we needed, but I intended to see what other arrangements could be made in the neighbourhood around the police station. I'd lived in a flat above the corner bakery until just a month or so ago; I believed that room was let now, but there might be another room available in the same building for Susie and me to use.

Certainly Astraia's home was more comfortable. But it really wasn't convenient for my work. Of course, as she pointed out, Astraia also worked in Whitechapel, in the library that was even farther away from her house than the police station was. But she didn't have to worry about book emergencies in the same way I had to be available to care for injured horses at any hour of the day or night.

The next morning after breakfast, Susie and Rutherford went into Astraia's coach barn to help John feed and harness the pair while Astraia and I enjoyed a second cup of tea in the parlour where the widow's letters were organised.

There were eight piles of paper and envelopes, the first two piles the tallest, the last two the shortest. In fact, the final one wasn't really a pile, it was only one letter in an envelope. The second-shortest looked to be several folded sheets of paper without any envelope. All the rest of the piles held six to a dozen full envelopes each.

"Each pile represents love letters written by a different man," Astraia said. She picked up the second-shortest pile. "These are letters written by Dr Dryson, that week they stayed at Nora's house. Séance week. Apparently he would sneak love notes under Mrs Tillis's pillow each day."

"Do I want to read any of them?"

"You do not. They do not provide any information of use to us, except they make it clear that he was besotted with her."

She set them down, and picked up the first, largest pile. "Most of the letters in the collection are dated and addressed. These are the oldest, from six years ago. They are from a Mr Morris Jenson, of George Street, Bath, to Miss Valerie Sitcup, a maiden lady taking the waters in that same city. Mr Jenson and Miss Sitcup met at an assembly, and he was immediately smitten. These letters from him to her document their courtship. She lived at a local hotel throughout their engagement. The last one was written just two days before their scheduled wedding."

She set them down, and lifted the next pile. "These are from Mr Brown, and document a three-month courtship four years ago. Mr Brown—or I suppose I should say Vicar Brown—was a clergyman who met Mrs Valerie Jenson when she was visiting a ruined abbey in his parish in Kent. Again, he was smitten; again, she remained in a hotel in the area during the whole of their engagement."

Returning these letters to their place on the desktop, Astraia made a grand gesture over the entire body. "And so it goes. Valerie Brown next became Valerie Bernard, but there must have been some problem with Mr Bernard's death because she is once again using the name Valerie Jenson when she meets Mr Aaron Thomlinson. She shifts between the names Brown and Jenson over the next couple of husbands. Perhaps it reduced the confusion for her. What's especially troubling for me is, the time between the first and second husband was two years. The time between Mr Thomas McAdams, husband number six, and Dr Richard Dryson, husband number seven, was only four months."

"Are we sure all of these men married the same woman?"

"Four of them ascribe themselves, 'Your loving Pookie-Bear'. Including Dr Dryson. Apparently she likes to use the same pet name."

"Were they all cremated?"

"I have no idea. We don't have any specifics about what happened to any of them after they married."

"Except that they died."

"Truthfully, we don't even know that," Astraia pointed out. "That's just my assumption. There isn't even any proof that she actually married any of them. There are neither marriage certificates nor death certificates in this collection of papers. I'll send a private enquiry agent to Bath and Kent and Cornwall to verify our hypothesis."

"Our hypothesis?"

"Yes. Our hypothesis that Dr Dryson is just the latest victim of a monstrous killer every bit as bad as the one who terrorised London a year ago. A Jill the Ripper, if you will."

As the world's foremost authority on that despicable fiend (though Astraia didn't know it), I couldn't let this statement pass without comment. "Valerie Dryson is not as bad as Jack the Ripper," I said. "He mutilated his victims. Mrs Dryson executed her husbands. Bloodlessly. Allegedly."

"Allegedly," she agreed. "But I would have to say that if our hypothesis is correct, and I'm certain it is, killing husband after husband is the worst sort of betrayal of the sacred bond of marriage. And though it's perhaps not as bloody, arsenic is a particularly painful way to die. And takes longer than mutilation."

I considered this, then noticed the last pile, the single letter in the envelope. "And who is that from?"

"I'm afraid it may be from her next victim," Astraia said, lifting the letter. "It was written two months ago to someone named Mrs Norbert Brown, at her hotel in Baden-Baden, Germany. Like most of the other earliest letters from her beaux, it's mostly about the weather, and social events, and enquiries about her health. Nothing sensational or amatory particularly, at least so far as I could interpret the handwriting. The author has horrific penmanship."

"Nothing particularly amatory?"

"The salutation is: 'My dearest Valerie'. And it's signed, 'Your loving Pookie Bear'."

She handed it to me. I removed the letter from the envelope, shaking my head at the almost unintelligible handwriting on the address, and then gasped when I opened it and read the name engraved on the formal stationary.

"Sir Peter Peacham!" I said in hushed horror.

She nodded. "Sir Peter Peacham."

***

Coachman John drove the children and me to the police station that morning on his way to deliver Astraia and his sister Letty to the Whitechapel Library. Astraia needed Letty to work at the library because she said she had better things to do with her morning than catalogue books. She intended to write letters to both of her brothers for John to deliver: to Mr Mycroft Holmes to find out what he had learned from Dr Dryson's financial records, and to Mr Sherlock Holmes to get a referral for a quick and dependable enquiry agent to uncover some marriage and death records for us. She also planned to send a letter to Nora to see she had copies of any of the photographs that had been taken of Dr Dryson's bride on their wedding day. We knew we needed to approach Sir Peter Peacham about his beloved, and thought a photograph from the woman's very recent marriage to another man might help us convince him that her intentions were not honourable.

We noticed Chan's blue head scarf as we drove into the precinct, and Rutherford hurried across the street to speak with his friend about all that had happened yesterday. The coach left for the drive to the library, and I sent Susie into the stable to see if Georgina and Old Toby had recovered from their scare.

I walked over to the ash heap that used to be my home and place of work. I had wanted to sift through the remains today to see if there was anything left to salvage. But smoke continued to hiss every time a drop of rain hit a pile of charred wood, and I realised that the ruins were still too hot to scavenge through. After a while I limped back to find Harry and begin the tedious process of setting up the new veterinary area in the stable.

In mid-morning PC Archibald Froest came by to see me, a pot of tea and a couple of mugs in one hand, a napkin full of fresh gingerbread in the other. We sat down in my makeshift hay bale office and tried to pretend we were just enjoying one of our normal tea breaks.

"We sent officers over to the Drysons' house," my friend said.

"Oh?"

"Yes. No one was there, apparently. The constables left a note in the door, instructing the householders or staff to contact them when they return."

"So that's that?"

"Until someone returns to the house," he said.

"Thank you, Archie." It didn't sound like the police had noticed or were concerned about the break-in. But this was a good reminder that I needed to send a letter to Mr Podmore straight away, suggesting he retrieve the psychical books and other items from Dr Dryson's collection before thieves stole everything of value. And ask him to keep an eye out for any books on the Asherah cult.

Archie took a notebook and pencil from his pocket. "So, Maddie, what do you need?"

"Need?" My mind was still on the Dryson house.

"To set up a veterinary surgery," my friend said. "Instruments. Supplies. Medicines. What do you need to get started again?"

I stared at him in delighted surprise. Until this moment, for some reason it hadn't occurred to me that the police force might pay for the replacement of their veterinary infirmary. I'd been thinking I'd need to scrape by with whatever I could scrimp up.

I spent the next hour as though in a dream, listing everything I'd ever wanted to have in order to establish a truly fine animal surgery. Archie wrote it all down, and although I knew I'd never see more than half the things I mentioned, even that half would be more than

I'd inherited when I'd taken over my father's practice upon his well-deserved demise.

I began to see the real benefits of the thing. If Zhu Wei had walked into the stable that minute, I would have thanked him. Before turning him over to the police, of course.

Mr Feinman, the owner of the bakery and flats on the corner, told me that there was a nice room available in the building on the same floor where his family lived. Since I had always been such a good tenant, he would be happy to rent it to Susie and me for no extra charge even though it was slightly bigger than the room I used to rent from him. I was particularly thrilled with this news, because I knew that the floor the baker's family lived in contained both an indoor water closet and a washroom off the landing. I told him we would take residence within the next few days, and when I returned to the police station I asked PC Froest if there were any camp beds that Susie and I could use until I could procure furniture. He agreed to add these to the list.

No sooner had PC Froest left the stable to hunt down these additional items on my list than he was replaced at my side by Samuel Rankin. I could imagine the two men passing each other at the door, each frowning as he wondered what the other wanted with me.

"Have you discovered who burned down my stable?" I asked DI Rankin.

"We have not," he said. "How are you feeling?"

I was touched by the note of concern in his voice. "I'm fine, Samuel." After all that had happened, the kiss and the embrace and all, I accepted that we were clearly on a first name basis now. "But I lost my cane yesterday, which is frustrating."

"I'll get another one for you," he promised. "Are you certain you're not injured? You were kidnapped yesterday—there isn't anything you're not telling me, is there?"

He looked so distressed that I realised he was worried that the kidnappers might have taken liberties with my person. I gave a small smile. "Really, Samuel, I am fine. Other than being hit in the face, I was not harmed. In any way."

He gently squeezed my upper arm. "I'm glad," he said. "We're scouring Limehouse looking for those men. They've spent enough time around here recently that we have officers who will recognise them."

So I wouldn't have to make an identification. "I'm glad," I said.

"I don't like you going into Limehouse, Maddie," he said.

"I shouldn't have to go there very often. I can make other arrangements to have my laundry delivered in the future."

"You're not going there to buy morphine any more, are you?"

In the past, I had bought horse medicine from an opium purveyor. "Actually, I'm concerned about that," I said. "I lost all of my medications in the fire. I don't know what I'll do if there's an emergency."

"You will not go into Limehouse looking for morphine," he growled. "The officers will make arrangements for you."

I didn't argue. I didn't like visiting opium dens. But I'd do what I needed to do when the time came. No need to fight about it now.

"I have a lot of things I need to get ready here, Samuel. Thank you for checking on my welfare."

"Did you really go to the zoo with that phrenologist?" he asked suddenly.

I stared at him, wondering how to answer. Someone had been tattling on me.

"I did," I said.

"I would have been happy to take you to the zoo," he said. "You had only to ask."

"I hadn't thought about it before," I said. "It's still a little cold to visit the zoo."

"But I understand you're planning to go to the zoo again with the children this Sunday," he said.

"I did tell them I would take them."

"Do you have the special Sunday tickets?"

I had to admit I did not.

He smiled in triumph. "I will get them," he said. "I will take you all to the zoo on Sunday."

I simply did not know how to refuse. And it wouldn't be the same as going to the music hall with him. The children would be with us. I'd be doing it for the children. "All right," I said.

"Have you and Astraia learned yet who killed Lady Deborah?" he asked, changing the subject so quickly I knew it had to be intentional. He wanted me knocked off my feet so I might slip and tell him something I might otherwise be careful to keep to myself.

"We think it was a suffragist," I said. "We're interviewing all of them who were at Parliament with Lady Deborah." I was confident Astraia would solve this case, but at the rate we were going and the number of women we still needed to interview, I wasn't sanguine that the solution would occur any time soon.

He smiled. "So you haven't settled on a suspect yet?"

"Our enquiries are continuing." I didn't care for the smirk on his face. "Have you found Rebecca Ravenwood Thornapple yet?" I asked.

He glowered at me. "I'll get the tickets for Sunday," he said, and left the stable.

I yelled after him. "And pick up an extra ticket, in case Chan wants to come along too." It wouldn't hurt for him to get to know Chan, if I needed someone besides Sherlock Holmes to help me get the boy a job in the police department.

Late that afternoon Rutherford and Chan returned, carrying a large basket of clean clothes and horse blankets between them. I was glad to learn Rutherford had changed the horse Annie's dressing without even being instructed to do so. After removing the horse blankets and enough clothes for Susie and me to wear tomorrow, I instructed the two boys to carry the basket of starched dresses and underclothing over to our new home above the bakery. I told Chan to let Mrs Ma know they would return the basket after I had a clean floor or other surface on which to set the clothing her workmen had laundered for us. Tomorrow I would send Susie over to clean the place prior to our taking residence.

From Chan, via Rutherford, I learned that Zhu Wei had been very displeased with his adult spies. He had not given them instructions to kidnap me; they had taken this action on their own initiative because they were worried when I recognised them and they did not understand the deep regard in which he held me; and he was deeply sorry such a thing had happened. I would not see the two men again, he said. I hoped this statement was not as sinister as it sounded.

Chan also said that Zhu Wei had not been the arsonist, nor had he ordered the fire. He did not think that living in the police station was appropriate for a fine lady such as myself, but he would never take any action that would cause me alarm.

I thought about the time only a month ago when Zhu Wei and a couple of his thugs had awakened me in the middle of the night by holding a knife against my throat as I slept, which had unquestionably been one of the most alarming things to happen to me during one of the most alarming weeks of my life. But I didn't remind Chan of this.

***

Dinner that night promised to be an uncomfortable affair. Astraia had written to her brothers, asking Mr Mycroft what he had discovered in his review of Dr Dryson's financial papers, and requesting Mr Sherlock to recommend a private enquiry agent to find out more about Mrs Dryson's past marriages. She had also invited both of her brothers to join us for dinner, a simple act of politeness she said she always included whenever she asked either of them for a favour, one which they could both be dependably relied upon to decline. But this time both had accepted her invitation, an unheard-of event which filled my friend with uncharacteristic dismay. Astraia was concerned that her brothers were planning to ally together against her.

"I'm glad you'll be there with me, Maddie," she said as we discussed the upcoming meal during the coach ride back to her home that afternoon. "You know how to control them."

I sighed. I knew nothing of the kind.

Letty was thrilled. She loved Mr Mycroft and Mr Sherlock, whom she had known ever since she and John served the family back when their parents were still alive. And she couldn't remember the last time they had both come to dinner together at Miss Astraia's house.

"Never," Astraia said.

"Then this *is* a special occasion!" the servant said gaily. I stared at her. I had never heard her speak gaily about anything ever, up to this moment.

"Will I really get to meet Sherlock Holmes?" Susie asked, joining in Letty's excitement. After hearing so much about him from Rutherford (so much for keeping the reason for Rutherford's presence in our lives a secret!), she'd been devastated that she'd missed him when he'd visited me on Sunday.

"You can meet him," Astraia said, "but then you and Rutherford will need to stay with John and Letty in the kitchen for the rest of the evening."

I was not surprised when Astraia said this. She wanted her brothers to be as pleasant this evening as they were capable of being. Forcing them to eat their dinner in the presence of urchins with poor table manners would not improve their humours.

One more thing I needed to teach the children...

"Mr Mycroft and Mr Sherlock love ice cream," Letty said. "I'll show you how to use the ice cream machine when we get home, Susie. You can make that while John and I prepare the rest of the meal."

"What can I do, Miss Letty?" Rutherford asked.

"You can set the table, Ruven," Letty said, using Susie's name for the boy. "I'll give you a picture that shows exactly where to place the dishes, linens and silver, and John will show you how to polish any pieces that are tarnished."

She sat back humming to herself for the rest of the trip, as she planned in her head the magnificent meal she would present in just a few short hours to her dear boys Mycroft and Sherlock Holmes.

***

After Rutherford set the table, John allowed him to accompany him to collect Astraia's brothers, Mr Sherlock from his home and Mr Mycroft from his club. This would give Mr Sherlock Holmes an opportunity to catch up with all the news of my life obtained by his spy in recent days. I didn't mind; it meant I wouldn't have to go over the details of my kidnapping and arson stories all over again.

Both of the men were gracious to the happy family retainer when Letty opened the door to them, allowing her to hug and fuss over them for several minutes without complaint. They solemnly shook Susie's hand, and then my own. Mr Mycroft Holmes bent down to kiss his sister on the cheek. Mr Sherlock gave her shoulder a semi-affectionate pat of acknowledgment.

I realised I had never witnessed the two of them together before. Seeing them standing side by side, matching in face and height, Mr Sherlock so lean and Mr Mycroft so stout, I was reminded of a cover of Punch magazine I'd seen once, comparing a socialist before he entered politics to how he looked after he had been elected to a life of graft and luxury.

Which was of course not fair to Mr Mycroft, whom I had no reason to believe was anything but a true and honest servant of the crown. And, of course, also unfair to socialists.

"I hope you gave the villain as good as you got, Miss Barquist," Sherlock Holmes said, peering at my face as he shook my hand. My nose was swollen and my eyes empurpled. I smiled but said nothing; I didn't want to get into a confabulation about my kidnapping, since we were here to discuss more important events.

We moved into the parlour for refreshments before dinner. After much discussion, Astraia and I had decided to leave the eight piles of widow letters out where they were sure to excite curiosity. Astraia thought this would help her to control the evening's conversation.

But Mr Mycroft Holmes had other matters in mind. "Why did you send me that fellow's financial papers, Astrie?" he asked. "He seems a very responsible citizen with a small trust and conservative tastes in investments. I've seldom read anything so tedious."

"He's dead," she said.

"Dead?" Mr Sherlock Holmes's engagement was piqued. "Was he murdered?"

"He was."

"By whom?" Mr Mycroft asked.

"By his wife," my friend said.

Both of the brothers lost interest. There was nothing intriguing about a woman murdering a tedious husband.

"Does this have anything to do with the case I assigned to you?" Mr Mycroft asked.

"Perhaps," his sister said. "There are connections to it, certainly."

"Astrie, I gave you a perfectly straight-forward case to investigate," the older brother said. "That was over three weeks ago. I had expected results by now. I must confess I'm disappointed."

John brought a tray of drinks into the room, glasses of burgundy for the gentlemen and mineral water for Astraia and me. I frowned as the bubbles hit my nose, and hoped there would at least be wine on the table with dinner. The clues thus far led one to conjecture a difficult evening ahead.

Astraia was more forthright with her displeasure. "John, Maddie and I would like to join my brothers in what they are drinking," she said. Stone-faced, John bowed and left the room.

Mr Sherlock Holmes began to leaf through the piles of letters on the desk.

"Are you collecting other peoples' billet-doux now, pet?" he asked.

"Now there's a story," she said. "After John brings Maddie and me our drinks, I'll tell you all about it."

Five minutes later, after bypassing several attempts by her brothers to derail her tale, Astraia launched into the narrative, beginning with the séance in Cambridge, the digitalis death of Lady Sotheran (which had nothing to do with the widowing as far as we knew, but was interesting nonetheless), and the quick engagement and then marriage of Mrs Tillis and Dr Dryson. She had just described the surprise appearance of Mrs Dryson at Sir Peter Peacham's home after our first visit to Lady Isabella's, the event that provided the first hint of a possible link between the two cases, when a well-scrubbed Rutherford came in to announce that dinner was served.

Astraia beamed at the perfect timing of this interruption and refused to say another word until the soup course was on the table.

During the rest of the meal and through the ice cream dessert, she described the rest of our adventures thus far, timing her tale so that at the very moment when it was time for the ladies to leave the gentlemen to their port and cigars, her brother were left hanging after she told them about running out of the Drysons' house in pursuit of the stranger, letters scattered all over the stairs.

"Come, Maddie," she said, rising from the table. She strode elegantly to the door, me lurching as gracefully as I could after her.

"You don't have to leave," Mr Mycroft Holmes protested.

"Maddie and I don't care for cigars," she said. Which was true. She walked back to the sideboard to pour each of us a glass of port and we left the room, carrying our drinks with us.

The Holmes brothers smoked the fastest cigars of their adult lives, joining us less than five minutes later. Mr Sherlock carried the decanter of port with him. Astraia held out her glass for a refill.

"So those financial papers you sent to me came from the victim's desk, I gather," Mr Mycroft said. "You took them from the house you burglarised."

"I did."

"And these letters on your desk are the documents that were dropped on the stairs?" Mr Sherlock said.

"They are. Maddie gathered them while I chased Mrs Dryson."

"So it was Mrs Dryson then, the person you surprised in the darkened house?" said Mr Mycroft.

"It was." Actually this had not yet been verified, but neither brother questioned her deduction.

"And what was in the box on top of the armoire?" Mr Sherlock asked.

Astraia paused, to build up suspense. "An oft-worn wedding dress," she finally said, in hushed tones.

Her brothers burst into laughter.

"Oh, that's just perfect," Mr Sherlock said. "Shades of Miss Havisham."

"But again I need to ask, what does all this have to do with the case I assigned to you?" Mr Mycroft finally asked, wiping his eyes with a large handkerchief. "Did you discover why Mrs Dryson was at Sir Peter's home that night?"

Astraia smiled. "That's where these letters come into the story," she said.

She went through the piles one by one, explaining what she had learned about Widow Valerie, her seven husbands, and the one man who remained alive.

Mr Mycroft frowned. "You're only assuming there's just one man left alive," he pointed out. "You don't really have proof that any of these men, other than Dr Dryson, has died. Or that any of the others married the Widow Valerie, for that matter."

"That's correct," Astraia said. "That's why I want Sherlie to give us the name of a good enquiry agent, someone who can search for at least a few of the marriage and death certificates for us, to verify our conclusions." I thought it was kind that she included me in this, though in fact the conclusions had been all hers.

"He should also investigate the gravesites and private crematoria near the marriage locales," Mr Sherlock said thoughtfully. "It would be interesting to know if there are any remains that might be analysed for arsenic."

"I assume you sent me the financial papers because you wanted to know how Mrs Dryson benefits from her husband's death," Mr Mycroft said.

"That is correct."

"Well, the sad truth is that Dr Dryson did not leave a large estate," he said. "His widow will inherit a small annuity at best. They were hardly married long enough for her to take out a life insurance policy on him, though I will look into that too. I suppose if she killed all those other men the money would add up—but really, it hardly seems worth it for all the trouble she's taken. Let me do a little more checking on him."

"I assume you intend to question Sir Peter Peacham about this woman?" Mr Sherlock asked.

"We do."

"When?"

"I've asked Nora if she has a photograph of the widow that she can send to me," Astraia said. "It will be more likely that Sir Peter will believe us if we can show him a picture."

Mr Sherlock nodded. "Be sure to let me know when you go to see him," he said. "I want to accompany you."

"Of course," my friend said.

"So how do you think this pertains to the actual case you were actually assigned to actually solve?" her oldest brother asked. "Do you think that Widow Valerie killed Lady Deborah in order to pursue her husband?"

"I don't believe so," my friend said, "but it's a possibility. Once we have a photograph, we can show it around to the suffragists to see if anyone recognises her."

"If she killed Lady Deborah, that would imply she might also have killed other women, in order to marry their husbands," Mr Mycroft said thoughtfully. "Was Dr Dryson a recent widower?"

Astraia looked at me. "No," I said, which may have been the only contribution I made to the conversation all evening.

Mr Mycroft Holmes walked over to sit by the piano. "Would you play for us, Astrie?" he asked.

She frowned, but walked over to sit at the piano. She played Chopin's nocturne in B flat minor, and then his nocturne in E flat, both without a musical score. I was flabbergasted to discover that my friend was a concert-level pianist. I had always considered myself to be a fairly competent musician. But Astraia's piano skill was at a level far beyond my own. Her playing was sublime.

Finally the room was quiet. Astraia closed the piano.

"That was lovely, Astrie," Mr Mycroft said.

Mr Sherlock nodded. "We should have a family concert night some time soon. It has been too long."

Mr Mycroft Holmes set his empty glass down on a side table and stood. "Are you ready to leave, Sherlock?"

"If you wish."

We walked the gentlemen to the door, where John assisted them with their coats and hats before leaving to bring the carriage around to the front.

"Astrie, how long do you think it will take you to solve the case?" Mr Mycroft asked.

"Which one?"

"The one I asked you to solve. The one the newspapers are calling *The Suffragist Murder*."

"I anticipate that we will have solved that one within the week," she said.

He nodded. "I'm glad. I have another one I need you to look into, but I don't want to discuss it with you until this one is completed."

His brother spoke up. "Mycroft, you're not planning to have Astraia and Miss Barquist work on that Lionel Rademacher case you told me about, are you?" he asked, disdain in his voice.

"I am," Mr Mycroft Holmes said stiffly.

"I cannot condone that," Mr Sherlock said. "He's a despicable villain, and I don't want my sister to have anything to do with him."

"He is a respectable industrialist and adviser to the Prince of Wales," Mr Mycroft said. "And this case would be perfect for Astraia and Miss Barquist."

Mr Sherlock Holmes turned to me. "Miss Barquist, do you remember when I told you why Rebecca Ravenwood Thornapple was sent to gaol?"

I nodded.

"Lionel Rademacher is the father of the woman she was threatening for alienation of affection. He's the man who bribed the judge into having her incarcerated. Please try to convince my sister to tell Mycroft 'no' in this instance."

"Astrie will be in no danger," Mycroft Holmes insisted, opening the front door. "And Rademacher has had the charges against Miss Ravenwood Thornapple dropped, as you well know." The two brothers left, continuing their argument as they walked down the steps to the waiting coach.

"Well, that went better than I expected," Astraia said.

"Do you and your brothers often have concert evenings?" I asked. I would love to attend such a thing.

"It's been ages," she said. "Sherlie is a competent violinist. But Mykie really should practise his cello more often. Ever since he moved into that club of his, his fingering has gotten rusty. Shall we go into the kitchen and see if there's any ice cream left?"

***

The morning post arrived the following day just as we were preparing to leave for Whitechapel. One letter in particularly attracted Astraia's attention, and she tore it open.

"Perfect!" she crowed. "This is perfect!"

Nora had successfully obtained the wedding photo Astraia had requested. The groom looked blissfully in love. The bride appeared less enthusiastic but the photographer had caught the image of her face in sharpest detail. No one would ever be able to mistake the face of the bride for anyone other than Widow Valerie.

"Are we going to try to see Sir Peter today to show him this picture?" I asked.

"We are."

"Are we going to let your brother Sherlock know we're going, so he can accompany us?"

She scowled. "Of course not," she said.

Chapter Twelve

Because someone needed to attend to our regular employment today, John drove Susie and Rutherford to the police station and Letty to the library, then returned to collect us. While we waited, Astraia and I discussed our plans for the morning. The main decision before us was: should we first visit the suffragists from the rush on Parliament to see if anyone recognised Widow Valerie from the photo, thereby taking at least some action with regard to *The Suffragist Murder*, or should we go directly to Sir Peter's home to explain the situation to him and unveil proof of the perfidy of his beloved?

"I think we should see as many suffragists as we can first," Astraia said, "at least two or three, and depending on what we hear from those women we can plan to visit more of them tomorrow. Mykie said that Mr Rademacher has dropped the charges against Rebecca, so I'd like to see if she is back at home. Also, let's see if Maria and Lydia recognise the widow. We can save exposing the widow to her paramour to the end of the day as a sort of treat for ourselves. It's unfortunate that we can't show the photograph to Lady Isabella today too, since she lives directly across the street from the Peacham house, but you'll recall that she mentioned she was leaving town last week to visit one of her other homes, Eastnor Castle. We shall have to improve our acquaintance with Lady Isabella when this is all over. I have always wanted to visit a castle."

But when we stopped at Rebecca's house we were not invited in. The maid who answered the door informed us that Miss Rebecca was at home but feeling poorly and wasn't receiving visitors. We informed her that we hoped Miss Rebecca would get well soon, and said that we would return on the morrow since the reason for our visit was urgent.

Although it was past ten o'clock, neither Maria Norton nor Lydia Percival were awake when we arrived at their houses (a reminder to us that the main complaint they had about Parliament was that it began too early in the morning). Maria was interested enough in our visit to have us sent up to her boudoir where a servant propped her up against her pillows, dishevelled and bleary-eyed, a lacy robe from an entirely different negligee set pulled over a thick woollen nightgown. We showed her the photograph of Widow Valerie; she insisted she had never seen the woman; she offered us a half-hearted invitation to join her for coffee which we declined; and as we left the room her snores accompanied our exit.

We did not receive even that much welcome at Lydia's home, where once again we had to inform a maid guarding a door that we would return the next day. When Astraia asked, in a somewhat snide tone, what would be a good time to call, we were advised that Miss Lydia was usually presentable to see company by four o'clock in the afternoon.

So when we arrived at Sir Peter Peacham's home, we didn't feel very optimistic that he would be available to see us. Which was indeed the case.

"I'm sorry, Miss Holmes," the housekeeper said at the door, viewing the card Astraia had handed to her. "Sir Peter is in the country at present. In fact, we are just now closing down the house for a month."

Astraia sighed. I shared her disappointment. What a disheartening trip we'd made today, after feeling such enthusiasm this morning when the photograph had arrived in the post!

We turned to leave, and the woman added, "Sir Peter's sister Mrs Broom is still here, if you would like me to see if she can spare you a few minutes."

"That would be fine," Astraia said, after a glance at me. Perhaps the sister would be open to gossip about her brother's lady friends. The housekeeper showed us into the drawing room.

"I'll just check to see if she's available," she said, and left.

We strolled around the room while we waited. No lamps were lit in the room, but happily there were several large windows open to the sunlight so we could see fairly well. No Freemasonry ritual manuals were available for visitors to peruse here; in fact, the room held no books at all. The walls were lined with taxidermied heads of exotic beasts, which one presumed were the pride of Sir Peter; beneath these monstrous maws sat shelves covered with dainty china gew-gaws which had no doubt belonged to the late Lady Deborah. I stood for a moment studying a little shepherdess which reminded me somewhat of my Mummy's treasured Grace, though Lady Deborah's was of much finer craftsmanship. And Mummy's lay buried now beneath a pile of ash.

After a long wait, causing me to wonder if Sir Peter's sister was also still abed, the door of the sitting room opened and Mrs Broom walked in, followed by the housekeeper bearing a tea tray laden with sandwiches and a steaming teapot.

"I'm so delighted you could join me!" the lady said gaily, then turned back to her servant. "Just set the tray down, Mrs Hannah, and then you and Herbert can leave. My friends and I will see to the clean-up before we go, don't you worry."

"Oh, Miss Valerie, I can't let you do that," the housekeeper protested. "It just wouldn't be right."

"You can and you will, Mrs Hannah," her mistress scolded. "I'm certain all of us have washed a dish or two in our time, haven't we girls?" she said to us with a wink. "And if not, it's high time we start!" She turned back to her servant, pushing her to the door. "I don't want you and Herbert to miss your train! So you just go now."

The housekeeper gave a tiny giggle. "Yes, Miss Valerie. And thank you, miss." She left, closing the door behind her.

We listened in silence as the woman walked away. Then the Widow Valerie gave a dramatic sigh. "Old family retainers!" she said. "Sometimes you don't know whether to hug them or shoot them, don't you agree, Miss Holmes?"

Then she looked at me, the malice sparkling in her bright eyes even from behind her widow's veil. "That's not something you'd know anything about, Miss Barquist, is it? Oh, I'm sorry to see someone has apparently punched you in the face. Have you and little Astraia been annoying people again?"

"I see you're wearing deep mourning, Mrs, er, Broom. Did someone close to you die recently?" Astraia asked, lifting a sandwich from the tray and studying the edges.

"Oh, you'll like those," Valerie promised. "Chopped egg and watercress. They're my favourite." She pulled the string to open the front of her black veil, plucked the sandwich from Astraia's hand, and bit into it. "And as for my mourning," she said around a mouth full of food, "well, you may not have heard, but," she turned to us and whispered, "my husband just died."

"Which one?" Astraia asked.

"Oh you naughty thing!" Valerie said playfully, tapping Astraia's hand with the sandwich as though it were a fan then handing it back to my friend. "I'm wearing these weeds for Mr Broom, of course. He died in Germany. We'd gone there for the baths, you know. But they just weren't enough to save him, what with his congestive heart trouble that has been bothering him for so many years. My brother is deeply distressed for me. He loves me very much, and is so sad for me even though unfortunately he never had a chance to meet Mr Broom even though we were married for ever so long. We eloped, you know; so romantic although dear brother Peter was a teensy bit angry at the time. He was my guardian, you must know; and so dedicated to that responsibility that he—well, never mind about that. Let's just say he always took very deliberate care of me and has never wanted me to be burdened by the weight of having to make too many decisions for myself. Peter and the staff left for Yorkshire today, gone to our childhood home to prepare the dower house for me to move into. I'll be joining him of course, to meditate in the country over my devastating loss. In isolation. Wearing black. Like a good widow should."

"You didn't seem very grieved over your loss when we saw you here entering the house the other night,"

Astraia observed. "And you certainly weren't wearing black."

"My widow's weeds weren't ready yet, silly," Valerie said. "All I had here in the house were my old gowns. And I so wanted to see the new Gilbert and Sullivan operetta that opened while I was out of the country—have you seen it yet?"

Actually we had, a month ago. But we didn't answer.

"So dear Peter agreed to take me. Finally. I assured him no one would recognise me. He's a dreadful stickler for the proprieties. He didn't want anyone to get the wrong idea about me. And it turns out, he was right, wasn't he? Because you two saw me, and Lord knows you got the wrong idea!" She burst into a peal of laughter. "It was a real lesson to me, though. To all of us, really. The man is always right. If I'd just listened to my brother, the three of us wouldn't be here together now."

"I think you're suffering from hysteria," Astraia said. "Or maybe from crepe poisoning."

Valerie sobered. "Maybe you're right."

I didn't remember a Mr Broom from the letter collection, and said so. "Which one was Mr Broom?"

Valerie giggled. "I'll let you in on a little secret," she said. "I've never actually been married to anyone named Broom." Then she looked thoughtful for a moment. "At least, I don't think so. Mr Broom was a useful pretence for getting money out of Peter without having to be under his thumb, you see—Mr Broom was a terribly bad financial manager, poor dear, and Peter was always happy to help us out whenever I wrote to him, particularly since we were willing to stay in Europe and not embarrass him with our impoverishment here in jolly old England."

Astraia frowned. "Then why did Sir Peter write to Mrs Brown when he wrote that letter to you in Germany?" And then she answered her own question. "He wrote to Mrs Broom, didn't he? I just read it wrong, because his handwriting is so bad. You've used the surname *Brown* so often, I just saw what I expected to see."

"We all do, dear," Valerie said, patting the blonde hair that poked out from her black veil. She set a couple of sandwiches on a plate and handed it to me. "Do eat up, Maddie. Tall girls like us need to keep up our strength."

I glanced at Astraia as I took the plate. She shrugged, and I took a bite of one of the sandwiches. The crazy woman was right. It was good.

"Let's all sit down like friends now and have a nice coze," Valerie said. "We have so much to catch up on."

"We're not even sure what to call you," Astraia said.

"Valerie, of course. I'm Valerie. You're Astraia. And you're Maddie!" She poured us each a cup of tea.

"Yes, but what is your last name, Valerie?" Astraia waited for Valerie to drink, then took a sip from her own cup.

"What difference does it make? All names belong to men, after all. We women are so unimportant in the scheme of things, even our names don't belong to us—we use our father's names, or our husband's names. And there's no point in trying to revolt and use our mother's last name instead, because she was also using her father's or her husband's. As far back as you can go, and none of us have our own names. Isn't that sad? I've always thought that was a teensy bit sad."

I'd never thought about it at all. But now that I did, I had to admit she had a point. Worse in my case than in anyone else's, perhaps—whenever anyone called me "Miss Barquist" they were commemorating a name that had belonged to the most notorious criminal in British history, even if they were unaware of the fact.

Valerie got up and walked to a wall, where she puttered about with the gas heater. "I'm feeling a bit cold; are you two cold? Peter had the gas turned off when he left, but I think we won't get in trouble if we run it for just a little while." She waited a moment, then said, "There. That's better, I think. It should warm in here quickly." She walked back to the table and sat the farthest away from the heater. "You two are my guests; you sit there, so you can get warm."

I was feeling a bit cold and so was happy to sit near the heater, though I couldn't feel the warmth coming through yet.

"Was it really necessary to kill Dr Dryson?" I asked. He'd been a friend of mine, in a way. Or at least someone I'd known for a while and hadn't disliked.

She gave a moue of distaste. "I am a teensy bit sad about that, I admit. He wasn't so awful. Certainly I've married worse. And he was devoted to me. Although he had started to ask questions I was unable to answer, mentioning people and ideas and interests he had been talking about with the other Mrs Tillis in their correspondence, which he really shouldn't have done because it embarrassed me, and I do so hate to be embarrassed. You should never embarrass your spouse—that's my number one rule. And then the two of you mentioned that you'd seen me here that night, with my brother. And that embarrassed me too—I really wish you hadn't done that."

"We apologise," Astraia said. "It was never our intention to embarrass you."

"Oh, well. Water under the bridge. Apology accepted. Just a little misunderstanding between dear friends. Have some more tea."

She poured us all a second cup and passed around the sandwiches again. Then she rose and walked to the other side of the room, sipping her tea as she stood beneath the stuffed and mounted head of a lion captured in mid-roar.

"Did you become embarrassed when you vomited on Dr Dryson at the séance?" Astraia asked. "Or was that just a part of your plan?"

Valerie laughed. "Oh, you know me so well, Astraia dear. That's the best part of having good female friends, don't you think? And I think the two of you might be the closest female friends I've ever had. You're right, of course. I can vomit at will. I learned years ago that men feel very protective toward vomiting females."

"I've always found tears effective enough," Astraia said slowly.

"Yes, but it's my experience that some men don't trust tears," Valerie said. "Vomit, though—they just can't argue with vomit."

"You were telling us why you had to kill Dr Broom...I mean, Dr Dryerson," I said. I took another sip of tea, to clear my head.

"Dr Dryson," she corrected. "Dear Richard. Yes. Well, I read in the newspaper that the real Mrs Tillis had arrived in England. There were just too many people who knew about my little masquerade, I'm afraid. It was time for that marriage to end."

"But did he have to die?" I repeated.

"Couldn't you just divorce?" Astraia said, then giggled. Then looked surprised at herself.

"Oh my dears, of course he had to die," Valerie said. "They all had to die. That was the whole point."

She walked over to a plant by the door, held her veils back with her hands, and vomited into the aspidistra. Then she settled herself, walked back over to her place by the lion head, and continued. "They were sacrifices to my goddess," she said. "They had to die for the greater glory of Asherah."

"Jehovah's wife," Astraia said with authority.

"She was not his wife," Valerie corrected. "He was one of her husbands. She came first. Before all else, the Mother Goddess came first."

"Are you a priest or something?" Astraia asked, her words slurred.

"Priestess, dear. Yes, I am the High Priestess of the Cult of Asherah."

"But why did they all have to die?" I asked plaintively.

"For so many reasons," Valerie said. "Not the least of which is the glaze."

Astraia frowned, and tried to stand. Her legs wobbled and she sat back down. "The glaze?"

"Let me explain," Valerie said patiently. "Asherah demands sacrifices. And she demands art. As her devotee, I provide her with both. You already know about my talent. I wanted to go to Italy or Paris to study with the great sculptors, but of course I couldn't. Because I was a girl. So that was that." She moved closer to the door. "Did you know that arsenic makes the best glaze for ceramics? And that human cremains also produce a very refined glaze? Anyway, ask and She will provide; over the years as I refined the recipe for my glaze, the interest in cremation in England has expanded as I needed it to. There is even a Council of the Cremation Society now, working for cremation acceptance throughout the country. And where others might see only a coincidence, I see the driving hand of my Goddess. And now I have the perfect glaze recipe, the sublime blend, and each sacrifice allows me to create one transcendent sacrificial bust to stand guard over the many sacred statues I manifest of the Mother in all her glorious and infinite faces.

"I am always conscious of the doors the Mother opens to me," she continued. "For example, I had never planned to marry Dr Dryson. It was a fluke that he was in Cambridge when I was there that week—I had actually been preparing to meet a professor or some other scholarly panjandrum; I've never yet married into the hallowed halls of academia, you see, and it seemed the right time. But I overheard Dr Dryson speaking with someone about his friend Valerie Tillis whom he had never met in person, and I knew that the Goddess had put me in that place at that time for a special reason. I knew, because of the name. Valerie. It was more than a coincidence. It was another Asherah opportunity, a sacred commandment from the Mother Goddess."

At that moment, Astraia collapsed onto the floor.

"Poor dear," Valerie said. "Poor frail, tiny little thing. You'll last longer, of course, Maddie. Although I can tell you're already unsteady. Even I am feeling the effects, though I am far away from the gas."

"Gas?" I said, shakily. I tried to stand, but couldn't.

"Yes, gas," Valerie said sadly. "I turned it on, but did not ignite the burner. Oopsie. This room is filling with gas."

It actually felt kind of nice. Like alcohol intoxication.

"In Germany, they've started adding mercaptan to the gas so that people smell something unpleasant to warn them if their gas is leaking. But the gas companies here have not put such a safety measure in place, which is unfortunate for you.

"You and Astraia will die, I'm afraid. Which is too bad, because I genuinely like you. You're my best friends. I've never killed a woman before. Except for that wretched Lady Agatha Sotheran, of course—but that was her own fault. She shouldn't have flirted with Richard when I had already staked my claim on him. And really, she was half-way dead from digitalis already anyway; who's to say that my little bit extra caused her demise? But our Mother Asherah brought the two of you here today. So she must want you dead."

"What about Lady Deboreborah?" I asked. "Your bruver's wife..."

"What about her?"

"Dint you kill her?"

I think she looked shocked, but I can't be sure because at that moment I passed out.

***

271

"Wake up, Miss Maddie!" an insistent voice said. I began to sputter as whisky was poured down my throat.

I woke slowly, my head spinning. I recognised that I was inside Astraia's coach. A man held my head in his hand and dribbled whisky into my mouth. I tried to focus. The man was Astraia's coachman John.

On the other side of the coach, I saw Astraia held in the arms of her brother Sherlock Holmes, himself dressed in rags like a beggar. I was gripped with anxiety until I saw that she was breathing, though not yet awake.

"I'm all right, John," I croaked. "Thank you."

"You can drive us home now, John," Mr Holmes said, his voice almost perfectly steady.

John left the cab to move into the driver's seat, and soon we were advancing down the cobblestone streets.

Mr Holmes allowed me to rest for a while, letting me take deep breaths and clear my head before he began to ask questions.

"Who is responsible for this, Miss Barquist?" he asked.

"Sir Peter Peacham's sister Valerie," I said.

"Ah," he said. "His sister." He glared down at his own for a moment, then returned to his questioning.

"Was Peacham there?"

"No, he and the entire household have left for their family estate in Yorkshire. I think Valerie is going to go there too."

"If she does, I'll catch her."

I could tell by the way Astraia's breathing had changed that she had awakened. I thought Mr Holmes probably noticed too, but he didn't say anything or shift his hold on her.

I nodded, then said, "What about the gas? Did you turn it off?" I'd had a sudden, horrible image of the entire block blowing up, including Lady Isabella's beautiful home across the street.

"John turned it off," Mr Holmes said.

"Was Valerie gone?"

"There was no one but the two of you in the house. We saw a woman bicycling away before we went in," Mr Holmes said. "That may have been her."

"Why did you go in?"

"One doesn't often see a woman dressed in mourning go bicycling through the streets of London. It seemed suspicious. And you'd been gone for too long," he said. "We knocked. No one answered."

"How did you get in then? Weren't the doors locked?"

He gave me a look, and I realised Astraia wasn't the only member of the family who thought nothing of breaking into other people's houses.

"Why are you dressed like that?" I asked.

"Because you didn't invite me to join you in your trip to interrogate Sir Peter Peacham like you said you would," he said. "I'm in disguise."

"You're spying on us."

"If you like."

I thought about the outcome of today's spying. "Thank you," I said. "For this once, I'm glad you spied on us."

"Was it worth it?"

"What?"

"Almost dying. My sister almost dying."

"Well, you don't have to find us an enquiry agent now," I said. "Valerie admitted to killing all those men."

"All of them?"

"We didn't ask after each of them by name, but that was the tenor of the conversation. She sacrificed them to her goddess."

He thought about that for a while, then said "We should get the specific details about each man's death anyway. To build the case against her."

"I suppose."

"Did she kill her sister-in-law?"

It took me a moment to realise whom he meant. Of course, I was still woozy from the gas.

"She said that Astraia and I were the first women she'd ever killed, other than Lady Sotheran who died during the séance in Cambridge."

Astraia roused herself at that. "She killed Lady Sotheran?"

"Yes. Apparently she fed her extra digitalis for flirting with Dr Dryson. But she looked stricken when I asked her if she'd killed Lady Deborah. I think. I was busy fainting at the time."

"I remind you both that she is a master liar," Sherlock Holmes pointed out.

"That is true," his sister said, her voice a whispered croak. "We cannot take her words at face value. Bu then again, perhaps this time she spoke the truth. We have not yet solved the case of *The Suffragist Murder*."

She slipped back into sleep and didn't wake up for the rest of the trip to her house, even when Mr Holmes shifted away from holding her.

He let John carry his sister into her home, then turned to give final instructions to me.

"I'm going to Yorkshire," he said. "Do not follow me."

"We won't," I said. He didn't need to worry about that. I hardly had enough strength to carry myself to my own room.

"The two of you can find something safer to do for a few days," he said. "Read some books. Interview some suffragists. I don't care. Just stay out of Yorkshire."

I reiterated that I understood, and entered the house where I collapsed in bed and slept for the next fifteen hours.

***

Due to the worst headaches of our lives, neither Astraia nor I could consume anything stronger than weak tea and toast the next morning despite having missed dinner the day before. Meanwhile, Susie and

Rutherford were excited to tell us all about what had happened at the police station the previous day.

"Harry and the lads let us do all the work!" Rutherford said.

"We had so much fun!" Susie said. "Even Chan got to groom the horses!"

"Please make those children be quiet," Astraia begged me.

I told the children to hurry up and finish their breakfast, and then we would go into the parlour where they could tell me all about how Harry had taken advantage of them yesterday.

"It was fun!" Susie insisted.

"Hush!" Astraia cried.

We hurried into the parlour to leave her alone in her misery. I sank into a chair in front of a cosy fire to hear all about the horse schedule, and the different shifts and different riders, and the types of horses they used to draw the Black Maria that carried prisoners around, and the different types of bridles they used for different types of activities, and myriad other horse-related details. As someone who'd spent practically every day of the last fifteen years in the police stables I knew all of these things already, of course, but I didn't object to their recitation because I thought this was good information for them to learn and repeating the lessons to me would help them to remember. I also deduced that Harry and his stableboys had more or less viewed yesterday as a holiday from work, instead showing Rutherford, Susie, and even Chan how to do the many mundane things that they themselves were paid to do.

I realised that if I did not spend time in the stable myself today, Harry and his minions would feel free to continue exploiting my charges. I returned to the dining room, where Astraia sat slumped in her seat, eyeing the fragrant eggs and ham on the sideboard with loathing.

"I need to spend a few hours at the stable today," I said.

"That's fine," she said. "We learned yesterday that there's no point in trying to visit any of these women before noon anyway."

"We're really going to interview suffragists today?"

"We are. I have a new angle I want to explore. I'll spend the morning working on the details. Go to work, but be sure to return here by twelve o'clock."

So John drove Letty, the children, and me to Whitechapel that morning, leaving Astraia home alone in her house. Letty informed me that she had made sandwiches for Astraia and me to eat for lunch, and she had brought along additional sandwiches for the children to have for their own mid-day meal. She asked me if we would all be returning to the house again this evening, as she didn't think there was enough mutton to feed everyone and she needed to know what to send John out to buy today at the market.

I felt mortified to realise how much work I had added to Letty's and John's shoulders.

"Oh Letty, I am so sorry!" I said. "You already do so much for Astraia—I shouldn't expect you to care for all of us as well. We'll plan to start spending the nights at our new home above the bakery very soon." I thought about how soon I could get the new flat ready for Susie and me and set up permanent sleeping arrangements for Rutherford in the stable. It wouldn't take too long if I wasn't so busy trying to help Astraia solve that blasted murder of Lady Deborah, as well as the other murders we'd stumbled upon. But Astraia seemed to think we would have *The Suffragist Murder* case closed soon. I would insist on a few days free from investigations after that, in order to take control of our living arrangements.

"We'll be out of the house by this next Sunday," I promised her. "In the meantime, is there anything we can do to help you out?"

"I can help in the kitchen!" Susie said excitedly. "And I can also help you with the washing and mending, Letty!"

I'd forgot about all the washing and mending Letty did, as well as the cooking and cleaning. And library work. At least we no longer expected her to launder our clothes.

"And I can help John with the horses and the extra shopping, since he's having to make so many extra trips around town now," Rutherford said.

I hadn't thought about all the additional trips John had to make these days. Before Astraia and I became detectivists, he'd had so much time on his hands most days he was able to make extra money driving one of his coaches around town as a cab for hire. This was certainly no longer the case. There were days he had to drive back and forth between the West End and Whitechapel four or more times. And much of that was in order to collect or deliver me to places.

Letty smiled at the children and thanked them for their help. "There is something you can do for me, Miss Maddie," she said.

"Anything, Letty."

"You can ask Miss Astraia to tell her brothers to hire a cook and maid to help me in the house," she said. "I'm a companion and housekeeper who cooks, not a librarian who's also a housekeeper and a companion and a cook. I need more than four hours of sleep in a night. I'm not as young as I used to be."

I winced at this, and said, "You don't want me to just tell her to hire an assistant librarian instead so that you can go back to your normal duties?" I asked.

She shook her head. "No, I like working at the library," she said. "I like helping all of the people, and finding new books to read. It's the cooking and cleaning that's become too much now, even though I've been doing such things all of my life."

279

Then she sat back in her seat, perhaps exhausted from doing so much talking at one time after only four hours of sleep.

I spoke sharply to Harry that morning, which took him aback since I rarely spoke sharply to anyone. But I needed him to understand that Susie and Rutherford were not there to lift the burden of work from him and his lads. They would always be happy to help, yes, but their job was to assist me with the sick animals (actually, Rutherford's job was to spy on me for Sherlock Holmes, but I could hardly let him know that).

Harry grumbled about this being his stable and the children didn't have anything else to do anyway and they never complained and other such things to justify his appalling behaviour, but eventually he returned to his work and I began mine. Old Toby had transitioned back to his usual duties with the other horses, which I knew wouldn't last. He had arthritis, and with the least amount of overwork would start limping again. He was replaced in the new veterinary box by another old nag with a swollen leg, and I had Susie start a poultice treatment on her.

An old desk had been found and set up for me at the side of the stable now intended for the veterinary services, with a replacement set of accounting ledgers and pencils. So I had what I needed to begin the rudiments of tracking cases and expenses. But that was not my most immediate concern: what I most needed were new surgical tools and medicines such as morphine.

This became critically clear when a horse was brought in with an enormous gash in its hindquarters from an accident on the road. I could superficially clean the gash, but I could not repair it because I didn't have so much as a surgical needle or thread. And I didn't have any chloral hydrate at hand to anaesthetise the poor animal, nor the tools necessary to administer such anaesthesia if I'd had it, nor even any morphia to alleviate the horse's pain.

PC Archibald Froest went out to a local opium den to procure sufficient opiate for this instance as well as a large hypodermic, so eventually the poor animal was able to rest in a box without distress, one of the fresh clean horse blankets covering his wheezing chest and upper legs, while I flushed out his wound a little deeper than I had before. It was critical, however, that I operate soon or else we would not be able to save the beast.

I was about to start crying in frustration when DI Samuel Rankin came in carrying two large medical bags. The annoying man had gone to every police veterinary service in the city to beg them for all of their extra equipment.

I could have hugged him, so grateful did I feel. Instead I thanked him, asked him to send a message to Astraia that I would not be back by noon today, and started boiling water to sanitise these replacement tools. Many were rusted and all of them old, but after a quick review of the offerings I realised with relief that I now had instruments adequate for the task at hand.

Susie and Rutherford watched and assisted as needed. I also noticed Chan's blue head scarf a time or two through the procedure. This was the first significant piece of veterinary work Rutherford had ever witnessed and he helped like a veteran; Susie had already experienced one or two of these types of operations with me in the past and she did her part with skill and fortitude.

We decided that Rutherford would spend the night near the horse's box, a hypodermic of morphine at hand in case it was needed in the night. I showed him several times what he would have to do, I watched as he gave the horse a dose a few hours after the surgery, and he continued to practise the skill by plunging the needle into a stuffed horse's head that Harry kept in his rooms. Rutherford felt deeply the responsibility he was being given, and said that he wouldn't need Harry to help him if he had to do it in the night. I insisted that he call Harry before he undertook the task anyway, and also ensured that Harry was prepared to help. Correctly injecting a large animal in distress is not always an easy thing to do.

I struggled with myself before deciding to leave the stable that evening. There was a chance the injured horse could die in the night from shock and blood loss. It was unlikely—otherwise I wouldn't have left

Rutherford to face such a tragedy on his own; the horse was young and otherwise healthy; but I warned the boy of the possibility and he insisted that he was prepared. When Letty and John stopped at the stable at five o'clock after the library closed, Susie and I returned to the house with them.

During the quiet ride back to Astraia's home I thought about the horses in my care. Old Toby was destined to be sent to a knacker's yard soon. I was fond of the animal, having treated him for many illnesses and injuries in his time, and would be sorry when he was deemed unfit for continued work. Most working horses only lived for three or four years, and Old Toby was already five, so he'd had a long life. During my years in the police station I had seen many, many horses similarly disposed of when they grew old and weak.

I wished I had enough money to create a retirement farm for horses, a place where they could spend their final months or years just eating grass and running around a field only as much as they cared to do. But I could not see any path ahead that could allow me to achieve such a dream. Right now, the best dream I could hope for was to procure a dresser and a bed for Susie and me to use so that we could move into our new home. And the best thing I could do for horses was to be kind to them and to care for them to the extent my skills as a doctor allowed.

As I sat back in the seat, I realised I had not spent one minute thinking about the Widow Valerie since arriving at the police station that morning. I wondered what kind of person I was, that someone should try to kill me one day and I'd completely forget about her the next.

When we reached Astraia's house, my friend held out a telegram from her brother Sherlock.

"Valerie has not arrived in Yorkshire," she said. "Sherlie thinks she might have stayed here in town to make sure she succeeded in killing us." She showed me the gun in her other hand. "I'm ready for her."

Chapter Thirteen

I recognised the gun, a tiny weapon of death which Astraia usually kept in her reticule. "Please put that away," I said.

"I will," she said, "now that you're here." For some reason, Astraia always viewed me as her protector. This didn't seem like the right moment to correct her misperception of my abilities.

John had procured additional servings of mutton, which Susie and Rutherford enjoyed in the kitchen with Letty and John while Astraia and I ate our dinner in the dining room. Susie had mentioned to me that Letty was teaching them table manners, which I thought was an excellent idea though it meant one more favour the good woman was doing for me.

I decided it was time for me to try to serve her in kind. "Astraia, could you ask your brothers to hire a cook and maid to help Letty? She is overworked."

Astraia looked at me in astonishment. "Why on earth do you think that? She hardly does anything."

"She does everything," I countered. "Cooks, cleans, laundry, library—there's hardly an element of your life that she doesn't help you with."

"Well, that's hardly my fault! I never asked her to do any of that."

"You asked her to help at the library."

"But she likes that. She gets to read all of those books."

I couldn't argue with that. Instead I said, "She isn't getting enough sleep, Astraia. She has to stay up all night doing the work around here that isn't getting done in the daytime when she's at the library."

"I could hire an assistant librarian, I suppose."

"She doesn't want that. As you said, she likes working at the library. She wants help around the house."

She was quiet for a moment. "She never told me that."

"She doesn't like to complain."

"Ha! You don't know her as well as you think you do." She thought for another moment. "Why doesn't she just ask my brothers herself? She gets along with them better than I do, for goodness sake. I hardly think they'd tell her no if she asked them directly."

"I think she's trying to respect the fact that she works for you, not them. Even if they do pay her wages."

"Ha. Well, that's a problem. Because I don't like to ask them for favours. They always want something in return. But you could do it, Maddie."

"Me?"

"Yes, you. They like you. They like you, and they like Letty. I'm sure they'd do it as a favour for the two of you." And having solved this problem to her satisfaction, she turned her fork to her mutton, ending that topic of conversation.

***

The next morning we agreed that I would spend the morning at the stable, but only the morning. "I'm going to come with John to collect you at twelve o'clock," Astraia warned. She suggested that I wear something decent to work and cover it with an apron, but I knew from experience this was an unsatisfactory solution to the horse faeces problem.

"I have clean clothes at our new flat across the street," I said. "I'll go over there and change before twelve."

The injured horse had slept fairly well through the night, and Rutherford had given him his only injection an hour before we arrived in the morning. I checked the wound, which looked good, and let the children handle the re-bandaging, which they managed fairly well, before sending them off to Mrs Ma's to check on Annie.

Sergeant Wilson had brought in some workers this morning to build walls and shelves for my new office. I decided to stay out of their way and instead spend some time digging around to see if there was anything to recover from the ash heap that used to be the veterinary stable.

I borrowed a pair of Harry's heavy gloves (another thing I'd need to add to the list) and began to burrow through the piles of my burned-up past. After a while a couple of officers joined in, deciding that searching through my detritus might make an interesting break from chasing after criminals.

It was satisfying work, because we were able to salvage much more than I had expected. Most of the metal items were intact—we would be able to reuse the stove, also many of my father's surgical instruments (which though they held tragic memories were nevertheless newer and in better shape than the replacements Samuel had brought to me). My bed was irredeemable, but I thought the small dresser could be restored to use. This almost made me cry; the bedroom set had belonged to my mother and to her parents before her, and I had been devastated to think I had lost them. Of course my lovely red celluloid comb and the little jewellery box in which I kept it were gone, along with the very few things owned by Susie.

I found Grace, who had another chip in her but was otherwise undamaged from the blaze. And as I was about to leave to go across the street to clean up and change my clothes, PC Perkins came running toward me. "Maddie, is this something you want?" he said, holding out a small object in his hand.

It was the little statue of Asherah. The goddess was completely intact; in fact, I couldn't even see any dust or smoke film on it. The glaze shone in the morning sun. I took it without a word, placing it in my bag.

At noon, Samuel Rankin came up to me as I stood waiting for Astraia on the sidewalk in front of the police station. "Miss Maddie, you look very nice today," he said.

"Thank you."

"I'm glad to see you. There's a problem in the gaol, with a girl. Could you take a look at her, see if you can help?" He seemed unsure of himself, awkward almost.

"I'm supposed to go on an errand with Astraia," I said.

"This won't take a moment," he said. He took my arm and steered me into the police station and down the stairs to the dark gaol hallway.

We stopped at cell 1, which was usually reserved for female prisoners since it was closest to the police office.

"She's having a problem, and there's no one here who can explain things to her," he said. He looked and sounded deeply embarrassed. He unlocked cell 1 and almost shoved me in, closing the door quickly, leaving himself behind in the hall.

A young girl lay crying on the miserable little cot that served as a bed, a girl who could not have been more than a year or two older than Susie. The bed and her legs were spotted with blood.

"What's wrong, my dear?" I said gently, walking over to her.

"I'm dying!" she wailed. "My guts are falling out of me!"

"I'm a doctor," I said. "Let me see what's happening with you."

It took me only a moment to glean that she had begun her menses. I told her there was nothing wrong with her, and that this would last for only a few days now but she should expect to have this same experience every month for many years.

I began to explain that she would need to prepare napkins to pin to a bandage or belt around her waist. This sounded familiar to her, and she told me that she'd seen such things on women before and wondered why they wore them. Learning that all women went through this, including women she knew, helped her to calm down.

She looked in disgust at the bloody mess that was her dress and bed.

"I don't have any napkins," she said, "nor anything to make them with."

I nodded. "I'll go get something for you, as well as a clean dress," I said.

Samuel Rankin had been standing outside of the door and opened it for me when I approached, his head down. He agreed to find a clean dress for the girl if I would make the objects the child needed. He could hardly look me in the face as he spoke. I told him to deliver her dirty clothes to me so that I could have them laundered for her before she saw the judge.

Astraia waited for me at the street, in John's coach. I explained that I needed to prepare something for an inmate, but that it shouldn't take very long. I went into the stable where there were plenty of clean rags and bandages, and manufactured a half-dozen napkins for the girl, which I delivered along with a few safety pins and a longer bandage she could wrap around her waist to secure the napkins.

She expressed her sincere thanks toward me, and I left. Samuel was nowhere to be seen, but I knew he would deliver the dress as he'd promised.

I joined Astraia in the coach, unsure if it was relief or gratitude I felt that the girl had not recognised me as the woman who had turned her over to the police at the zoo just a few days ago, when she had attempted to pick the pocket of Dr Inskip.

***

Yesterday when I had failed to return to Astraia's house, she had used the time to write letters to Lydia Percival, Clara Finchley, and Rebecca Ravenwood Thornapple, three of the women who'd been at the rush on Parliament, asking if we could stop to see each of them this afternoon on a matter of business. Each had written back an affirmative.

We decided to see Clara first, since she seemed the most likely to be up and about near noontime. I knew Clara Finchley by sight from meetings of the Fabian Society; members of that group and the Society for Psychical Research were almost interchangeable, and I was somewhat hesitant to visit with her since I feared she would want to gossip about the new scandal facing the SPR—the death of Dr Dryson and disappearance of his wife who was not whom everyone had believed her to be.

This concern of mine proved to be valid.

"Did you hear about Dr Dryson?" she asked, almost first thing after we sat down in her parlour and she served us tea.

I looked at Astraia, who answered for us. "No. What about Dr Dryson?" she asked.

"You had heard that he married, didn't you?"

"We did hear something about that."

"Well, he died the same week he wed. Mr Podmore thinks that his new wife killed him. And guess what?"

"What?"

"No one knows who his new wife is! She had pretended to be Mrs Tillis the famous psychic medium, but it turns out she was an imposter!"

"You don't say!" Astraia said in a shocked tone

Clara continued going on about this for a while, but eventually we were able to get to the point of our visit.

Astraia took Widow Valerie's photograph out of her purse. "Have you ever seen this woman, Clara?"

Clara carefully studied the image. "I don't believe so. Who is she?"

"She's a person we're trying to find, to help us in our enquiries. You read that Maddie and I are investigating the death of Lady Deborah?"

"I did! So exciting! And you think this woman was the killer?"

"We don't know that. Right now we're trying to determine whether or not she was present during the rush on Parliament last month. You don't remember seeing her there?"

Clara looked at the photograph again, then shook her head regretfully. Clearly she would have given anything to be able to say she remembered this woman from that fateful day. But she opted for honesty. "I just don't think I've ever seen her," she said.

Astraia and I left a few minutes later. Back in the coach, with instructions to John to deliver us next to the home of Rebecca Ravenwood Thornapple, Astraia said, "I feel sorry for Clara."

"Sorry for her? Why?"

"She was so excited about the mystery of the imposter who married Dr Dryson. And here we were showing her a photograph of that very person, and we didn't even let her know."

We had decided next to visit Rebecca Ravenwood Thornapple in order to give Lydia Percival as much time as possible to wake up before we arrived. Rebecca's maid showed us into a darkened parlour in a small but elegant house. Drapes were drawn against the windows and only one or two weak gas lamps were lit.

"Miss Ravenwood Thornapple will be with you shortly," the maid said, and left us to our own devices.

While we waited, we looked around the room as was our wont on these occasions. Rebecca's parlour was fairly standard; she practised the too-much-furniture and too-many-knickknacks style of décor that was so popular with many people these days, a style that had made me nervous ever since I broke my foot and my agility had become undependable. She had a piano, the first I'd seen in any of the numerous parlours we'd visited recently. I walked over to examine her taste in sheet music, but quickly turned when I heard Astraia gasp.

"Maddie, come look at this!"

I hurried over, stumbling only once on a foot cushion, to review the collection of china statuettes on a shelf in front of my friend.

We might not have noticed her before. But today, even amidst all the china Venuses and Dianas, she was unmistakeable.

"Asherah," I said.

"Good afternoon, ladies," a hoarse voice whispered behind us. We turned to see a figure heavily swathed in mourning veils, almost drowning in the weight of all the black, from the black bombazine dress brushing the top of her black shoes to the black veil and large black hat covering her face and head. Black silk gloves enshrouded her hands.

"Rebecca?" I asked. I really couldn't identify her under all of the material. And that voice didn't help.

"Hello, Maddie. I'm sorry I couldn't see you the other day when you came by, but I've suffered a great personal loss and I just wasn't up to having visitors."

"Oh, I'm so sorry, Rebecca," I exclaimed. "We had no idea you were in mourning." I looked at Astraia. Unlike the Dryson home, there was no mourning decorating the exterior or interior of this house. Nor had the maid been wearing so much as a black band on her arm or black ribbon in her hair.

Rebecca understood our confusion. "I don't believe in public displays," she said. "My sorrow is buried inside. I don't feel like talking about it." Her voice was so hoarse, I imagined her spending the last few days crying until she ruined it. I felt overwhelmed with sympathy that she should be experiencing so much sorrow.

Though she too was dressed in widow's weeds, Rebecca couldn't have looked more different from Widow Valerie. Her mourning was real.

"We won't keep you very long, Rebecca," Astraia said. "We have a photograph we'd like to show you, if you don't mind."

"A photograph?" Rebecca asked, her voice confused. "You came over here to show me a photograph?"

Once again Astraia took the image of Widow Valerie out of her reticule to show it to a veteran of last month's rush on Parliament. But she held it back, not handing it to the woman yet.

"It's so dark in here, Rebecca. Do you think we could have more light?"

"No, I'm sorry—my eyes are very sore. I just can't tolerate bright light right now," Rebecca said.

"Then let's go over closer to the gas lamp so you can see it better," Astraia said. She walked over to stand by the lamp.

Rebecca hesitated.

"Just as close to the flame as you can bear," Astraia said. Rebecca moved a little closer to Astraia and the light.

When they were about a foot apart, Astraia held out the photograph. Rebecca brought it close to her face to study it. Astraia moved nearer to her. "Do you recognise the woman?" she asked.

"I don't know," Rebecca said. "Perhaps. She looks familiar."

"She is the woman who sculpted that statue of Asherah that you have on your shelf," Astraia said.

"Oh, of course," Rebecca said, relief in her voice. "Lady Valerie. I met her at a meeting of devotees once. A very talented woman. Maddie has one of her statues too, I noticed." She lifted her veil just enough to show the enamel pin she wore on her breast. "Are the two of you devotees of the Divine Mother?"

"Not precisely," Astraia said. "We have a fundamental theological problem with any religion that encourages its followers to kill other people."

"I can understand why you would feel that way," Rebecca said. "But when you understand Asherah more, you learn that her worship is not about killing but about death itself, death as transition, as an integral step on the path from birth to death to rebirth. Just as we celebrate birth, so too should we celebrate the death that opens the path to the next birth. I have some literature I can share with you, if you'd like."

"Not today, thanks," Astraia said. I thought she was going to say something more, but she was busy staring at Rebecca's head, almost as though she was trying to peer underneath her veil.

"Rebecca, was Lady Valerie one of the suffragists at the rush on Parliament last month?" I asked.

"I don't thi—"

But Rebecca never finished that sentence, because Astraia interrupted her.

"Maddie, open the drapes on the window!" she ordered. "Now!"

I had no idea why she was telling me to do this, but I never disobeyed Astraia when she used that tone of voice. I reached over to the window and pulled open the drapes. At the same moment Astraia raised the gas on the lamp to full, and then reached up to pull off the hat and veil covering Rebecca's head. Rebecca shrieked and fell in on herself.

"Oh my God!" I said, staring at the cringing woman's head now displayed full in the light both natural and gaslit.

Rebecca's face was red, swollen and blistered. And her eyebrows, lashes, and the front of her hair was burned off.

She turned away from us. "Don't look at me!" she cried. We saw that the back of her head had also suffered damage—burnt bits of hair stuck out from her head, her former beautiful chestnut mane gone, leaving frayed and crisp strands of dark burnt straw haloing her sore pink skull.

"Oh, Rebecca, I am so sorry!" I said, reaching out automatically to the pitiful woman now slumped on the divan, crying in her hoarse, damaged voice.

"I wouldn't feel too sorry for her, Maddie," Astraia said coldly. "After all, she injured herself trying to kill you."

"I didn't try to kill her!" Rebecca objected through her tears.

"You started a fire in the building where she works," Astraia said. "You could have killed her, the children who work with her, and the animals she treats. It's a miracle that no one was hurt. Except for you, of course. I assume your beautiful celluloid hair combs caught fire while you were setting the stables ablaze?"

Rebecca just started crying harder.

I stared, unbelieving. "Rebecca started the fire? But why?"

"She read in the newspaper that we were investigating the death of Lady Deborah. And we'd even told her when she was gaoled in your stable that night that we knew the murderer had been one of the suffragists, who had struck that day at Parliament using a very thin blade. She was afraid we were getting too close to her. She thought that she'd digress us from our investigations by starting a fire at the police stable."

"Too close to her?" I was still befuddled, still lost in my pity for the woman.

"Maddie, don't you understand yet? Rebecca Ravenwood Thornapple killed Lady Deborah. I wouldn't be surprised if she doesn't also intend to kill Lady Isabella."

At this accusation, Rebecca finally responded the way a murderer is expected to respond. She pulled a gun out of a pocket of her dress, and pointed it at Astraia.

And I responded the way I usually do. I struck the gun away with one hand and punched Rebecca in the face with the other. The murderer collapsed onto the floor.

Chapter Fourteen

Astraia sent me out to tell John to fetch the police. When I returned, it was to find that she had ordered Rebecca's maid to bring us all tea and cakes.

"I haven't had my lunch yet," she said. "And I feel like eating something sweet."

By the time the maid brought the tea in, Rebecca was calmer and had returned her veil and hat to her head. She explained that the maid was unaware of her injuries. She had put on mourning in order to cover up what had happened to her beautiful face and hair.

"These weeds belonged to my mother," she said. "After my father died, she wore heavy mourning for years."

"Has your mother passed away herself?" I asked, trying to engender a tone of sympathy. It should have seemed strange to be having this type of social interaction with someone who had tried to kill me just a few days ago and Astraia not fifteen minutes past, but since meeting Astraia I was getting used to such odd things as a matter of course.

"No, my mother is on her honeymoon," Rebecca said. "She married a man twenty years her junior. Just before they left for Paris, she told me she intends to sell this house when she returns. I don't know where I'm going to live after that."

"You don't need to worry about that," Astraia said.

Before Rebecca could start crying again or again try to kill one of us, the maid returned to bring the rest of the tea items and we changed the topic to something more innocuous. The weather, perhaps.

But once she'd left the room for a second time, Astraia decided to get as many answers as she could from Rebecca before the police arrived to take over the interrogation.

"How did your head catch fire?" she asked. "Our information was that someone—we assumed a man—had thrown a bomb of some kind into the stable and left before anyone realised what they'd done."

"It was a glass hand grenade that my grandfather brought back from the Crimea," Rebecca said. "He kept it as a paperweight on his desk. But he always said we had to be careful around it because it was still full of gunpowder. I had been thinking of throwing it into Walter's home, sometime when he was away and his wife was there alone, but realised a better use would be to make you quit your investigation."

I assumed Walter and his wife were the reason she'd been arrested recently. She certainly had a penchant for extreme behaviour. "How could your head catch fire from throwing a grenade?" I asked.

"It didn't," she said, and began sobbing again. "If I'd just left then, just got back on my bicycle and ridden away after I threw the grenade, I would not have been injured. But no, I had to stay and watch, and when the crowd grew, I moved in closer to see better. Dressed as a man, I suppose I felt invincible. And then sparks started falling into the crowd—and that frightened me, so I left then. But apparently a flying spark got caught in my hat, and I guess the wind from my bike ride blew the spark into a flame, and the flame burned through my hat to my hair and touched one of the celluloid combs—and that was that. Like a flash, my head was on fire. I covered my head with my cloak to smother it out, but it was too late."

Between her sobs and her hoarse voice we could hardly understand these last words.

"Calm down, Rebecca, calm down," Astraia said. "I have only one more thing to ask you. All you have to do is nod or shake your head. Do you understand?"

Rebecca nodded. I heard noise at the street in front of the house, and knew the police had arrived. We had only moments left to question the murderer before our investigation would be taken over by others.

"I want to be clear in my mind about your motive for murdering Lady Deborah," Astraia said. "It was because she was a temperance suffragist, wasn't it? You were afraid that because she was so influential and so passionate about it, the issue of suffrage would be conflated with the issue of temperance in the minds of the people, and men would never give women the vote."

Rebecca nodded, then spoke again. "You know what's really funny about all this?" she said through her ragged tears.

"What?" Astraia asked. I heard DI Samuel Rankin's voice at the door, demanding entrance.

"I don't even like alcohol, myself," Rebecca said. "That night at the stable with the two of you—I had to force myself to drink that wine you served. Nasty stuff."

***

After an hour spent explaining to Samuel the details around our capture of a woman the police hadn't been able to find even though she'd apparently just been hiding in her own home, a woman who was both the murderer of Lady Deborah and the arsonist who'd set fire to a police building, John drove us home to Astraia's house, then left to bring Mr Mycroft Holmes over so that we could report to him the resolution of the case. We sat in Astraia's parlour while we waited for her brother, all alone since Letty and the children were still in Whitechapel performing our daily work.

"There is still some port left in the decanter from the other night," Astraia said. "Would you like a glass?"

I told her I thought that was a fine idea. We settled in front of the fireplace, discussing the case.

"Astraia, how did you guess?"

"Which part?"

"How did you guess that Rebecca had started the fire?"

"That was good, wasn't it?" She smiled in self-satisfaction. "It was her hat, you see. That huge mourning hat. I'd observed that Rebecca never wore hats indoors. Remember? At Lady Isabella's and at the stable when she was arrested—the first thing she did when she entered a place was remove her hat. Because she had such glorious hair. She might say she loves hats—and maybe she does, for when she's outdoors—but she certainly doesn't wear them inside."

I began to understand her point. "But she was wearing one inside her house."

"Yes. She was wearing one inside her own house."

"But Widow Valerie wore one inside her house too," I pointed out.

"Yes—a small mourning cap pinned to her veil, because she needed her veil to help her avoid ingesting the gas. Remember? She wore a veil, she vomited, and she stood as far away from the gas heater as she could. She did not want to suffer the same disaster she planned for us." She sipped her wine. "In both circumstances, it was suspicious that the women decided to wear their black hats and veils inside their own homes. I should have been more careful at Widow

Valerie's. But I was expecting her to poison us through the food or drink. I missed the potential danger of using an unlit gas heater as a weapon."

"You anticipated that Widow Valerie was going to poison us?"

"Certainly. I didn't eat or drink anything that she didn't eat or drink first. She knew I was suspicious too—that's why she made a point of trying the sandwiches and sipping the tea before we could."

"I did think it was strange when she vomited into that plant," I said.

"That actually didn't surprise me too much," Astraia said. "When I was in college, lots of the girls would retch after eating. They did it in order to avoid putting on weight."

I had never heard of such behaviour. All my life, a major focus had been to obtain enough food to survive. Food was not something you intentionally vomited away.

"But when we were at Rebecca's," I said, "it seems to me that you were taking a big chance when you just pulled her hat and veil off her head."

"Not really. I knew there was something wrong with her hat, you see. Although it was a big hat, and she always had so much hair, there weren't any hatpins holding the hat to her head. After I noticed that, I looked more closely at her face under the veil, and I saw the pink skin and blisters, and then I realised she'd been burned. And when I knew that, everything else fell into place.

"Even at Parliament—I'll bet she removed her hat when the ladies entered Westminster. She was carrying her hat, and her hatpins, and at some point in the jostling of all the ladies she was pushed close to Lady Deborah—and maybe she didn't even plan it in advance. I imagine she just gave into temptation and pushed the thing up into her victim's rib cage. In and out, over and done. To quote Widow Valerie, another Asherah opportunity. In fact, if I was Rebecca's barrister, I would claim it was an accident—and I'd say that Rebecca never even knew she had been the murderer of Lady Deborah until she was informed of it by the police."

"You'd probably have made an excellent lawyer," I said.

"Probably."

"Why did you say you thought she was intending to kill Lady Isabella too?"

"Because it seemed clear at the joint meeting of the suffrage groups at Lady Isabella's house that she is the next leader of those women, for both the temperance cause and for suffrage. Lady Isabella is simply a nicer version of Lady Deborah. Rebecca would have had to kill both of them to achieve her goal of keeping temperance and suffrage separate."

***

Mycroft Holmes was pleased with the outcome of *The Suffragist Murder*. He seemed particularly glad that the murderer of Lady Deborah had turned out to be Rebecca Ravenwood Thornapple.

"Maybe Sherlock won't be so judgemental now about your assisting Lionel Rademacher," he said. "Clearly the man knew what he was doing when he attempted to keep Miss Ravenwood Thornapple from harassing his daughter. He was protecting his family from a madwoman."

"I don't think I can take on another case right now," I said.

"Maddie! Why not?" Astraia said.

"There are so many things I have to do to get the veterinary stable set up," I said. "And I need to get my new home in order as well." I also wanted to rest my body for a few days, but decided not to bring that up. I was tired of always complaining about my injuries.

"That reminds me," Mr Holmes said, "I've been in conversation with the police commissioner, and it's been decided that when the new police station is built, it will include a modern veterinary stable and a women's gaol wing. They'll be needing a matron for the women's gaol. I've given him a hint that you might be the best person for that, Miss Barquist. It would be an administrative position, and you'd have assistants to handle the workload when you and Astraia are busy with one of your cases."

He clearly expected me to be grateful for this opportunity. "What about the horses?" I asked. It would be grand to work in a modern veterinary office, one where rusted surgical implements weren't the norm and you didn't have to rely on local opium dens for your horse medicine.

"Oh, we'd hire another veterinarian," he said. "You wouldn't be expected to be responsible for both offices."

"Or you could let her administer both offices and pay her more money," Astraia said. "She could supervise the new veterinarian."

"Er, yes, or we could do that," her brother said. "It's early days yet. They're still in the precinct design phase."

Astraia and her brother agreed that I could have a few days to settle my new situation before he would brief us on our new case involving the industrialist Lionel Rademacher.

***

As the children had been reminding me all week, the following day was Sunday, the day we would go to the zoo with DI Samuel Rankin. I was glad that we were still at Astraia's, because Letty and John were available to help Susie and Rutherford get cleaned up for their big day. I had taken special care with my own dress and hair and thought I did not look unrespectable. But I did not know what to expect with the children—neither child owned the type of clothing usually worn by youth in social settings—and therefore I was flabbergasted by what I saw when they emerged from the kitchen to stand in front of Astraia and me for our inspection, Letty and John proudly hovering behind them.

Both were dressed in velvet, Susie in a blue dress and Rutherford in a black knee-length suit. Both wore white stockings and shiny leather buttoned boots. Starched lace trimmed both outfits. And both wore their hair in perfect ringlets, topped with broad-brimmed sailor hats.

"He's the very image of Little Lord Fauntleroy!" Astraia breathed. Rutherford beamed. The book by the American Mrs Francis Hodgson Burnett had inspired a particular fashion among boys of Rutherford's generation but not his social class. Dressed this way, no one would ever take him for a lad of the streets.

I was impressed to see that both children had blonde hair. I had always suspected it of Susie—but never even considered such might be the case with the boy.

"You both look absolutely splendid," I said. "I will be very proud to be seen with you." Which was the truth. However, before we could leave for the zoo we first had to go to the stable to check on our animals. This morning's challenge would be to get them both to the zoological gardens without Jamie and Little Teddy beating them up first. The stableboys were unlikely to be tolerant of their fellow manure-slingers dressing like toffs.

John read my mind, bless him. No doubt he'd had the same worries. "I will keep the children in the coach, Miss Maddie, until Detective Inspector Rankin collects you all for the outing."

I nodded. "Thank you, John. Now, what about their coats?"

Letty had also procured good wool coats for them both, and as she and Astraia walked us to the door she helped the children to put them on. After I had put on my own less impressive coat and pinned on a hat she handed me a very large apron and a gaiter to take with me. "You'll want to cover your dress and shoe when you go see the animals, Miss Maddie. I know that stable isn't as clean as the one you used to have."

I bent down and kissed her cheek. "Thank you, Letty. You and your brother are both the kindest people I know."

"I paid for all of it," Astraia said. I bent and gave her a peck on the cheek as well. "Thank you too, Astraia. What will you do today?"

"I'm going to visit Florence Balgarnie," she said. "I'm hoping she might have something in one of her books about the cult of Asherah."

"Excellent," I said. "I like her."

"I do too."

John stopped the carriage at the police station long enough for me to alight. "I will drive the children around the block a time or two, Miss Maddie," he said. "I expect Mr Samuel will arrive soon." I was taken aback by John referring to Samuel by his first name, then remembered that Samuel had grown up in the same neighbourhood as Astraia. John and Letty had no doubt known him when he was a boy.

I told the police constable in the station house to watch my coat, reticule, and hat while I ran back into the stable to check on the horses. He was surprised by such an unusual request from me, but I wanted to keep them clean if I could. I tied the apron around my dress, slipped the gaiter over my one good shoe (the other foot still encased in plaster), and hobbled back into the stable, trying my best to avoid the muck that covered most every walking surface in a horse yard during the winter. I would wipe down my cast before entering Samuel's coach.

The injured horse was doing well, and I changed its dressing without incident. I discharged Georgina back into the regular horse rota. Bluebell and Charlie were just fine. No other animals had appeared in the veterinary boxes overnight. I fed the dog Old Vic, gave him a pat, and told him he was in charge for the day. I informed Harry that the children and I would be out today (which he already knew—everyone who worked in the precinct knew that DI Rankin was taking Miss Barquist and her two stable workers to the zoo today); and I also said that tonight would be the last night we would be staying at Miss Holmes's house, because our camp beds were ready and Susie and I would be moving into our flat tomorrow.

I walked back to the station house to wash my hands, remove my apron and gaiter, and replace my coat and hat, then went out front to await John and Samuel.

An elegant one-horse enclosed landau pulled up in front of the police station. The driver came down to open the door and a boy exited, followed by a man. The boy was dressed much as Rutherford had been, only his Little Lord Fauntleroy suit was in burgundy velvet instead of black, and he wore a tam on his head instead of a sailor hat. The man wore rich Chinese robes, and a long queue down his back.

The boy was Chan. The man was Zhu Wei.

I stood staring for a moment, my mouth agape. But finally I got my wits together. "You look splendid, Chan," I said, holding my hand out for him to shake. Shyly, he did. "I'm so glad you can go with us to the zoo today." He nodded his head, but still didn't look at me.

"I am gratified that you are taking Chan with you today," Zhu Wei said. "Anytime you wish him to escort you in future, he will be honoured to do so."

"Thank you," I said. What I wanted to say was: 'Help! Police! Murderer here! Come make an arrest!' But mostly I was concerned about Chan, who had traded in his blue head scarf for a Little Lord Fauntleroy outfit in order to go with me to the zoo. I took Chan's hand in mine and pulled him over to stand beside me. "Thank you for bringing Chan to me, Mr Zhu," I said. "He has done me many services, and I appreciate him."

Zhu Wei bowed, and said. "I have two other things for you, Miss Maddie." He reached into the coach to bring out a bundle and a stick. He held the bundle out to me. "I wish to return this article of clothing to you."

I took it. It was one of my nightgowns. I had last seen it when we took the laundry to Mrs Ma. I had not noticed it missing.

"That is the gown you were wearing the night we met," he said.

We had met one night when he and a few members of his cohort had broken into my bedroom and threatened me with a knife.

"Thank you," I said, bowing back, Chan's hand still firmly held in mine. I wondered: had Mrs Ma given the nightgown to him, or had one of the men who worked for her? Probably the latter. I would tear the thing to rags, and use it for horse bandages.

"And I also wish to give this to you," he said, handing me the stick. "You lost your cane due to the recklessness of my former employees. I beg you to accept this in its place. I hired the two men to watch over you after you were attacked and stabbed on the street. I was very angered when they caused you additional harm." The fierce way he looked at me, I knew he noticed the faint bruises still healing on my face.

I released Chan and took the stick. Made of a dark reddish wood, richly carved with animals and symbols, heavily lacquered, it had a curved handle of gold. Heavy gold.

"Mr Zhu, this is much too expensive," I said. "I cannot accept such an important gift."

He shook his head, scowling. "No!" he asserted. "It is my fault that you lost your cane! I insist that you take it!" Beside me, I felt Chan begin to shake.

"All right," I said. "Thank you." Down the road, I saw John's coach coming up the street. I also heard noises coming from the stable, indicating that a coach and horses were leaving. "Mr Zhu, our ride is here," I said. "I do not believe you wish the police to see you."

He bowed. "Good-bye, Miss Maddie."

I did not answer. The man entered his landau, and it left just as John pulled his coach over to the sidewalk. As Chan walked over to welcome the children spilling out of John's coach, I observed him. He carried a small cloth bag, which I assumed held his other clothes and the blue scarf he usually wore on his head, so that he could change into his regular garb before going home this evening on his own; Little Lord Fauntleroy in Limehouse would excite unnecessary attention, I was sure. But now, seeing him from the back in his velvet British boy's suit, for the first time I understood why he normally draped his head in the blue scarf. Chan's hair was worn in a queue, now pulled up and pinned, hidden for the most part under a tam. When he turned, I glanced at the front of his head and noticed from the edges I could see under his hat that he also wore the front part of his head shaved, as Zhu Wei did. I realised he probably wore the blue scarf in order to keep the fact of his queue hidden while he lived amongst British people who would no doubt have treated him harshly because of his hair. His usual street clothes were the same as those of other urchins; he was certainly not the only child who kept his head wrapped up in a scarf; and as a half-British child wearing rags and covered in dirt it was not hard for him to be mistaken for one of the other thousands of children similarly situated in London. Except that his head scarf was bright blue.

The police coach neared us. I quickly put the cane and nightgown on the floor of John's coach, then returned to the station house in order to bring the gaiter and apron to add to the pile to return them to Astraia's house.

Chan had taken the Zhu Wei cane back out of the coach and held it out to me. "Chan, I can't keep that," I said. "It's worth so much money. I'd be afraid someone would steal it." I tried to push it back into the coach, but he stubbornly kept hold of the thing, wanting me to take it. Finally he actually looked me in the face, for the first time ever, and in his eyes I saw both fear and ferocity. I knew that if I did not use this today, Chan would suffer for it. And if anyone ever dared to steal it, they would suffer. "All right, Chan," I said, "how about I use it today, since this is a special event, but most days

I keep it aside with my best things, just to use when I have something important to do; would that be all right?"

He thought a moment, then nodded. I took the cane from him, and tried to balance my weight with it. It was the perfect height, much better and more sturdy than the cane it was replacing. Which did not surprise me.

"Chan, would you like to leave your bag in the coach?" I asked. "Then you can change at Miss Astraia's house, after we have dinner there this evening." I knew the children would want Chan to join them for the evening meal, in order to tell Letty and John all about their day at the zoological gardens.

He looked at Rutherford in uncertainty. Rutherford took his friend's bag out of his hand and set it on the floor with my items. Then the blonde boy removed his warm wool coat and placed it on the seat of the coach. "If Chan isn't wearing a coat today, neither am I," he announced.

And of course Susie had to join them. "Me neither," she said, taking off her own coat.

I did not argue. Happily the day was reasonably warm, for a February. And after all, the animal houses in the zoological gardens were heated. And ventilated.

Samuel had paid an off-duty officer to be our coachman for the day. Riding in a private two-horse carriage was certainly quicker and more comfortable than going by omnibus with three changes; and having three children along made for a much less awkward trip than the hackney ride I'd taken last week with the phrenologist.

Samuel proved to be an excellent companion to children. His father was a Fellow of the Zoological Society, and Samuel had been to the zoo many, many times. He knew just what would thrill children, and during the long trip to Regent's Park he talked about all the different snakes and lizards in the reptile house, and the antics they'd see in the bear pit, and imitated the sounds they'd hear in the monkey house. He insisted that we would certainly be in the lion house today at four o'clock to witness their feeding, when we'd hear them roaring and running around in excitement over their daily meal.

"And you know what else we're going to do today?" he asked the children in a hushed tone.

"What?" they said excitedly.

"We are getting a special chance most visitors never get, to go to the back of the houses to visit with the zookeepers and learn what they do with all that animal poop!" he said.

They roared with hilarity and excitement—these children who spent hours of their own days shovelling horse excrement and moving it into piles at the edge of the police precinct to eventually be carted away to a dump outside of town when the size of the piles grew dangerous. I just smiled, and relaxed for the first time in weeks. For the moment, no one was trying to kill

317

me or anyone I cared about. For the moment, there were no crimes I had to solve. For the moment, I did not need to worry about food or shelter or safety. Today, I could relax.

In their excitement, the children almost leapt from the coach when we arrived at Regent's Park. Then Samuel got out and helped me to alight. When my standing was secure, he reached in to get my cane, as well as a second cane he pulled out from under the seat.

"I told you I would get you a cane," he said, showing me the sturdy piece of smooth oak he had brought out after handing me the Chinese cane. "But I see you have acquired a much more elegant staff."

He waited for me to explain where I had obtained the expensive piece. Instead, I reached out for the one he had brought for me and stroked it. "This is lovely, Samuel. Thank you. And much more practical than this other one. If you don't mind, I will use the other one today, and keep the one you have given me to use as my regular everyday cane. I cannot tell you how grateful I am to you for giving it to me. It has been so hard for me to get around, and this will serve me perfectly." I was no doubt more effusive in my thanks than I would otherwise have been, just to keep him from questioning me about the other. And truthfully, I was grateful. I was tired of always being on the verge of falling down. And I could hardly use a gold-tipped cane when traipsing around a stable full of sick horses.

He nodded, pleased with my response, and returned my new everyday cane back into the coach. "Let's go see the bear pit," he said loudly. "I've brought some fruit that you rascals can throw to them." The children cheered, and we entered Regent's Park to walk to the zoological gardens.

While the children exclaimed over the bear climbing the post in the centre of the pit, growling at the people throwing food at its face, Samuel updated me on the police search for Widow Valerie.

"We have been able to verify that there are marriage and death certificates for all of the men you and Astraia suggested that we investigate," Samuel said. "In each case, the men married a woman named Valerie. In a few cases, it appears that this Valerie was probably the same person—she retained the name of one husband when she married the next. But other than that, we know nothing about any of these Valeries, including whether or not they are even all the same person. We have reviewed all of the letters you obtained from Mrs Valerie Dryson of course, and we recognise that the fact that she had possession of all these letters might indicate that this was the same woman in each case, but your hypothesis is that she killed all of these husbands, and you must admit that it is unlikely in the extreme that just one woman could have managed to kill so many men with no one noticing. Yes, these men are all dead. But there is no indication that any of them were killed by their wives. Or that they even died under unnatural circumstances. In no case did the medical certificate or the coroner's inquest question the cause of death."

"Could an autopsy be conducted on any of the remains?" I asked. "We really do believe that each of these men was killed by arsenic poisoning." Actually, the only reason we thought that was because arsenic was an ingredient in Widow Valerie's glaze recipe, which she had been refining over the years; it might not have been used in her earliest murders.

He frowned. "Unfortunately, the police in those communities have been unable to ascertain where any of the men were buried," he said. It was clear he felt this sloppiness in losing dead bodies was an indication of poor police practises in the rural counties, something that would never occur in the modern London police force.

"Do we know where Mrs Dryson took Dr Dryson to be cremated?" I asked.

"We do not," he said shortly. "Barbaric practise, cremation."

"If Astraia gives you a photo of Mrs Dryson, could you send copies to each of those other towns to see if anyone who attended the weddings recognises her?" I asked.

He nodded. "We could probably do that," he said. I was not convinced he felt it would be worth the trouble, since there was no proof that any of the men had been murdered. But I felt sure that if someone started asking questions, people who'd known the men would come forward with information or to express their own concerns.

"What did you do with Rebecca?" I asked.

"Miss Ravenwood Thornapple is being kept in confinement under a doctor's care at a women's hospital," he said. "Her family is able to pay for the best treatments. I doubt that she will ever be incarcerated in a gaol, as there is no proof that Lady Deborah's murder was intentional—and in fact, it would even be hard to prove in a court that she was the suffragist who wielded the murder weapon. But it also seems unlikely that she will ever again be a free woman. She has been horribly burnt. Under the circumstances, she will probably not want to return to society anyway."

By now the children had grown tired of the bear pit and expressed themselves ready to see the rattlesnakes and cobras in the reptile house. They hoped they'd be lucky enough to see one of the animals eat a rat or suck an egg, both feeding activities having been described in detail by Samuel on the drive over.

We headed over to the next animal house, and nothing more was said during the rest of our visit about murders or widows. I had to admit to myself, Zhu Wei's cane made the hours of walking I did that day almost pleasant. Less pleasant was the thought that came to me over and over: *I wonder which of the other people here at the zoo today is only here at Zhu Wei's direction, to spy on me?*

At least I wasn't worried that Sherlock Holmes was at the zoo today, spying on me disguised as an old man or a fat woman or maybe one of the grouchier lemurs in the monkey cage. As far as I knew, he was still in Yorkshire, waiting for Valerie to appear at her brother's estate to move into the dower house like a good widow.

As it happened, Zhu Wei did not send his spies to follow us to the zoo. He came himself.

I first noticed him in the monkey house. I almost didn't recognise him in his smart British clothes and hat. Only for a moment did I consider telling Samuel who the man was. But I worried about what would befall Chan if I informed on his master. For the same reason, I was glad I had decided to carry the lacquered cane into the zoo, rather than Samuel's oaken gift.

I turned my back on Zhu Wei and smiled at the children scampering around in front of the monkeys. He may have then followed us into the lion house to watch the 4 o'clock feeding. I do not know. I kept my eyes on the animals, and on the charges in my party.

Chapter Fifteen

Samuel agreed to join us for dinner at Astraia's, saying that afterward he would take Rutherford and Chan back to Whitechapel so that John wouldn't have to make another drive. Under Letty's direction the children changed their clothes then went to the kitchen to join Astraia's two servants and the police officer who'd driven the coach for a meal featuring a great deal of meat, pudding, and ice cream. Samuel sat down to eat in the dining room with Astraia and me, where Astraia did her best to ignore him. She had not been the person who proffered the invitation to him to join us (Letty had done that), so she didn't see why she needed to be a gracious hostess to him even if it was her house.

"Did you enjoy your visit with Florence?" I asked my friend.

"I did. She hasn't found out anything about the Asherah cult yet, but I'm confident that if anyone can unearth anything it will be she."

"What cult?" Samuel asked.

"Florence and I took the train to Woking today, to visit the crematorium there," Astraia told me. "Apparently that's the only place in England the public can use if they want to burn up their loved ones. The managers swore they never heard of Dr Dryson or of any of Widow Valerie's other belated spouses."

"The police already did that," Samuel said.

She pointedly ignored this interruption too. "However, we learned that there are private crematoria dotting the landscape everywhere. You might remember, Maddie, that Widow Valerie mentioned the Council of the Cremation Society. I've learned that there are dozens of members of the Cremation Society, most of them wealthy, and many of them have built crematoria on their own estates for the sanitary disposal of their dead grandmothers. It seems likely that Valerie uses one or more of these. Or perhaps she has her own estate and own crematorium—with all of the money she's inherited over the years, not to mention money she's obtained through her brother and God knows how many other men, she might have accumulated sufficient funds to build her own family furnace."

"Why are you so sure that Dr Dryson and the other men were cremated, anyway?" Samuel said.

I answered him. "Because Valerie said they were. And not just to us—she wrote letters to Nora Sidgwick and Frank Podmore telling them that there would be no funeral for Dr Dryson, and that she had already had him cremated. She did not tell them where that cremation was done. What she said to us was, she uses the ashes from the cremated bodies of her arsenic victims—"

"Cremains," Astraia said helpfully.

"Thank you, the cremains, as ingredients in the glaze she makes for her ceramics. She said that arsenic and human cremains result in a particularly nice glaze."

"And her glazes are very fine," Astraia said.

"That's true," I agreed. "Exquisite, really."

"She makes ceramics?" Samuel asked. "With human bodies?"

"She's not a nice woman, Samuel," I said.

"She's an excellent artist, though," Astraia noted.

"Oh yes," I said. "A really excellent artist. Brilliant, even."

"So where does she do her ceramics?" Samuel asked.

"She makes her ceramics in her home," I said. "All she needs is a load of clay and a few tools, really. The difficult part is, she needs a kiln to bake the pieces—"

Astraia and I stared at each other.

"Oh my God, Maddie—we forgot about the potter!" Astraia said.

"What potter?" Samuel asked quickly.

"Do you really think she would have used the potter I mentioned to her?" I exclaimed in excited horror.

"What potter?!"

"Of course she would!" Astraia said. "There's no end to the gall of the woman!"

"WHAT POTTER!"

I was about to give him the name, then saw Astraia glare at me. "A potter I know in Whitechapel," I said.

"What is his name?"

"We aren't going to tell you his name," Astraia said, carefully enunciating each word.

"Why not?!"

"Because then you would go there without us," she said sweetly.

He looked at me, and I shrugged.

"You know she's right," I said.

He railed, but I refused to give in. Instead we made arrangements to all meet first thing the next morning at a particular pub in Whitechapel. I said that once there, I would take us to the pottery.

To further protect our interests in the case, Astraia and I arrived at the pub an hour before the time we told Samuel we would meet him. We sat down at a table and straight away ordered food and drink, since we'd left home too early to eat there.

Astraia had never had a pub breakfast before. "Florence would be horrified to see us sitting in a pub, swilling small beer with our eggs and bacon at seven o'clock in the morning," she said.

"You could tell her you didn't like it really," I said. "That you only partook out of duty."

"I could tell her that," she agreed. "But you and I both know it wouldn't be true." She took another sip of her beer.

Samuel arrived fifteen minutes later. He was surprised and not happy to see us already ensconced. Three other officers followed in behind him. They were out of uniform, so I knew the plan was that they were supposed to be here before we arrived, hiding in the corners of the place, and they would then follow us to the pottery where the four of them would take over the investigation and push us out.

"Hello boys," I said. "You might as well settle in and order something to eat. You won't be going with us."

"Yes, they are," Samuel said, but without much force. He knew he would lose this fight.

We waited until the three other officers had started in on their bangers and beer, and then Samuel, Astraia and I left the pub to walk the two blocks to George Woodward's pottery shop.

George was delighted to see me. He wasn't surprised, though, because Mrs Dryson had told him I would probably come there to check on her progress.

He told us that she had picked up all of her pieces on Friday.

"That was the day after she tried to kill us," Astraia whispered to me.

"What kind of pieces did she have?" Samuel asked.

Astraia and I knew the answer already, but the information was new to Samuel. "One exceptional male bust, plus a dozen goddess statues of various sizes," George said. "Truthfully, I have never seen the like, in artistic skill or quality of glaze. Maddie, I am really grateful that you sent her to me. It was an honour to fire her work. Plus she paid well. Do you know what she uses in that glaze? I've never seen the like."

"Arsenic is one of the ingredients," I said.

"Oh yes, I had guessed that," he said. "I sometimes use arsenic myself. But there was something else, too." I said I didn't know the complete recipe.

We turned to leave. "I'm sorry we missed her," I said.

"Just a moment," he said. "She left you a letter."

All three of us turned quickly toward him, practically slavering like a dog waiting for his bone. George went behind his desk and returned a moment later, an envelope in his hand.

Samuel reached for it, but Astraia slapped his hand away.

"It's Maddie's letter," she scolded him. "She gets to read it first."

I opened the letter with trembling hands.

> *'Dearest Maddie,*
> *If you are reading this letter it means I was unsuccessful in my attempt to kill you. Good for you! And in that case, I hope our little friend Miss Holmes survived too. I am so sorry to have*

missed you today, but I applaud your resourcefulness in figuring out that I took your recommendation to have your friend George fire my work in his kiln. What a lovely man. And you know I don't use that type of praise lightly!

I urge you both to avoid me in future. Since you're alive to read this letter, I can still say that I have never yet killed a woman except for that one time which I can hardly be blamed for. But I cannot make any promises about it going forward. And since you are both my dearest friends in the world, I would hate for something to happen to you.

You can do me a favour, though, as a friend. I accept that I will probably never get my letters back, because the police no doubt have them now and they won't understand the sentimentality of a poor widow's heart, the brutes. But can you take care of my lovely wedding dress? I have worn it so many times, in so many places, and I'd like to think that someday I will find a way to reclaim it again.

I have made two little Asherah with your faces on them, to remember you by. They will substitute for the two that Astraia stole from me, the naughty girl! I hope

you will cherish those as I will these replacements.
Much love to you, my dearest darlings.
Don't forget me!
Your Valerie'

Astraia and Samuel had huddled around me as I read the letter, so I didn't have to do anything after I finished it but put it back into the envelope and hand it to Samuel. After all, it was evidence.

George Woodward had been more polite. No doubt he'd been curious about the letter, but he hadn't hung over me uninvited to read it.

"George, if she ever comes back, can you do me a favour?" I asked him.

"Of course. What?"

George's wife had run off with a peddler a few years back. "Before you decide to marry her, please talk to me," I said.

"She has a bad history with husbands," Astraia said.

"Very bad," Samuel chimed in.

I looked at him. "So you believe us now?"

"I have to, don't I?" he said, patting his pocket with the letter. "This is practically a confession."

***

Three weeks later

The doctor had not wanted to remove the cast, since he doubted that my foot was entirely healed, but it had been over two months now and the thing was extremely nasty, embedded with horse manure and ash grease and the general offal oozing on every London street. I just wanted it off. I went to Astraia's house for the procedure, because Letty had offered to help me wash my foot after the thing's removal. I did not look forward to seeing the poor twisted thing. Or smelling it.

Astraia was not at home. She and Florence Balgarnie had gone to visit Lady Isabella at Eastnor Castle in Herefordshire, to discuss the future of the British Women's Temperance Union. I knew for a fact that Astraia travelled there with a bottle of whisky secreted in her portmanteaux. I did not accompany them, because I was not a hypocrite. After her return to London next week, Mycroft Holmes would brief us on the details of our next case. All I knew now was that it involved industrialist Lionel Rademacher and a girl's school he was being asked to endow.

Letty's new maid Harriet had let me into the house this morning. She was young, a girl not more than a year or two older than Susie. Young, but enthusiastic. I knew straight away upon meeting her that Sherlock Holmes had interceded personally to hire her, since otherwise she would have been sent to a reformatory or worse. He would have remembered her from that first day at the zoo, when he was witness to my capturing her after she had tried to pick Dr Inskip's pocket. I was glad he had taken an interest in Harriet's future. And that he had decided to accede to Letty's request for assistance, although I questioned how much actual assistance a young girl would be when Letty would have to train her, which would only add to the poor woman's burden, at least for a while. She was already spending hours each week teaching Susie to sew, embroider, and cross stitch.

Susie's cloth dolls filled our new flat. Now she had started talking about tatting doilies. She said we could frame them and hang them in our new office when it was built. Which would make a much prettier veterinary surgery than the one I had grown up in, a draughty old building replete with rotting leather, rusting tools, and corroding jars filled with moldy animal foetuses. Now that I had got past the sorrow of losing so many of my mother's things, I felt grateful to Rebecca for burning the place down.

I had told Mr Holmes about Letty's request for a cook and a maid after he returned from Yorkshire, where apparently Valerie had never arrived to move into her brother's dower house like a respectable widow. Mr Holmes had come by the stable to see how things were progressing, and to bring me a cane to replace the one I had lost in Limehouse.

I showed him the cane Samuel had given me. "I already have one now," I said. I did not mention that I actually had two. I did not wish to be berated for my failure to turn Zhu Wei in to the police that day he'd delivered Chan to visit the zoo with us.

"Then you won't need the one I brought," Mr Holmes said. He took it home with him, and I never saw it again.

Rutherford was excited to see Mr Holmes and grabbed his arm to drag him to the veterinary box to see Hazel, who had been brought in with a serious hoof crack. I had called in Bill, the farrier from a neighbouring police precinct, since the crack was worse than I normally treated. Before I consigned the poor horse to the knackery I wanted to see if Bill had a better idea. The farrier thought it might be possible to stitch and clamp the crack, and he and Rutherford had spent hours working on Hazel's foot together. I could see Mr Holmes's disappointment when he realised how much Rutherford loved doing the farrier work. The poor man had hoped that the boy would want to be a policeman when he grew up.

"There's always Chan," I told him when he returned from the horse box to tell me good-bye. "I think he would make an excellent officer."

"Possibly," Mr Holmes said. "If he doesn't become too invested in his master's criminal enterprises. Which reminds me: I wanted to tell you that you don't need to worry about those foreign spies any more."

The way he said this gave me discomfort, even though Chan had already told me the men were no longer watching me. "Why do you say that?"

"Their bodies have been found," Mr Holmes said. "Their throats were cut."

I shivered. I knew these deaths were because of me, even if I wasn't at fault.

"Zhu Wei is a very dangerous man," Mr Holmes continued. "And he has replaced those men with two others. You must be careful. He seems fixated on you."

I considered telling Mr Holmes that Zhu Wei had hired the two men to watch over me after I was attacked and stabbed on the street. But I kept mum about it, because then he would want to know how I found that out, and I didn't want him to know I had actually talked to the crime lord without turning him in to the police. So I changed the subject. I mentioned that in addition to wanting Mr Holmes and his brother to hire a cook and maid to help at Astraia's house, Letty was thinking about taking up another career.

"She asked me if she could be a police matron," I said. "When the new women's gaol is built."

"Why on earth would she want to do that?" he asked.

"She thinks all the years she's spent watching Astraia has given her the experience she needs," I said. "Frankly, she thinks guarding criminals in gaol would be an easier job."

"I can understand that," he said, and walked over to look at the little goddess statue I had sitting on a shelf above my desk in the new office.

He lifted it, peering closely at the workmanship. "This is one of Mrs Dryson's Asherah statues, I take it?"

"Yes."

"Why do you keep it up here? All by itself like this, it's almost like a shrine."

I shrugged. "She seems like an appropriate focus of devotion for me," I said. "Or a reminder of past sins." I didn't have to explain myself to him. He was the only person in the world who knew that I was guilty of patricide.

I was thinking about this visit to the stable while I waited for Mr Holmes to bring the doctor to Astraia's house, to remove my plaster cast. He had sent a message to me through Rutherford yesterday, saying he would accompany the doctor because he had something he wanted to show me.

I was so excited to have my cast removed. I knew my foot would never be what it had been before the horse had stepped on it. I suspected I might always have to use a cane. But the freedom of having the weight of that plaster rock removed—just thinking about that made me happy.

And I was happy about something else as well. I had received my first remuneration for solving a case! Mr Frank Podmore had been so grateful to learn what we had discovered about Widow Valerie that he had paid me for my time, even though she had not yet been arrested for killing his friend. Once my cast was removed, I planned to use the money to buy a Rover safety bicycle with pneumatic tyres. I would join the Cyclists' Touring Club, and start wearing "rational dress".

Although both women were villains, I felt very inspired by Valerie and Rebecca, who had each ridden bicycles and worn men's clothing in effectuating their criminal activities. Why shouldn't detectivists do the same?

Sherlock Holmes and the doctor arrived at Astraia's house. While the doctor was preparing his cast removal tools and going over the after-treatment with Letty, Mr Holmes discussed his new concern with me.

He wanted to know if I had a photograph of Widow Valerie. He knew his sister had one, but she was with Florence and Lady Isabella in Herefordshire. I told him that unfortunately I did not, but that I believed that Astraia had given the photograph to Samuel Rankin to have copies made to send out to the rural counties where Valerie had victims strewn hither and yon.

"Then I had better find Samuel," he said, replacing the hat and coat he had just removed minutes ago. "I need to take a photograph of her with me to Oxford."

"Wait," I said. "Why do you need a photograph of Valerie?"

He reached into his coat pocket and handed me a newspaper article. "That clipping is from this week's *Oxford Times*," he said. "The banns must have been read for the first time only three days after she tried to kill you. She certainly works quickly. I hope I get there on time."

MARRIED

In Trinity Church, Oxford, on 12 March, by Reverend J Hepplewhite, PROF HIRAM DANGLE, MA, Litt. D, of Christ Church College, to VALERIE, relict of REVD H BARQUIST, of London.

"Valerie Barquist, eh?" I said.

"Indeed. She must have thought that 'Valerie Holmes' might incite questions."

"It could be a coincidence."

"I doubt it."

He left, and the physician came in to remove the bane of my existence from my damaged foot.

Mr Holmes sent me a note two days later to tell me that the bridal couple had left immediately after the wedding service for their honeymoon on the continent. Several of the wedding guests thought our Valerie resembled the new bride, but Mrs Dangle, nee Barquist, wore glasses and had a prominent mole on her chin, similar to the one that disfigured the face of Professor

Dangle. It was, in fact, that very shared feature that had caused them to realise immediately upon meeting that they were Soul-mates.

A month later Astraia's brother sent me another news clipping from the *Oxford Times*. Professor Dangle had died tragically while mountain climbing in the Alps. No funeral service was planned. He had been buried abroad.

THE END

Printed in Great Britain
by Amazon